Grane
Book 2 of the
Luna Chronicle

by

S. C. Dane

Published by
Melange Books, LLC
White Bear Lake, MN 55110
www.melange-books.com

Grane ~ Copyright © 2013 by S. C. Dane

ISBN: 978-1-61235-700-3 Print

Cover Art by Caroline Andrus

Grane
S. C. Dane

In the northern Maine woods, a wolf pack unlike any other reigns the landscape. With the ability to shift into human shape, they are the supreme rulers of their territory. Until the real humans threaten their secret realm…

A seasoned fighter who has murdered too many of his fellow wolf-men to bear counting, **Grane** is long past salvaging, no matter the reason behind his lethal campaign. But then he meets **Suma**, the white wolf who wields the power to heal his emotional scars.

But Suma is not a wolf-woman who can easily forgive Grane his horrific deeds. She mistrusts him, and seeks every opportunity to remind the wolf-man of the pain he's caused her pack.

Yet it is through this fire that Grane's redemption is forged, and as he heals, Suma witnesses the unfolding of a generous heart, and learns there just might be passion and loyalty to be found in forgiveness—if they can survive long enough to find out.

Dedication

Like the first book in this series, this story could not have been written without the safety of the den, generously provided by the original S.C. To him I owe a world of gratitude.
A special nod of thanks goes to my little pack of women, who always heal my heart—no matter where I roam.

Chapter One

The Luna with her mate. I kept my nose tucked under my tail and feigned sleep so I could watch them. Their bodies belonged together. It showed in the way they folded in and around one another. I lay still, and when they finished talking and Luna fell asleep, I could see their bodies rise and fall as their breaths harmonized. They were beautiful. And I was a fool to have ever taken her.

Alec, her mate, watched over her while she slept, his tender vigilance illuminating just how much he had missed her, and how ardently he protected her. From the likes of me.

Yet, they offered me consolation when it was I who had stolen Luna from her family, seizing her from this fierce love. How could they overlook my crimes? My mauling by Meron's pack of wolves would have been a fit ending to my wretched life. They should have left me to endure the justice of a cruel death.

But no. Instead they protected me, and offered sanctuary to my little group from the violence of their daily existence. For that kindness alone, given to the old wolf-women Ane and Elga, and my little brother Armand, I owed the alphas more than my loyalty. I revved my spine and shot the blood to my skin so I could speak to my new leader with words and not my wolf body language.

He watched my transformation with a quietude born of confidence. "You do not sleep, Grane," he whispered.

His mate stirred, but did not open her eyes. She smiled in her sleep, and looked nothing like the frightening creature I had witnessed earlier that day, when she had fisted Meron's head in her hand for us all to see.

I turned my attention to my new pack leader. Like his mate, he was smiling because they were whole again. Truly, I did not deserve to witness such affection, and I answered before my self-disgust overwhelmed me. "No, we are too close yet to Meron's pack," I admitted. "If they followed us…" I let my sentence trail away. If these two creatures were harmed, I would never forgive myself.

"I do not think they will come," he predicted. His confidence was not misplaced. My sister would not send anyone, nor would they come voluntarily. The Luna's threat, and utter dominance of Meron, had shaken the hearts of every wolf present. I had seen it in their eyes, their bodies. To be under her protection? I spoke to quiet my thoughts.

"I believe you are right, Alec. But still, I tend to be cautious."

"It is a trait that will benefit our pack, Grane. We welcome it."

I dropped my eyes. He said the word *we* as if he spoke for them all inclusively. My heart fluttered with hope. I would need time to grow accustom to this fellowship, and I asked for my leave before I revealed too much of myself.

I retreated into the woods where I could let my heart crack without witnesses to watch it. I was a disgusting, spiteful wolf who did not deserve this opportunity for redemption. For too long I had been under Meron's sway. How could I let myself hope? I was undeserving. Armand was the one. As were Ane and Elga. It was they who needed deliverance. My atrocities against my fellow wolf deserved no forgiveness.

I inhaled to calm myself. It was not safe to let my emotions best me, and I gripped the silver stems of a cluster of alders that offered their shelter. I would humbly serve this pack. I would bow to each and every member to repay them for my barbarity, and for their kindness to mine. I let myself go and burned into my wolf form so I could hunt to distract my thoughts. We had far to go before we returned to the territory where I had stolen Luna. *Great suffering!* We were returning to the origin of my crime. I moved my paws to silence my brain and quell my heart. I had a debt to pay and I would own it if it killed me.

* * * *

When I returned, my new pack had already awakened and were

shaking off sleep. I dropped the partridge I had killed at Beth's feet. She watched its descent and then lifted her blue-green eyes to me. Her face warmed with gratitude, and my tail wagged in spite of my resolve to shutter my heart. I sat down out of her reach and yawned to cool myself. Alec stood behind her and complimented my gift, but he took none of the bird for himself. I turned to greet my dear friends who also dared to leave Meron's pack. I waved my tail and kissed Ane and Elga. Armand was in human form, but he dropped to his knees to kiss me. I rubbed my face against his, the scent of him reminding me of his sister, my fallen mate. He was growing into a fine wolf-man, and I was pleased to be rid of the influence of Meron's pack. Our alliance with Alec and Beth came at a crucial time for the young wolf. I hoped my gamble would pay off, and the forgiving attitudes of my new pack leaders were the same as those they left behind.

Beth came toward us to share her meal. I maintained my wolf form so I would not have to speak. Her kindness rattled me, and I trembled in spite of my best efforts. It had been so much easier to hide my emotions when she had been chained. I could leave, hide away, or not go near her. But here? I had nearly destroyed this generosity of spirit. The old women Ane and Elga knelt and accepted her offering while Armand and I stood away.

The poor wolf. He was as unnerved as I was, but for different reasons. His heat radiated against my fur and then he slipped into wolf, too. I leaned into him to offer my comfort. Like me, he had seen the Luna when she healed him and he had been frightened then. I hoped he did not see too much of her confrontation with my sister. I am a seasoned wolf, and I shuddered at the sight of her.

It did not take long for the partridge to be devoured, and we got under way before the pin feathers could settle. Beth, I was sure, was anxious to return to her pups. As was Alec. We made good time, with Elga and Ane proving themselves to be dogged travelers as they had done when I offered them a place with me after we decimated their pack. Like then, they put their noses to my tail and followed without complaint. Their tenacity for life warmed my heart in my cold times. I never regretted taking them on, and I hoped our new leaders would not either, as I had grown fond of the sisters and wished them only happiness in their waning years.

I lost myself in my thoughts as we trotted along and was glad Alec led the way. Beth finished our line at the back, protecting us from anyone or anything that might follow. The fact she was there bore testament to the confidence the brown wolf had in his mate. I, too, was comforted by her presence there, even though I kept my ears on the forest around us. If wolves did not bother us, there were other creatures who would. I had not smelled humans, but that meant nothing. I had not smelled them when they had killed my mate. Their treachery knew no bounds and there was no honor in their taking of life.

My throat constricted, and I was glad to be moving, for I had no honor either. I had killed my fellow wolf-men as callously as any human. For a time I welcomed the release of my rage. Fury was the only emotion I felt after my Misha's death. I later understood how Meron used it and shaped it for his own use, but by that time, I was too far gone.

Yet, Armand held onto the wolf he knew before the slaying of his sister, and every time he greeted me with his affection he reminded my heart it had once been joyful, rather than vengeful. I owed Luna my life for saving him. I foolishly put him in harm's way when I asked him to help the day she injured him. If I had lost my little brother? I kept my nose down and shifted my focus onto the trail before me. It did no good to think about what might have been.

We did not stop moving until well after the sun had set.

* * * *

The six of us manipulated ourselves into our human forms before gathering in a circle and settling down for the night. Beth and Alec were concerned for the older women, and they asked each in turn how they were holding up with the pace.

"We are doing fine, Luna." Elga winked at her and said, "Do not worry."

Everyone laughed but Armand and me. I confessed I did not get the joke. Alec grinned as he explained. "Beth cannot help herself, Grane. She is predisposed to worrying. It is her Luna shining through her." He rested his long hand on her thigh and turned his smile to his mate. She returned it with a mock sneer, and I smiled in spite of myself. Their affection for one another was infectious, and I looked at Armand to see even he could not resist them. He wore a friendly grin and his muscles were relaxed. It warmed my heart to see him getting comfortable with Beth.

But my warming heart threatened to split. I excused myself and walked into the woods away from well-meaning eyes.

I had nearly destroyed such affection! I gripped a birch tree and pressed my forehead to its trunk. My immersion into this pack was not going to be easy for me. I would have been better off had I stayed and taken my beating until my death. My spine stiffened against the thought. It was not my way. I knew when I accepted Luna's protection what it would entail, and I would endure it for everyone's sake.

"Grane?"

Beth. As if by reflex, I turned and dropped to my knees.

"Please stand up, wolf-man."

I obeyed her and rose to my feet, but kept my face lowered. She had witnessed me in my private moment. "Luna," I croaked, my voice betraying me. I inhaled before I spoke again. "I just needed…"

She stepped close to wrap her arms around me, and placed her hand on the back of my head. I laid my face into her shoulder, the same one Meron nearly tore apart, and my knees buckled. I fell upon the ground before her and clasped my own arms around her strong legs as if I were drowning. My heart was a tumult of my disgust, my regret, my grief. My body seared and I tumbled into wolf. I swung away from her and dodged deeper into the trees, and ran until my anguish could not catch me.

No, no, no. I had already grieved. I had slain fellow wolves in the name of my despair and I would not resurrect it. I stopped long enough to release the pressure of my distress with a short howl. *No!* I would not let her work her healing hands into my heart to unearth what I fought so hard to shroud. She understood too much already.

I lowered my nose to the ground and sped off through the woods. I hunted with grim determination, presenting each successful kill to the little pack before I retreated back into the forest, where I fled from my heart and my thoughts, and killed anything edible in my path.

I finally tired enough to get myself under control and returned in silence to the group, without a meal this time. I circled a few times before I settled down into a tight ball and then cast my glance toward my pack leaders. Luna was laying on her side with the brown wolf behind her knees. I peered at her face and her blue-green eyes opened onto mine. My heart flipped, and I shut my own eyes against her knowing stare, then burrowed my face into my tail to make myself as small as possible.

Who was captor now? And yet, I did not sleep, but kept my senses peeled for any outside threat that would bring harm into this close circle.

Chapter Two

By morning I recovered myself, and greeted everyone with sincerity, especially Armand. His plunging and tail wagging as he licked at my face told me my foray into the woods had not gone unnoticed by him. His concern touched me as usual, and I rubbed my face along his mane for another stolen whiff of Misha. I would not live long without my little brother beside me to steady my heart.

Alec circled to ready us so we could follow him. We trotted behind him at a steady, ground-covering clip, and I was glad then for having provided meat for everyone the night before, as we did not stop to rest until the sun arced high in the sky. We took our respite under the branches of the heavier trees where the sun could not penetrate.

The brown wolf coalesced into his human form. "We will stay here for the rest of the day and keep cool in the shade." Our leader nodded at Ane and Elga. "We will travel again later when the air is not so hot. Armand, I would like it very much if you would come with me to find water." Alec's invitation to the young wolf seemed affable enough, yet I suspected it was not without its purpose. I assessed my new leader, but found him to be as relaxed as his voice had indicated. My own muscles softened in kind. He would not abuse the young wolf-man, and I watched them disappear behind a thick wall of leaves without worry weighing upon me. I nestled onto the cool soil and fell into a heavy slumber.

I awoke to the drone of feminine voices and cracked an eye toward their humming. The three wolf-women were gathered so close their knees kissed and their foreheads nearly touched. Then I watched with a stilled heart as Elga and Ane positioned themselves alongside of Luna as she lay her body to the earth. They covered every inch of her skin with quick slaps of their hands and my breaths stopped.

The wolf-woman on the ground convulsed and trembled, and still the old women did not cease the cuffing of their palms against her flesh. A groan escaped her throat and she rolled her head so far back I could see her face. Suddenly, her eyes flipped open and stabbed me.

I leapt backward, alarmed by the Luna's uncanny penetration, then dashed off into the woods with my tail tucked and my heart heaving. I galloped until I had put a safe distance between myself and the women, and then turned my panting self back toward the direction I had just fled. Unwilling to get too close, I hung at the perimeter of our little encampment, even when the three wolf-women dozed, and did not dare go near until Armand and Alec returned.

The sun had lowered considerably by the time they got back. Their voices wafted light upon the air as they joked amongst themselves, and I shivered into my human form to greet them. As soon as Alec looked from Armand to me, he stiffened.

"Brother, what is wrong?"

I shook my head to allay his fears. "Nothing. All is well."

Beth strode right over to wrap herself into her mate's waiting embrace. He looked from her to me, his brow not losing its crease. He peered back down at his wife and his sharp grin spread across his face and brightened his eyes. He started to laugh and shake his head.

"Grane, my brother. Judging by my wife's current condition, you have witnessed something best left unseen by us men folk."

"How did you know?" I gruffed.

The tall wolf-man before me did not lose his smile or his laughter, and pulled his mate tighter to himself. "I have had my own dealings with the Women, and I have learned that they can shake the bones of any wolf-man."

Beth squeezed him, and he lowered his face to kiss her. Then she stepped back to rest her hand on Armand, who bravely held his ground. He had been relaxed on his return until he had seen my agitation, and the close proximity of the Luna ruffled him. I watched him breathe to steady himself, and eased my own body for his sake and offered him a steadying smile.

"You have found water, my heart?" Beth's voice carried a slight scratch. The old women rose to join the circle and we all looked to Alec. He answered in the affirmative, and led us in the direction he and Armand had just come from. Elga and Ane positioned themselves on either side of me and took my hands in theirs. They were very warm, and I peered from one face to the next. They said nothing. They merely grinned with a shared contentment and that was enough to feed my heart. My step lightened as I strolled along between them.

By the time we reached the little brook, I felt steadier and wondered what secrets these two old women harbored. If previous experience indicated anything, I would follow Alec's example and leave them to their mysteries. I knelt at the bank of the brook and drank long and deeply. The cold water snaked a path to my empty belly and cooled my whole body. As I raised my face to the blue sky, my stomach growled with hunger. I glanced around to catch five pairs of eyes staring at me. Beth arched one eyebrow, conveying her thoughts with that slight gesture.

I had not eaten the night before because I was upset. My reaction over her concern for me did nothing but jeopardize my health, and therefore, the welfare of our pack. Message delivered and received. Chagrined, I pursed my lips in an apologetic grin, and she rewarded me with an understanding smile. I would need to keep a tighter rein on my emotions.

We lounged by the brook for a short while longer, and then headed back onto the trail at dusk, just as Alec said we would. We fell into the same rhythmical trot with the brown wolf leading, but this time Beth ceded her spot at the end of the line to me. I was happy for the position. It was easier on my nerves if I could keep my eyes on the red wolf, and not the other way around.

The cadenced pace settled my nerves. I kept my ears alert for Elga's and Ane's breathing, but they had no difficulties as we sliced through the forest. By daybreak, the red wolf grew fatigued. I had witnessed it before when we had traveled with her as captive, and I stopped to shift so I could speak to her. I jogged up behind her to catch up.

"Beth?"

S. C. Dane

She turned her furred head and halted. Then she, too, shifted, her chest heaving with her exertion.

"You are tired and we should rest."

She smiled her appreciation at my concern and then spoke. "I know, Grane, but I am anxious to see my family."

The rest of the group stopped and returned to us. Alec homed in on his mate. "Luna-Beth," he breathed. "You are tired and we will stop here."

She protested and gave her same excuse to her mate.

He shook his head. "No, Beth. They can wait another day. We will stop here." He did not wait for her to protest further, but scooped her up into his arms and carried her to a large birch. He nestled in with his back to the trunk and cradled her, and my heart fetched at the sight of them. I turned away.

Yet, still I needed a distraction. "Armand, we should hunt while everyone else rests."

My little brother looked at me with expectation shining in his yellow eyes.

"Ane and Elga? You will stay?" I always asked them and never gave them orders. I deferred to their wisdom of age, always. They nodded and snuggled together to rest. Armand and I headed into the woods for food, my heart tripping like a sudden rainstorm even though I was not running hard enough to make it do so. I knew the image of the two pack leaders together caused it to beat its quick staccato in my chest, and I accepted it as another lash of the whip to my spirit.

Luna had grown exhausted before any of us because she had been my captive, chained to a tree and fed the scraps Kayla retrieved for her, and then physically abused. My ears burned with my shame. Yet she forgave me simply because I had kept her mate alive and allowed her pack to live. I silenced my thoughts and concentrated my nose on the ground in front of me. I would not go where my anxiety taunted me, to where she had another reason to overlook my transgressions. My heart. As if she could heal it and I would let her.

Armand's tail stiffened, and I followed the course he set. Yet, once I smelled the rabbit, I branched away from him in case it out-maneuvered him. When I heard it scream my heart swelled with pride for my little

10

brother. Rabbits were not always easy prey. They were nimble, and our legs were long and we missed more times than we struck successfully. I followed my nose to the sight of the kill, and arrived just as Armand shook the rabbit to break its neck. He clamped it in his jaws, stuck his nose into the air with a deserved bit of pride, and trotted back to the little group by the birch tree. I watched him go, remaining behind to finish hunting.

It was not long before I picked up the musty scent of a mouse hole, and shoved my nose in and clamped my incisors around the soft flesh within. I flipped it around in my jaws, crunched twice, and swallowed, then resumed my search and returned to the group with a plump gray squirrel. I offered it to Beth, but she declined and gave it to Armand and Alec instead, who had not had any of the rabbit, I assumed.

I curled up in a ball, my own fatigue catching up with me, and fell asleep while the others were still awake.

* * * *

We traveled along in the same way for a couple of more days. No rain fell, so we moved at night and rested during the heat of the day. We hunted only when the scent of game was strong and the chance of a kill was strongest. I maintained my wolf form for most of the time, hoping to skirt discussions as much as I could. I simply did not trust my voice. Seeing Luna and Alec together was a painful reminder of all I nearly destroyed. Yet, I never hesitate to show my affection, or my gratitude, with proper greetings. I just would not remove the wall around my heart, and remaining as wolf was the easiest way to avoid conversations on the matter.

However, by the last leg of our journey, I could withdraw no longer. Alec and Beth called our little group together in the muted, orange light of the dawn.

"We are nearly at our home," Luna announced, her voice tight with a thread of squeak. Her husband rested his hand on her shoulder and she smiled automatically. Still mesmerized by their ease of affection, I trained my eyes on them.

"Grane, I would like to speak with you before we get there."

I knew what she needed to say.

She gripped my hand with a gentle squeeze, and led me away from the others. Her palm radiated warmth, and it soothed my heart despite what I knew was coming. She finally stopped us when the others were beyond the range of hearing. I knelt before her, then leaned back to expose my vulnerable underside to her.

"Grane, please."

I raised my face, but still did not speak. Yet, she understood my silence as if I had spoken.

"I know you have avoided me, but I'm not fooled," she announced. "We will mend that heart of yours eventually." She smiled at me and her eyes danced impishly. Then her face grew serious.

"I know, Luna. We approach your sister, and I have harmed her." I dropped my head and closed my arms into my chest. I knew I would face her, and wondered about the white wolf, what her reaction would be. My heart raced with my memory of their capture. Suma had fought with courage and intelligence. I understood what it had cost her to leave her sister behind to be taken away. I would receive no polite welcome from the white wolf.

"Yes, Grane, and I don't know how she or my little brother will react to your presence. All I can ask from you is your understanding and patience?" She tilted her head.

"You ask me for it? Luna, for what I have done to you and yours I will endure it all. It is my penance," I admitted, and hung my head under the weight of my shame.

Beth knelt down beside me. Her body radiated against my own and it was difficult to know whose heat was the greater. "Your heart gives you away, and I know I do not need to ask. I do so because you deserve the honor of being given the option. I can't promise they will not try to hurt you." Her honesty with the situation rested well on my nerves.

"I will be aware of it, Beth. I will receive what I must," I promised, then dared look into those mercurial eyes. "I will cause no more harm to you and Alec."

She did not push herself into me as I expected her to, yet still my body flared in anticipation of her dominance display, which never came.

Luna shook her head. "Grane," she whispered. "Too long you have been under Meron's fist." Tears welled in her beautiful eyes and my spine tingled. I inhaled deeply to see our conversation to the end. "I know you are mine, and we are yours."

Her words were like shots fired into my heart, and my body erupted into flame so I could contain my human form no longer. But I did not leave my place beside her, and remained on my furred stomach, awaiting her release.

"Come," she said, as she bent down toward me. She lifted my chin with her tapered fingers and smiled at me. "We have a short ways yet to travel and I am anxious. You will walk back with me?"

I placed my flank as near to her as I dared, and kept pace with her. She rested her fingers upon my shoulder, entwining us in solidarity, and my heart quickened. How was I to endure this kindness? A beating I could take, and I looked forward to the meeting with her siblings Suma and Eaen.

* * * *

It was nearly dusk when we arrived at their den. We had hiked through their territory for a full day, and the scent of Eaen and Suma was strong. I settled enough to revert to my human form so I could speak to the brother and sister when I greeted them, and hung back to allow Beth and Alec their homecoming without my interference.

Alec gave a quick shout up toward the mouth of the cave, and it was not long before their siblings emerged. They each held a babe. I knew Beth mentioned her pups, but I thought them older. My spine tingled as the pack leaders ran toward their family. The four of us stayed back to watch the greeting, and I was pleased to see not one of us stood unmoved. We four were growing fond of Beth and Alec.

I returned my gaze to the reunion. Luna's yelps and cries as her family swarmed her seized my heart. It screamed for me to flee, but I planted my feet and felt two hands coil around each of my own.

Ane and Elga.

"This is the joy you stole, wolf. Pay attention." Elga raised her yellow eyes to my face, her jaw set. I nodded my response, acknowledging her truth, yet I would have preferred the lash rather than bear witness to the tearful reunion. Still, I did my duty, and welcomed the tight fisted grips of the old women to steady me.

13

The four adults before us huddled into a tight circle and hugged, caressed, kissed and cried. They all touched one another, buried their faces close. The little babes squirmed into wolves, and their ecstatic yips twisted my stomach. Beth fell to her knees, her little pack dropping with her, and wrapping their arms about each other as if to tie a knot with their bodies. I had never seen such an emotional display of solidarity in my life. If not for the physical pressure of the old women, I would have sparked into my wolf form and fled.

It was too much. I had taken too much, and I looked from one old woman to the other and saw their tears track down their faces. They had lost at my hand and would receive no excited homecoming from their pack. Elga, as if reading my thoughts, gripped tighter, and her hand crushed like the squeeze of ice from a frozen lake. The chill moved up my arm and my spine cooled under its glacial presence. There would be no avoiding this pain.

Finally, Alec pulled away from the tangle. He carried the two pups in his arms because his mate could not. She had lost her control and slipped into wolf. Eaen and Suma shifted as well, and they rubbed their furred bodies together as they reclaimed each other.

As if by silent cue, they all turned toward us in unison. The wolves sat on their haunches, and yawned themselves into their human forms again. Beth turned to wipe her face and the faces of her siblings before removing the brown and silver pup from her mate's arms. She kissed his little furry head and the pup lapped at her face. Luna glowed, and she beamed a toothy wolf smile as they approached.

I scanned a rapid assessment of the other two. Eaen stood tall like his brother, and I glanced over at Armand to catch his reaction to the other young male. He stood erect, eager and excited. Armand had never greeted another wolf-man who was close in age and physicality. Most of those we encountered during our travels had been too eager to prove themselves, and we had slain them. Those who submitted were immediately enfolded into Meron's close posse and not allowed to be foolish young wolf-men. Armand witnessed it without complaint. Here was his chance, and my heart fluttered in my chest. I held my breath for him, hoping his instincts would emerge.

Eaen approached, his body stiff and upright. The four of us dropped to our knees, but Armand kept lifting his head to better see the other young wolf-man. He could stand it no longer and he jumped up and flashed a fantastic wolf smile in greeting. Suma and Eaen stiffened in defense, and Alec let out a comforting laugh.

"Eaen, it seems you have a friend. This is Armand." At the mention of his name, Armand extended his arms and bent his knees in the human equivalent of a play-bow. The other wolf-man relaxed, and took Armand's hands in his own, then flashed a wolf smile back at his new friend.

My heart skipped like a rock across a pond, and I pressed my hands into the earth to steady myself, making sure I did not rise. Eaen politely acknowledged Ane and Elga, and then bristled up to me. I dropped onto my back in complete submission, and bared my throat in anticipation to his anger.

I did not get it. Suma flew at me, instead, and I nearly sprang to my feet to defend myself against her assault. I flinched, but accepted her weight as she clasped her long fingers like a band around my throat, and lowered her face to within inches of mine.

My stomach clenched as I rolled my eyes away from her glare. My body burned, but I dared not breathe, and fought to hold my submissive posture. Her grip tightened around my throat, stopping my blood. Suma roared into my ear, and I convulsed involuntarily.

No one interfered. I sweated and writhed to maintain my human form, but did not get off my back or twist to remove my neck from her crushing grip. My vision faded, and finally I could stand no more. I rolled my body from beneath hers, yanking my head back before I blacked out. Her hand slipped from my neck, but she recoiled and grasped again as I fought for air. I still did not rise, but pushed my body away from Suma. She was relentless, and straddled me to keep me in place. I yielded but she did not, and held her ferocious position above me.

"Suma." Luna's voice coaxed with soft sincerity.

The wolf-woman who held me relaxed her choke hold and turned her ear to the plea behind her. She did not take her brown eyes off from my face.

"Suma, please. He has submitted." Her voice grew louder as she neared, and I felt my aggressor's body lift from my own. I jerked away as soon as Suma's weight was off from me and crouched with my head low. I sweated, and my skin tingled as my fur crept to the surface. I clenched my jaw and trembled, then lifted my eyes to Suma and Beth.

The white wolf stood proud and immovable in front of me. I burned and succumbed to my wolf body, too, then bolted for the tree line, where I stopped to look back to see the reactions of those I left behind me. The flicker of a white tail caught my eye as it disappeared into the trees on the opposite side of where I stood.

I dashed away, blazing my own disappearance into the deeper woods so I could grieve unseen. I had not expected my visceral response to Suma. She blew my heart into tiny bits, and I curled up onto the forest floor to stifle my wails. Never had I had such a reaction to another wolf. Ever. Not even to Luna, who could kill me easily, yet saw into my heart. She was my witness, not my destroyer. But Suma? I threw my head back and howled my agony into the evening sky.

SUMA! Enemy!

But the only one who could splinter my heart into a thousand shards, then piece it all back together.

I spewed my torment at the stars.

Chapter Three

I did not return to the pack until the middle of the night, and I did not enter the den. I snuffled to take a body count, and settled myself for the rest of the night once I was satisfied everyone was there. Including Suma. I tucked my nose into my tail and dozed until the sun cracked orange across the gray sky.

When I woke, I stretched my arms and legs and yawned, then sat with my elbows resting on my knees to survey the area. The cave hid itself well amongst the trees, and would remain so even when the oaks and birches shed their leaves. Plus, it sloped high enough to remain dry in the wet months, and gain a vantage point from any approaching intruder. It would be a pleasant spot to make a home and my chest tightened with the prospect.

Alec emerged from the den and sat down beside me.

"I am sorry for Suma's reaction to you," he said, his voice still raspy from sleep.

"It is all right, Alec. It was well deserved." I peered at my new pack leader as he stared out over the tree line.

"She will come around," he predicted.

I did not know whether to believe him. The wolf-woman's wrath had been brutally intense and would probably remain so for a very long time. I would have to tread too carefully.

I nodded anyway. "Perhaps. But if she does not?"

Alec turned his face to me, his golden eyes pressing. His jaw tightened. "Grane, please do not leave. As you can see, we are a small pack and in desperate need of new members." He spoke his heart, and I liked him all the more for it.

Still, I protested my inclusion. "Alec, you could have chosen any number of wolves from Meron's pack. You did not need to return with the one who had your wife and sister at the end of his pole." The image of the two wolf-women in their struggle for freedom crimped my guts, and sweat prickled across my shoulder blades.

"That is where you are wrong, friend. I recognize regret when I see it, and you exude it." His nostrils flared as if he could smell it even then, but he kept his eyes on me and continued his argument. "You managed to save my life, and the life of my mate, even though you were subordinate. You also took on the care of two elderly women on top of your duties to Meron. No one else in that wretched pack could have, or would have, done these things. We need you, Grane, and that is the truth of it."

I turned toward him and raised my face to his, challenging him without physical threat. I refused to let his compliment reside in my heart, and my voice rose with my exasperation. "Alec, I harmed your women and took the mother of your pups. How can you overlook it?"

He snagged my forearm like a striking snake. "I have not forgotten what you did, wolf, but I am willing to forgive it. Beth and I both like you, as odd as that may seem, and I trust what she has seen in your heart." His grip eased as a warm smile spread across his face, and my body heated in response to his affection. His openness unnerved me, I could not fathom it. Was he not afraid I would try to hurt him, his little family?

"No, Grane, I am not afraid. I am sorry. You have been stripped of your decency, and yet you risked your life to reclaim it. That courage is what we nourish in our pack, and you would do us a great honor by sticking with us no matter how difficult your path to redemption might be."

His words stripped me, and I abandoned my objections. The mate of the Luna wielded just as much power in his own right. They both had an uncanny aptitude for assessing their fellow wolves, and I could not help but wonder if Suma, too, had the same talent for it.

In joining this pack, I stepped in over my head and felt myself drowning. Harm them? They were safer than a porcupine in a tree. I was the one in trouble here, and I did not know if I could do what my pack leaders expected of me. But I would try. For them, and for Armand. I put my hand over Alec's, and lifted my eyes to his.

"I will do whatever is necessary," I promised as my heart flopped around unfettered in my ribcage.

Alec grinned and pulled me to my feet. "Good, gray wolf. Now, let us go check out your new home and reclaim our space." He bent himself toward the ground, and effortlessly adopted his wolf form, his tail riding high and waving loose. The brown wolf's happiness stuck my heart into place. I shifted onto my paws to start a brand new day.

He led us in a southerly direction and then east. There was plenty for my nose to observe, and the terrain varied enough to accommodate an array of species we could hunt. Moose foraged at the most eastern point of Alec's territory, and I did not doubt the six of us could take one, provided we could learn to work as a team. We would not go hungry here.

I caught the scent of Eaen and Armand loping up behind us. They had been running hard, their heaving sides and lolling tongues giving them away. I stiffened, worried something had gone wrong back at the den and they were sent to find us. Yet, as I watched their approach the tension in my muscles eased. They were simply out romping as young wolves do, and my ears and lips pulled back in a pleased grin. Armand had a friend.

The brown wolf embraced their playful attitudes and bounded over to them to nip at Eaen's long legs in jest. The black wolf plopped onto his rump, then lunged for his brother's belly. Alec bounced away and slid in sideways for Armand, who leapt straight up into the air and twisted in bewildered surprise. When he landed, he dropped to his back and presented his throat. The brown wolf's jocularity astounded and perplexed him. The young wolf had never witnessed such impish affection from a pack leader before. I trotted over to him with my tail waving, and nudged Armand under the chin. With my mind so focused on reassuring my little brother, I never noticed Alec swoop in from behind, and he caged his long teeth around my lower leg. I spun, coiled my paws beneath me, and torpedoed us into a somersaulted tumble of

S. C. Dane

fang-flashing fur.

I had not had such great sport since Armand's age, and when it was over I gave a vigorous, carefree shake. The brown wolf quivered a great shake, too, and I spontaneously nudged him under his chin. Then cowered at my transgression and flattened myself for his reprimand. In our fun, I had forgotten my place.

He ignored my apologetic reaction, and dashed over to where Eaen and Armand were laying. He slobbered them both as he waved his tail high and loose over his back, then sprawled with contentment beside them. I lay on the ground where I had prostrated myself, buoyantly stunned that our pack leader allowed such outward displays of affection.

His leadership behavior was unlike anything I had ever seen. He was so fraternal, so easy-going. The brown wolf rose, stretched his lean body, and trotted off toward the woods. Armand and Eaen followed him without hesitation, and my own body moved magnetically after him. My heart gushed as if it were pregnant with blood as my brain unfolded the truth like a fiddlehead unfurls into fern.

Alec did not lead by imposing himself. He was pack leader because we were happy to follow him, and I would fight with far more heart for this wise and friendly wolf-man than I ever had for Meron, of that I was certain. And I knew why: because I wanted to please him. Because to receive Alec's gratitude and affection fed my spirit and made me glad to do it. I had made the right choice in betraying Meron. The brown wolf's pack was where my dear Armand belonged, and I would do anything to make sure I did not jeopardize his place here. Which meant enduring Suma no matter what she confronted me with.

I turned my thoughts outward, away from the white wolf, to dispel the angst brewing with the slightest thought of her, and assessed the two young wolf-men trotting ahead of me. It was then I noticed Eaen's slight limp. Armand appeared oblivious to it, and as the young wolves cuffed and chomped on each other as they trotted along, I suspected he had not challenged his new friend.

I was proud of my little brother for that, and was again struck by my unexpected reaction. Ordinarily, a wolf should have taken every advantage to elevate his status. I should not have been pleased by Armand's oversight. But Alec's pack was different. Here they played,

20

and laughed readily, and my chest tightened with the joy of seeing the young wolf-man with his first friend. I tingled with the promise of what the coming days would reveal, and for the first time in many years, my heart pumped with the blood of hope.

* * * *

The four of us arrived back at the den in the middle of the afternoon lugging a small, white-tailed deer between us. Beth and Suma, along with Elga, Ane and the pups, strode out to greet us. Then the women slid themselves in beside us to heft their share and lighten our load. We had carried the deer far, and the extra hands were appreciated. The pups toddled along beside us, and nipped at their father's bare heels. Spirits were high, and I could not contain my smile, even though I was excruciatingly aware of Suma's proximity. Her scent taunted me, and sharpened the experience of the packs' intimacy as we shared our burden. I gripped the bone of the stag's leg tighter to disperse the emotion swelling within me.

We carried our bounty up the slope toward the entrance of the den so the pups could be bustled inside if protection deemed necessary, and our group wasted no time in descending on the carcass.

I held back and waited until everyone positioned themselves before joining in. Alec and Beth had the place of honor at the abdomen, with Eaen just above them. Suma and Armand shared the flank, and Elga and Ane situated themselves at the deer's shoulder. My mouth watered in anticipation, but I would not proceed. With seven wolves on the carcass, there was nowhere for me to go but next to Suma. Instead, I minced my paws on the ground and licked my lips as I watched everyone eat.

I could not move in next to Suma.

Beth turned her head to me as if she heard my silent protest. It was very possible, and if she had, then I knew everyone else had heard it, as well. Including Suma. My stomach twisted and growled with hunger, and the urgency to feed ultimately won over my cowardly heart. It was ridiculous to starve because of my turmoil for the white wolf, and I stepped tentatively toward the back of the deer. Ane moved closer to her sister to give me room, but Suma snarled her warning and bared her fangs. I halted and whined. My stomach growled its protest, but I

21

ignored it and retreated to where the pups, Gor and Terra, were playing.

My agonized heart regained its footing while watching them. The fuzzy pups' antics soothed me. I snuffled them and lapped their rounded bellies, and as they chortled my tail wagged, signaling my happiness. The growl behind me froze my heart, stilling the blood in my veins.

Suma.

I scuttled away as I turned to her. Her brown eyes narrowed, pinching her beautiful face in a vicious countenance, and she vigorously cleaned the puppies as if to erase my scent. I skulked away with my tail between my shaking legs.

She was impossible, and incredible. I was a grown wolf-man, not a sickly coyote, and yet I acted like a wounded pup around her. My reactions to her were frustrating. I had never been so shaken in my life. Not even with Misha, and the image of my dead mate rose in my head, settling my heart like a stone in my chest and recalling me to who I was. I had forgotten for a while because I was suffused with hope. It felt like swaying in the sun atop the uppermost branches of the tallest tree, then getting crushed by the weight of my fall back to earth.

I curled my body around my empty stomach and pressed my back into the base of a large pine tree. The warm, pungent aroma of sap soothed me like a balm, and I closed my eyes to wallow in my thoughts.

My Misha. Dead now two years, and I had been running with Meron and my blood sister since, destroying lives and doing dishonor to our species by warring with our own kind, instead of against the humans who had pushed us out of our territory.

Luna's scent banished my thoughts until I could retrieve them during a private time. I sat up, then shivered my spine so it crackled with heat so to greet Beth in my human form. She carried a well fleshed deer leg in her hand.

"Grane, you can't go without food." She handed me the venison, which I accepted as I bowed my head in thanks, but did not eat it in front of her. She stayed as if she had more to say.

"Suma is being difficult. I am sorry." Her voice warmed me like the sun I felt earlier, dispersing the cold clouds gathering around me. I did not move away from her.

"You seemed rather happy when you arrived this afternoon," she observed. "You wolf-men had a good day in the woods?"

"Yes, Beth. Your mate is an exceptional pack leader, and he put my heart at ease for a time."

She beamed with my compliment. "He has an easy way about him," she agreed. "Truth be told, Grane," Beth leveled her blue-green eyes on me, "he makes us laugh all the time. You might as well get used to it." She winked and grinned as if she had revealed a great secret.

I picked right up on her mirth, and adopted her grin on my own face, then leaned into her and whispered, "Truth be told, Luna, he is well paired, and I will do my best to get used to it."

She laughed outright, slapping her thigh. "See, it has caught you already. That is the first time I have heard your attempt at humor." She arched her eyebrow and kept laughing.

I settled myself as I watched her, but remembered my position within the pack and dropped to my knees. Yet, I kept my eyes on her when I spoke. "Thank you," I breathed. "You give me more to digest than just my dinner."

She giggled. "Excellent, Grane. Now, I will leave you to your musings and your meat." She fell back to leave but caught herself, and held up a tapered finger. "One more thing."

I nodded for her to continue.

"You did not come into the den last night. I hope my sister did not keep you out?"

I shook my head. "No, Luna. I have been sleeping under the stars for more than two years now. I have grown rather used to it." I reassured her with a small grin that I felt in my heart.

"Very well, then. We will see you soon? Alec plans to tell us stories while we digest our full bellies."

"Yes, I will come later," I promised, and watched her return to the others.

My day left me with plenty to think over. It grew easier to forget all I had done when I was with Beth and Alec. In spite of everything, they reconciled themselves to me without restraint. They even let me play with their babes, which in itself revealed how much they were willing to trust me. With them, I felt like a new wolf, only better. I felt like the old me before I had ever had the misfortune of becoming a member of

Meron's pack. I thought I had lost that part of myself, despite Armand's belief to the contrary. Yet, it had not taken long for it to surface. It was as if my old self had been ready and waiting all along.

Then there was Suma, who did not hesitate to remind me of who I had become and of what I had done. With a single curl of her lip she resurrected the shadowed creature I had become. It was just as well. I should not get off so easily, or forget my reasons for agreeing to go along with Meron in the first place.

I ate my deer leg as my thoughts muddied my head and my heart. When I finished, I turned toward the pack, which had gathered in a close circle. I hovered at the edge of the trees to watch them.

Their voices were murmurs and their laughter twinkled upon the evening's warm air. I did not approach for fear of interrupting their joyful mood, but squatted and listened with my eyes closed and my nose alert for their individual scents. Suma's trill lilted on a breeze, and my chest tightened so that I found it hard to breathe. Just her voice sent my heart galloping.

Suma.

I dug my hands into the dirt while my muscles contorted in a flush of heat, then quit fighting the inevitable and slid into my wolf form. Yet, I stayed at the tree line for the rest of the night, gazing up at the ocean of stars until my lids grew heavy and I fell asleep with the hummings of my new pack caressing my ears.

Throughout the night, I awoke out of habit, just to assess our surroundings, and make sure nothing ventured near. Spending two years without a proper shelter had honed my survival instincts, and I had not slept a full night since leaving the mountains. Waking periodically was now second nature, and I was not aware I even did it until I had arrived at a real, permanent home. The revelation became just one more stark reminder of how far I had fallen.

Chapter Four

The summer days passed by, and the nights grew cool as autumn approached. My little group slipped into their new roles within Beth and Alec's pack with ease. Elga and Ane spent a lot of time with Suma, Beth and the pups, and seemed to relish their new status as respected elders. They were sitting with the pups one day while Suma and Beth went on their own hunting excursion, so I took the opportunity to visit with them. I knelt down with the babes and hefted Terra. She lolled plump and heavy in my arms, and gurgled with laughter. The faces on the old women shined with open pride and merriment. I grinned back at them.

"You seem to be doing very well, my ladies."

Elga lowered her lids over her yellow eyes and lifted them.

"We are happier than we thought possible, Grane. Thank you."

"It is not me you should thank for your good fortune, Elga," I deflected.

She was not put off, but pulled herself over to me to kiss little Terra on the crown of her fuzzy head. "It was you who found our Luna and brought her to us."

I shook my head in denial. "You forget, my friends. It was me who kidnapped her and nearly got her killed."

Ane sidled up next to her sister, and transferred Gor into my other arm so I held both babes. Their scents tickled my nose. "Grane, our thanks to you is not misplaced. You should not be so quick to denounce yourself."

"Your role was more important than you realize," Elga added to her sister's admonishment. "Now, if you would please, take these little ones somewhere so we old women can have some rest in the sun."

They shooed me away with the waving of their long hands, but their faces were still lit up with their smiles. Accepting defeat with a lightness of heart, I secured Terra and Gor and stood up. Their round, squirming bodies nestled right into the crooks of my arms, and my throat constricted with affection for them. They rested their almond shaped eyes on my face and chortled with glee and bubbles. My heart soared, and I cooed back, then dribbled baby talk at them as I nuzzled my nose onto their downy heads and smothered them with my kisses. The world evaporated around us.

"You are quite a sight, wolf-man."

I spun around to face Suma, dropping to my knees as I did so. Yet, I cradled the babes tighter to me as their eyes widened with the sudden drop in elevation. "Suma," I breathed and dared not look at her.

"What are you doing with the pups?" Her voice cut my skin, sparked my spine.

"Do not, Suma," I gargled. "The pups." My muscles singed, yet I had to step toward Suma to give her the babes before I dropped them when I shifted. I raised my eyes to her, and my heart fluttered as my stomach lurched.

She stood over me, imperious. Her skin against mine rippled a shockwave into my guts, and I struggled to control myself until I could secure the babes in the wolf-woman's arms. A groan escaped my throat and Gor giggled. I clamped my jaw and held my breath.

Suma's brown eyes widened as she realized how close I teetered to losing control, and she rushed to place the pups in her arms. I slid my hands away as I contorted into wolf, my stolen moment smashed like the fragile thing it was.

I thought I heard my name pass through the wolf-woman's lips, but I dashed away toward the tree line as my guts rolled in shame, the scent from her spoken breath lingering in my nose. She was killing me. Why would she not just leave me be? She had to see how she unhinged my self-control, how she stripped me to my basic level. Of course, she did. It was why she did not let up. I was not to be forgiven for my transgressions against her family, and moments of happiness were not mine to steal.

I settled into a ground-covering lope, and did not stop until I was several miles away, until my heart steadied into a rhythmical beat to feed my fatiguing muscles. My breaths evened and I slowed to a walk, until I found myself on a grassy ledge overlooking a small pond.

I remained on that beautiful spot, whiling away the rest of the day, and gazed upon the dark water until the air around me expanded with the threatening buzz of an airplane. I lifted my face to the sky as I retreated to the dense cover of the trees so I could witness its progression across the sky. It flew low and my heart heaved. Humans in planes. A lethal combination for wolves, and my mind catapulted to the pack I left back at the cave. I minced my paws, but dared not move. I knew what it would mean if I were sighted, death to me or my family. I bolted as soon as the plane shrunk to a speck in the sky, and raced for home.

I rounded the den from the back of the entrance and nearly smacked into Alec, who filled the mouth of the cave with his bulk. His tense posture told me he already knew about the plane.

"Grane, did you see it?" Worry weighted his deep voice.

I sat back on my haunches, shifted into my human form, and did not wait to recover to answer him, but responded with the residual gravel in my voice and the heat of my heaving breaths.

"Yes, but they did not see me. And ours?" I peered up at him, anxious that any of the others had been seen.

My pack leader shook his head. "No one was seen. Suma was the only one outside, but she hid as soon as she heard the plane's approach." Alec's entire demeanor darkened. "I do not like it," he growled.

"A plane only means trouble," I agreed, but needed to press him further. It had not escaped me that he and his pack were the only wolf-people in this region. Age's and Elga's pack was the last one Meron's had seen for some time before we settled this far to the northeast. Did humans even know that wolves resided this far? I voiced my thoughts.

Alec shook his head. "Not until recently, friend. We had been here for a very long time without any human or wolf interference, but it has not been the case in the past year. We are no longer so isolated," he snarled.

I understood, and inhaled to rein in my guilt. Meron and his pack brought wolves this far east, and to Alec that had been both a blessing and a bane. The cost of new pack members ratcheted upward with the sighting of the plane. Eventually, someone would be spotted. There were too many of us in the eastern woods, where previously there had been just a few.

He snatched onto my guilt with that uncanny accuracy he shared with our Luna. "It is not only your fault, Grane. It is mine, as well." The tall man consoled me, but I did not understand his part in it, nor would I ask. "Let us go sit down, and I will tell you." Alec rested his hand on my shoulder as we walked, and we made ourselves comfortable on the ground not too far from the den. We stayed close to the tree line, as well. The passing of the plane grated too harsh on our nerves to let our guards down.

Alec pinched a smile and sighed. Whatever he wanted to say would be worth hearing. I felt honored he would share his story with me. I waited with respectful patience.

He inhaled again, then pressed on. "Myself and a member of my father's pack have been held in human captivity, and Eaen has been the victim of a steel trap. We have made our presence known." He drilled his almond eyes onto mine, and my stomach wrenched. His implication rang clear, but his hurried summary left me with too many questions. None of which I would ask out of respect to him. I felt certain that with time, I would come to know the full story of these loving wolf-people.

"Then we will keep our senses sharp for human intrusion and do what we must," I offered.

"Grane." Alec did not acknowledge my reassurance.

I searched the wolf-man's face as his heat emanated around us. He would reveal more sooner than I expected.

He inhaled, held his breath, and then let it out very slow to calm his trembling muscles. "I am afraid of humans."

"As we all should be," I answered quickly, and leveled my stare on my pack leader to drive home my intention. "I am not unlearned in the lengths humans will go, friend. We will deal with their interruption if it arises." I could not suppress my need to ease him, and proffered my own wink and conspiratorial smile at the wolf-man beside me. "We are better off in our wolf forms anyway, do you not think? We would look mighty conspicuous running around the forest as naked humans."

Alec laughed, and it warmed my heart to hear it. He was too great a wolf to let something as trivial as the fear of humans lower my estimation of him. Any smart wolf would do well to keep such fear close to his heart, lest he forget how dangerous humans were.

My pack leader stood up and offered his hand. I clasped it, and he helped me to my feet. "We are ready, and will do what we must." He repeated my sentiments as if to reinforce our alliance against our common enemy, and smiled wide, revealing all of his luminous teeth.

The sense of well-being enveloped my heart again. I really liked this wolf, and the satisfaction that I betrayed Meron in order to protect him returned once more to squeeze my heart like a warm hug. We headed back to the den together, but I halted at the entrance.

Alec looked back over his shoulder. "Come inside and sleep within the safety of these walls, gray wolf. There is room for you here."

I took a deep breath, stepped forward, and snapped one more tie to my life with Meron. The sweet smell of earth bombarded my nostrils, and I took quick little puffs to locate the warm bodies in the dark. The den felt large, the ceiling of it high. It seemed very much like the one I had been raised in, and memories flooded into my head.

My puppy-hood had been too long ago. Back then I romped full of myself, bursting with life and its promise. I had been so naïve, and never imagined myself as the wolf I turned out to be. I squashed my thoughts before they closed in to crush me. Alec bid me good-night, then retired toward the rear of the cave where Beth and his pups awaited him. I continued to poke my nose around to single out Armand's scent. Eaen lay right next to him.

I would not bother them. Instead, I made myself comfortable near the entrance, and fell into a restful sleep with the mingled odors of my new pack rolling across my palate.

Chapter Five

Eaen and Armand were the first to stir when dawn arrived. They stretched, and Armand came right over to hug me as soon as his sleepy eyes spied me at the entrance of the den. I welcomed his embrace.

"Good morning, little brother," I whispered. A smile warmed my face and my body. "Good morning, my other little brother," I joked as I peered over Armand's shoulder. I was caught up in the feeling of camaraderie, overwhelmed from only one night of shared shelter. What was the matter with me?

Eaen put his arms around me as Armand had done. I squeezed him back, and then held him at arms' length to get a good look at his face. I smiled up at the tall, young wolf-man and uttered a thick thank you. "Your acceptance of me is—"

"Worth teaching me some fighting moves?" he interrupted, his hopeful grin stretching across his face and illuminating his brown eyes. He had the eyes of his sister.

"Of course," I answered quickly to switch my thoughts. "Start today." We exited the den so as not to wake anyone else, and stretched the sleep from our limbs. My eyes were not accustomed to being in shadow for such a long time, and I squinted against the soft shine of the morning sun. I had also not slept so sound in such a long time, either. I would trade a good night's sleep for squinting any time, and I smiled my greeting to the day. I rested my gaze on the two younger wolf-men who exited the den with me.

Grane

Eaen had his bare leg stuck out in front of him while Armand bent over it, studying it with appreciation. I strolled over to them.

"That is quite a scar, little brother," I complimented.

Eaen looked up, and the shadow fled from his eyes so that they glowed with pride instead.

I jutted my chin toward the old wound. "Your brother said that you received that beauty from a steel trap. Is that so?"

"Yes, Grane. It was awful," he admitted. "I almost did not survive it."

I widened my eyes in respectful awe. There were not many wolves who could boast they had survived such an injury. "It was bad then?" I coaxed.

"Yes. I would not have lived if it had not been for Beth." His voice oozed with gratitude for his sister. "She stopped the bleeding and reset the break."

"Your sister is a healer without match," I admitted, and took the plunge. If Eaen meant to accept me, I wanted there to be no secrets. "I know because she healed me. And Armand."

I glanced at Armand, whose face wilted. He had obviously not revealed what he knew about his friend's sister. I smiled encouragement to my little brother, and then returned my attention to the scarred wolf-man in front of me.

"See this?" I pointed my finger at my upper arm where a thin, crescent-shaped scar pocked the flesh. "That was a wolf bite from Luna that would have killed me."

Eaen looked skeptical, a shy grin graced his lips.

"Truly. Armand, show Eaen where Luna bit you, too."

Armand looked crushed and utterly reluctant.

"Come on, let me see," Eaen's muscles firmed with his excitement as he faced his friend. "I showed you mine," he challenged.

Armand heaved a resigned sigh, then stretched his torso to reveal the white scar on his side. Eaen reached out to touch it, but Armand winced as his yellow eyes darkened.

"Armand," I soothed. "We must share everything. There will be no secrets here. Perhaps you may find Eaen has seen the Luna, too."

Eaen nodded as he appraised Armand. His voice dropped to a

31

reverent hush when he spoke. "She bit you and then healed you? She let you see?"

Armand dipped his chin in shame, and his ears reddened.

"It was my fault, Eaen, that Armand had been harmed. He tried to restrain Beth only because I had asked him to. The blame is not his."

Eaen's face darkened. He clenched his fists and spun toward me. Immediately, I dropped to my knees in a submissive posture, and Armand did the same. Eaen stood between us like a tree in a growing wind.

"I will confess all if you would hear it." I kept my tone low, apologetic, and absolutely did not look him in the eye, and waited for him to either recover himself or hit me. I prepared for both, but kept my senses alert to make sure that the offended wolf-man aimed his aggression toward me, not Armand.

Eaen's breathing evened, but his voice remained rough. "Tell me."

I raised my face to his, but did not make eye contact. "Can we sit somewhere comfortable while we talk, brother?"

Eaen narrowed his eyes but acquiesced, and Armand and I took the weight from our knees and settled onto the ground.

"This is not an easy story to tell, Eaen. I am indebted yet again to your charity." I let my gratitude saturate my tone, knowing full well the importance of him understanding that we were not going to cause his family harm ever again.

"Your sister is a generous creature," I started. "And fierce. She fought like no one I have ever seen. She is stronger than most wolf-men," I boasted.

A small grin tugged at her little brother's mouth as he glanced sideways at me. I continued with his quiet encouragement.

"She was very cunning. I let my guard down, and that is when she attacked me. If I had not had so many years of fighting experience, she would have killed me on the spot. I am sure of that." I hung my head in deference to my defense against her. I had knocked her out with a hard punch to her face, and the memory of it made me sick to my stomach. My hands shook and I sweated, and I decided to gloss over that detail for everyone's sake. Including my own, I admitted, but my stomach still constricted, and I pressed my palms in the dirt to steady myself.

"Her bite made me sick, though, and it would not heal. If I was going to survive her poison, I had to accept her offer to help. She scared me very much at first, and I was not sure if I could trust her to heal me and not kill me outright."

Eaen's grin expanded, his pride for his sister evident.

"She laid her hands on me and started to sing." I stopped there to assess the young wolf-men, who nodded their heads in mutual reverence. I continued on with my story. "Her song was powerful and heavy, as if it were made from the weight of the ages. Yet light and sinewy, as if it were born of the strongest trees on the earth."

"Yes," whispered Eaen, his brown eyes wide with its memory. But then he shook his head, as if to rid it of water. "She poisoned you?"

"Oh, yes. I thought you knew?" It was my turn to be jolted by new information. I searched the young wolf's face for some clue of his foreknowledge. There was nothing but amazement. "You did not know?"

"No, we did not. But, then, how would we? She has never had cause to harm us."

The young wolf-man had a wit as quick as his brother's, and his words stung Armand and me both. I cast a quick look at my little brother and could see his muscles trembling.

"Armand, breathe," I coaxed, ignoring my own pain. I hurried to address Eaen to diffuse the tension. "You speak truth, brother, and I would do anything to undo the hurt I have caused." I tilted my head to the side to expose my throat, offering him my utter submission and his total dominance over me.

Eaen sat still for many moments, and the strengthening sun warmed my bare back, but I did not move. Nor did Armand, except to breathe in his effort to see this through to the end.

"It was never Armand's fault," I repeated in a whisper, and dared to raise my eyes on my brother's behalf. "He never laid a hand on your sister, Eaen."

His brown eyes locked on mine, and I froze. One wrong move on my part could crumble this tenuous bridge toward complete fellowship. His voice had a thread of a quail, and it hammered into my heart how important his friendship to Armand had grown. "Armand never touched her? Ever?"

"Never." I did not lower my eyes from his. "He is innocent of any crime, Eaen. Ask your sister if you must." My heart raced with promise. He hovered so close to having a thoroughly open friendship, and my nerves scraped for them both.

Armand's voice slid through the tension. "She bit me before I could," he freely admitted, and his muscles tensed in expectation.

Eaen turned to his friend. "But you did not, brother. So there is nothing to forgive." He grasped Armand's hand and pulled their bodies together in a close hug, and then turned back toward me.

"You, on the other hand," he growled, "deserved everything my sister gave you, and more."

He was right, of course. I lowered my eyes.

"But, my sister saw it in her heart to heal you and share her song, and that means something, too." There remained a slight edge to his voice, but at least it had warmed somewhat. His hand emerged before my lowered eyes, and I reached for it without hesitating. He hugged me to him, as well, and my throat caught. I could feel his heat against me, revealing how difficult it was for him to extend his forgiveness now that he knew the details of what I had done.

"Thank you, Eaen," I croaked and pursed my lips. He was as generous with his heart as Alec and Beth, and I gripped him hard in my arms, overcome by his nobility of spirit. When I stepped back, I glimpsed Suma out of the corner of my eye. She was standing about thirty feet away, her face an unreadable mask. My spine vibrated, and I nodded a silent greeting to her, as I did not trust my voice. If she had heard? Anxiety revved the blood through my veins. It was one thing to confess to Eaen, who had not been my direct victim. But to have Suma know? My shame burned my skin. I was not ready for her. I could barely keep my human form around her long enough to speak two words, how was I going to confess everything?

I felt her near, the hair on my neck prickling.

"What am I missing, little brothers?" Her voice may have been the song of the morning birds who greeted the day, but I heard the scratch of her claw in it.

I stared at the ground, not missing the plural inclusion of who she thought of as her brothers. I was not her little brother.

"Grane has revealed some of what our Beth did to him and Armand," he crowed.

"Is that so?" The birds in Suma's voice trilled, and my stomach knotted. "And what did you tell them, wolf?" The skin on my face felt the scorch of her eyes.

I searched my swirling head for the right words. Eaen and Armand were both staring at me. It was obvious I had had far more composure when I was speaking just to them, and they picked up on it. I squeaked past the knot in my throat to address Suma's question. "I told him that Luna had poisoned me with her bite and that she healed me."

Suma stood silent.

I inhaled, and held my breath until my pulse throbbed in my ears, then turned my face to her. The mask she had been wearing slipped; her brows furrowed over absent eyes, as though she was lost in thought.

"Suma?" I dared, even as my spine vibrated and burned.

She focused her eyes on me, yet I did not know what I should say to her; my mind eddied and darted. She still had not opened her mouth to speak.

Eaen filled the vacuum around us. "Beth can kill a wolf-man with one bite. How great is that?" His excitement did not let him see the danger. I knew too little of the Luna legend to make conclusions, but I could only guess some were immune, like her mate. The idea that all of her loved ones would be, too, myself included, floated across my heating brain like a wisp of fog, but it didn't last. My muscles twitched with the growing heat in my body.

"I have to go," I croaked, and before I could step away from them I buckled into wolf. I shook the remaining tension from my fur and trotted off toward the stream. I did not dare look back at the three I had insulted by my abrupt departure. It was just one more time my actions offended the white wolf, and I was sure it would not be the last.

Chapter Six

"So, am I going to get those fighting lessons, Grane?" Eaen, Armand, and I were stretching the sleep from our muscles in front of the den the following morning. I had spent another night in the cave and had rested well again. I felt up for anything.

"Not today," Armand answered in my stead, his excitement quickening his words. "Alec wishes for the whole pack to go on a hunt for moose today."

A steady rain had fallen during the night and I breathed in the damp morning air. The wet earth already steamed from the rising sun. "Excellent, I look forward to it." Armand's enthusiasm echoed in my response. I could not wait to see how our new pack would cooperate on such an important hunt.

"Even the grandmothers and pups are going," he added.

In jest, Eaen shot a punch at Armand's shoulder. I prickled, ready to interfere, but then relaxed. This was boy play, and I had forgotten what it was like. Armand muckled Eaen's head in the crook of his elbow, and wrestled his instigator to the ground.

I laughed as the feeling of good-will spread throughout my body and lifted my heart. "You both could use some help by the looks of things."

They turned to me as if sharing a single thought, and charged. I held my ground until they were nearly upon me, then ducked to wrap my arms around Armand's waist to swing him in the direction he already traveled. I circled him into Eaen's path, colliding the two young wolfmen, who tumbled to the ground as I leapt away.

36

"Not fair," Armand protested. He beamed a wide wolf smile, swelling my heart with the sight of it.

A disheveled Alec came out of the den. "What is not fair, Grane?" He looked as if he had slept with the twins tousled in his hair, and I could not help telling him so. He laughed readily in spite of his sleepy countenance. "You are very observant, wolf. That is exactly how I spent my night."

The rest of the pack emerged from the den, and we shared our morning greetings. I was careful to mind myself around Suma, keeping my eyes lowered and not daring to breathe in her scent. For her part, she said a curt good morning and left me alone. I appreciated her indifference, as it allowed me to remain with the pack as human. I wanted to discuss the up-coming hunt and would not be able to do so if she rattled me into wolf form.

Fortunately, our pack leader brought up the subject of our hunting right away. "We will all go, including the grandmothers and the pups. If we are successful, then we will stay with the carcass until we have cleaned it, or we have been driven away. There is bear sign where the moose are, so I ask that everyone be wary."

His warning pierced every one of us. Everybody stiffened in preparation. A black bear against six adult wolves would not hang around long, but we would have the pups and they would be vulnerable. It would be up to us all to keep an eye out for them during this necessary foray. We had to eat. If we were lucky, we would find bear cubs and make our own meal.

I scanned our group, pleased by what I found. Every eye rested on Alec, and each pack member glowed with anticipation. Heart reigned supreme in this little group, and my spine tingled with it.

We headed southeast straight away, while the forest could still wet our bare skin, and steam rose in pockets wherever the morning sun penetrated the thick canopy above us. I breathed in the pungency of the freshly cleansed forest. I always loved how the rain released the scents that had been dried into staleness. Even the water tasted better after getting mixed with the falling rain. Luna's soft voice broke through my daydreaming.

"Grane?" Beth stopped to let the others pass. She had Terra in her arms.

"Yes, Luna?"

"Will you carry my girl for a while? I will take your spot at the back."

I accepted with pleasure. After having the chance to hold the pups a couple of days before, I itched for every opportunity to be with them. "Of course, I will." I scooched down to lift Terra from her mother's arms, honored by Beth's trust, even though it heated my skin.

She raised her brow. "You will be able to, won't you?"

I nodded. "Yes, Luna. I just get overcome sometimes with all of this, that you would trust me with your offspring."

For a reply, her blue-green eyes swirled, and she lifted her lip from her teeth in a menacing snarl. I braced my feet as my body rounded in a protective arc over Terra.

The wolf-woman relaxed her posture, and pointed an accusing finger at me as she smiled to set me at ease. "You just instinctively protected my babe, gray wolf. I do not worry about you. Now, let's catch up with the rest of the group."

I turned down the trail and followed the others with my stomach knotted in my throat. How quick the red wolf cut to my core. With a single gesture she forced my instincts to the surface, exposing my true heart. Living with a Luna had snags I had not foreseen.

Yet, the weight of Terra in my arms grounded me. Living with this Luna also had its advantages, and I nuzzled the black fuzz on Terra's head. She gurgled and coalesced into a fat pup.

I turned to show Beth, and she nodded her approval for setting the pup onto the ground so she could romp. Terra ambled her way forward, and Beth and I picked up our pace to catch up with her.

She led us straight to Suma and Gor, and I had been too caught up in her plopping trot to pay heed to who she hurried to see. I stopped short, and the wolf-woman behind me nearly ran up my back.

"What are you doing?" she laughed, and then quieted. She had forgotten, too. She rested her hand on my bare back and I flinched. Ignoring it but not its reason, the wolf-mother slipped past me, and caught up with her pups and Suma to navigate them onward. Suma cast a glance my way, but it flashed too quickly for me to read it. I fell in behind them, but maintained a slight distance.

* * * *

The sun arched high in the sky by the time Alec halted our hunting party. We gathered around him to await his instructions, and I made sure to keep myself away from Suma. Eaen and Armand stood on either side of her. Alec made eye contact with each of us. The musk of moose wafted in the hot air; we were in their feeding territory.

Ane and Elga snuggled the pups into their arms and settled down next to an enormous uprooted tree trunk. The root system, which had been ripped from the earth when the mammoth fell, stood at least eight feet high. It provided excellent protection that the old women could back into if the need arose. Beth gave her pups quick parting kisses, and then we all shivered and convulsed into our wolf forms for the hunt. The sooner we got our moose, the sooner we could have the pups back amidst the larger pack, and better protected.

We followed the brown wolf as he struck east, and stayed together until we spotted an ancient bull grazing on the sedges at the edge of a small pond. He raised his giant head from the water and rivers cascaded down his face and from his expansive antlers. We fanned out to drive him away from the water. Suma and Beth trotted the farthest back to approach from behind to get him running. The rest of us lined the shore to direct his route and to make sure he did not spin around and rush headlong through the other two wolves, toward the safety of the deeper water.

The white wolf waded deep enough into the brackish water so her tail floated behind her as she circled in on the rear of the bull. The red wolf closed the gap, and then the two females plunged toward his rear. The great bull guffed, bolted, and charged onto the bank. Eaen and I herded him toward Alec and Armand, who had retreated a bit to make certain the old beast kept moving forward and sideways.

The bull's sinewy legs churned beneath him, but the strength to thrust his body with vigorous power had waned as he had aged. Still, he gamboled toward the woods within several strides. I dashed ahead to slow him down, and to close our circle. The brown wolf lunged for the thick rump, and the bull twisted and kicked, his sharp hoof just grazing our pack leader's face.

The brown wolf retreated, recoiled, and sunk his teeth deep into the bull's muscled hindquarters. I snapped at the soft tissue of the bulbous nose while Eaen lunged for the side of the thick neck. The white wolf swept in at the exposed flank and thrashed her lethal fangs. The bull bellowed his outrage, and my heart raced as he planted his feet.

Run him! Alec's voice thundered in my head.

I released my hold on the bleeding nose, arced around to the hind of the moose and bit at his heels, the rot of mud on his legs clogging my senses. The bull kicked and ran, and Alec leapt again for the muscular rump he had already punctured and slashed. The red wolf launched herself onto the beast's neck to hang her full weight, while Eaen latched on beside her. The mammoth staggered, and Armand slammed into his shoulder, sending our prey stumbling.

My pulse quickened as we mobbed the brute to keep his bulk dropping to the ground. Suma slipped in between his thick, thrashing legs to eviscerate the bull. His blood oozed from the great, severed artery that ran the length of his stomach.

The sight of his life's fluid gushing frenzied us. We stabbed at the bull's bulk and darted away from the flaying hooves until their thrusts weakened. Alec positioned himself at the thick neck of the moose and clamped his jaw across the long windpipe. The old bull thrashed weakly with his front legs, and glanced a blow against the brown wolf's hip. Alec cringed, but did not release his hold. The bull flailed, helpless against the intense onslaught of exuberant and hungry wolves.

We had taken him! We descended to shred the moose, to pull him apart, and exalted and brushed our bodies on one another as we moved around the hulk of our kill, boisterous as pack. Immersed in the moment, I forgot myself, and received a quick snap from the white wolf. But we were all triumphant, and her reprimand delivered no sting.

Once the beast lay still, I lowered my tail and stepped away to watch, even though the fresh blood on my muzzle and tongue thrilled my heart. We were missing four. I spun away, putting my nose to the ground to follow our trail back to Elga, Ane, and the pups. My heart expanded as I rushed along. I did not need to alter my form when I came up on them.

Grane

The old women picked right up on my excitement and the scent of blood I carried. They gathered the pups, and we headed toward the kill as a tight group.

We met the red wolf on the trail. I shambled up to her and yipped, and her mouth widened in a happy wolf smile as she rubbed and greeted the four we had left behind. She gusseted up the rear of our little troupe as I led the way back down the trail. Electrified as I was with our success, I kept my senses homed toward any threat from coyote or bear, even after we arrived back at the carcass. I remained on the outskirts with the pups while everyone ate. I did not mind my duty as pup sitter, and culled much joy from watching them fight over the scrap of hide Alec tossed to them.

They snarled their possessive ferocity, and Terra pounced on her brother until he released his end of the pelt. She toddled off triumphant, until Gor chased her and sent her rolling with a bumbling body check. She snapped at him, then pouted as he strutted back under my legs with his prize. My tongue hung in a happy pant because they warmed my heart, and held my dark thoughts at bay.

I kept my eye on the rest of the pack, too, and did not mind that the best parts of the moose were being consumed. I was content with my lot. Luna, sated, removed herself first. She stretched and lay beside me while the pups licked at her face in supplication. She retched their dinners and they lapped with their tails wringing, and then begged for more within seconds. Their generous mother could not refuse, and offered them one more pile before leaving the pups to themselves while she cleaned herself.

Satisfied the pups were under their mother's watchful eye, I trotted up to the carcass and tore bloody, bite-sized strips of flesh. The bull moose provided plenty of meat for us all, and soon even Ane and Elga glutted themselves, and plopped down by Luna and her pups. I was the last one left eating, and watched the others while I filled my stomach.

Armand sniffed a cautious, yet exploratory approach to Suma, and my mouthful sat squished in my molars un-swallowed.

Oh. No.

The white wolf basked in the warm sun as my little brother slunk up to her, his tail swishing low. She ignored him, and my heart stilled.

Armand circled his paws twice, and then lay down beside Suma while he cleaned himself.

My stomach dropped. I had no more appetite, and the joy I had been wallowing in evaporated like a rain puddle in a grooved rock. Armand was courting Suma.

I left the moose and positioned myself away from everyone so that I could redirect my jealous stare onto scavengers. I stretched my body out under the sun and wrestled with my emotions, while I forced my heart to beat as if it had not received a rattling blow. I panted to soothe myself and my churning thoughts. Armand deserved to have a mate, and I knew for certain their pairing would be encouraged. Alec and Beth made no secret of their wanting the size of this pack to grow.

I kept myself calm by rationalizing the options of a second breeding pair, and corralled my envy. If I allowed the pain of seeing Suma and Armand together bore itself into my heart? I refused to even contemplate the outcome. Armand deserved every happiness. And myself? I had had my mate. My share of opportunity. I refused to begrudge my little brother his chance, and swallowed my selfish fear, and buried my needs.

* * * *

Later that day, our guts stuffed and our bodies languishing around distended bellies, we gathered around Alec for a story. I welcomed the distraction from my earlier alarm, and looked forward to the storytelling. I had not had the pleasure of an entertaining tale in years, and I knew these times were still a novelty to Armand. I sat back, but waited with eager pleasure.

Alec shared with us the time he and Luna first found one another, and we all laughed with the way he described it. We laughed even harder when Beth interjected with her own version. Regardless of either account, they had both been startled out of their wits. My heart swelled as I listened to the two of them, my body warming in their presence. I took stock of the faces in our pack, each one open and radiant. My tears fell with little warning, and I drew away from the group so they would not see. I trembled, and slid into wolf, then skulked off into the trees. No one followed, so I did not have to go far for my privacy.

Or so I had thought. Armand had tailed me, and I coalesced back into my human form to greet him.

"Armand, you should be with the group," I admonished him, my voice scratching from my recent change.

"No, brother. I am where I should be right now." He grew more independent with each passing day. Soon, he would be a full adult and my protection would no longer be necessary.

"Did you enjoy your story?"

His face lit up. "Oh, yes! Alec is a wonderful speaker. But, I did not realize Luna was so new to our world."

He spoke my own sentiments. Their humorous tale of finding one another had not been told without its revelations. For all of her strength, Beth was heart-wrenchingly vulnerable. And I had brutalized her, delivered her to Meron. I sat down to ease my shaking legs. Armand came to me, draping his strong arm across my shoulders.

"Grane, you did not know. How could you?" Armand's voice dropped to a soft whisper as it thickened. "She is fierce, brother, and very powerful."

I offered him a weak smile. He was right about that. She was fierce and incredibly powerful, but it explained why her little group was so ferocious in their own right. They protected her as courageously as she did them. Which split the wound in my heart even wider. I inhaled through my constricting throat. "You should go back to the group now, little brother," I recommended.

The young wolf-man stood to leave, but before he did, he looked down at me sitting on the ground, his brow creased with concern. "You do not even realize how you saved their lives, do you?" He shook his head, then returned to the pack, leaving me to chew on his parting question.

He had been spending time with the old women, I was certain of that. Saved their lives? They were all delusional if they thought that. Suma could set the record straight. They could ask her if she felt like I was saving her life as she struggled on the end of my pole.

I covered my face with my hands to hide another wash of tears that sprang from my battered heart. Armand and the old women were right. If it had been one of Meron's posse who had led our hunting party? My spine shuddered. They would not have stopped after they had captured the Luna, but would have sought out her family to make certain they were not followed. They would have prevented Meron's death by doing so.

That little nugget checked me, and I raised my face to the sun. Did I even dare to acknowledge such a truth? For the moment no, and I refused to read farther into it. I rose and made my way to the pond where we found the bull moose, and waded into the deep water to relieve the burning engulfing me both inside and out. When I emerged, I felt like I had on new skin, and stretched out on the bank to dry off. I dozed as the insects buzzed in the warm, late summer air.

* * * *

I awoke to the sound of voices approaching and picked right up on Suma's trill, her giggles mingling with the others' joking and teasing. The pack had come for a swim, too. I stood up to greet them with a welcoming smile, even as the sight of them all together twisted my stomach. They were a beautiful pack, and that ever-present shadow floated across my heart. I did not join in when they dipped into the pond.

Once refreshed, they clamored out to sit around the bank with me. Their show of solidarity chased away the shadow, and I felt warmed again by their sun. I gazed up at the sky and watched as two ravens swooped into the area; they had caught the scent of the moose carcass.

"Our forest kin have arrived," I announced to no one in particular, but seven faces turned to the sky.

"They will rat us out to the bear," Suma added, but she smiled just the same.

"At least they return the favor of a meal every now and then," I managed to rejoin. The large, black birds announced the presence of food, and smart wolves were quick to pick up on a free meal. The white haired wolf-woman nodded in agreement and my heart tripped in its cage. Suma's scent, a blend of spicy mosses and the dark soil, swirled on my tongue, and my belly constricted. Yet, I could not move myself away from it, and I breathed her in as I sat in the sun.

The commotion to my right bounced me from my reverent perch. Eaen and Armand were wrestling again, and Armand had gotten the better of his black haired friend.

"Grane, now would be a good time to show me some fighting techniques," Eaen hollered from under Armand's leg. I stood up, laughing at his predicament. A quick nip to the thigh would give the young wolf-man the second he needed to loosen his head, but he did not see. He really did need a few tricks. I raised my eyebrow to Alec, who had stood to watch with an indulgent grin. He nodded his approval.

I shouted my idea to bite to Eaen, who did not hesitate to try it out. As predicted, Armand flinched just enough for his opponent to slide away. They squared off, and then my little brother dove into the pond with his friend tight on his heels. They splashed and carried on for a while longer until they tired and returned to the shore.

The sun lowered, and cast a golden haze upon the landscape. A light breeze picked up and it looked as though thousands of golden stars twinkled on the ruffled surface of the pond. I sat with my elbows on my knees and drank it in. The brilliant display illuminated the ending of a good day. I must have spoken aloud because I received acknowledgment from just behind me.

Suma.

Her voice ribboned dreamy and thick. "It is very beautiful, Grane."

My heart flew around in my chest from the purr of my name in her voice. My core revved and I heated.

No, no, no. Not now. I held my breath, put my hands to my head as her scent fetched along the breeze and teased me. My back muscles undulated, and I wanted to howl from the pressure of trying to stave off my shift. I stood up and promptly fell to the ground in a rush of fur, then shot the white haired wolf-woman a look of regret. Although I would not be able to speak to her, and her scent would be that much stronger in my wolf nose, I did not leave, but sat on my haunches to finish watching the sunset with her.

I sat for some time with my heart slapping in my chest and my stomach rolling. Suma had finally initiated polite conversation, and I could not take it. That was just great. I cast one last look at the disappearing sun, and the captivating wolf-woman sitting behind me, then trotted off. It felt as if her eyes singed my skin, and I suppressed the urge to dash into the protective cover of the forest. Once there, however, I could not resist looking back at her. She had moved to be with the other women. My groin pulsed, and I clamped my jaw. Had she purposefully sat with me all that time? I dared not hope such a thing.

I turned away from Suma and my thoughts, and put my nose to the ground. Dusk descended. It was a good time to scout the area and pick up on any visitors that might be enticed by the smell of the moose carcass. Our pack leader warned of bear in the area so I poked around to double check for safety's sake.

My scouting yielded nothing, and I returned to the site of the kill for more to eat. I was not the only one who had a growling belly. Everyone had returned to the carcass, including Terra and Gor, and my heart squeezed at the sight. I decided to take my chances and moved in to feed beside Ane as I had done with the deer. This time, Suma did not drive me away, and I closed my eyes against the bliss of it even though my stomach flitted with butterflies and I could not eat. I opened my eyes and found myself looking straight into Luna's blue-green gaze. She lowered her lids then lifted them in a slow blink. Her simple gesture relieved me, and my unsettled stomach. I bit into flesh and ate my fill.

Chapter Seven

By the end of the next day we had gleaned the carcass of most of the meat and left the rest for the bears and ravens. We wended our way home, as we were all sated and at ease. This time, Alec let Eaen lead the way as he brought up the hind. I positioned myself just ahead of Ane and Elga, and kept my ears and nose alert for bear or coyote. Having the pups out in the open made me nervous, and my comfort evaporated. I did not relax until we were back at the den and confirmed nothing had troubled the place during our absence.

Beth and Alec retreated for the remainder of the evening, as did Ane, Elga, and Suma. Even Eaen went in and left Armand and myself to while away the rest of the night at the entrance to the den. My brain twirled a spiral of mundane thoughts, and I felt soothed by their innocent ramblings. I had had enough adventure to last me five life times, and did not even yearn for my home in the west. Too much had happened since I had left it, and I was content to stay in this place to do battle with myself instead, or with bears and coyotes.

But not wolves. No more. My deeds had left me broken, and I no longer hungered for or needed pain. Armand picked up on my mood.

"Big brother, you are musing." He grinned, warm and cheeky.

"You are right, Armand," I sighed, then coughed a chuckle.

He laughed with me until we both fell silent. After a time, the young wolf-man spoke again. "It is good to be here. I did not know it was so easy to be happy."

I turned to look at my young wolf brother, who had grown so fresh and handsome. He had shed Meron's influence, and his demeanor was one of ease and affability. I thought my heart would burst.

"I love you, Armand." The words flowed from my full heart and out of my mouth before I realized what I had said. The wolf-man beside me cocked his head, then beamed, and I found myself returning his expression.

"I love you as well, brother. I am glad you are back." He hugged me to him, and the weight of his arms caressed like a salve to my sore heart. "I am glad, too, that you found Luna. She has healed more than your arm." His words were a breath in my ear, but they carried the firm bite of truth. I gripped the wise, young wolf in my embrace and then released him.

We said nothing more, and as the sky darkened, Armand said his good-night and went into the den. I remained under the stars for a while longer until I grew sleepy. I rose to my feet, stretched, and retreated to the protection of the lair. I made myself comfortable just inside the entrance, and fell into a deep sleep. I did not wake until the patter of rain on the dusty ground stirred me. It was just coming dawn, but the darkness from the heavy cloud cover still shrouded the world, and I felt in no hurry to go out in the rain. I readjusted my position and fell back to sleep.

* * * *

I woke a while later and noticed the rain had slowed to a misty drizzle. I stretched and stepped outside. Ane and Elga came out behind me, shaking themselves into wolf. I knelt and greeted them before they scampered off into the woods together. I watched their departure until Suma emerged from the den. I knelt straight away, and greeted her while my heart pounded in my temples. I did not dare look up.

"Good morning, gray wolf." Her greeting may have been formal, but to me it sang like the forest birds.

I managed to choke out my own hello. I felt her eyes on my head and peeked from under my lowered brow.

"Suma."

She did not answer, nor did she move away. She raised her eyes to the tree line and snuffled.

"May I rise, Suma?" I did not know if she left me on my knees on purpose to push me, or if she did not realize I would not move without her say so. She lowered her brown eyes to my face, and I swear the rain stopped.

"Please. Yes, Grane."

I rose slowly, and then squatted beside her. I could smell her spice and it thickened inside me. "I am sorry," I managed to say.

She looked my way, resting her brown eyes on my face; yet, I could not read her expression, so her words surprised me. "Beth and Alec say you saved their lives. They say if it had not been you who had caught us, we would all be dead right now."

I dropped my face and shook my head, then inhaled deep, her scent winding itself through me. My stomach wrenched, and I could not respond, or acknowledge the truth of her words.

Unperturbed by my choked silence, she spoke on, her voice soft as the hair on Terra's little head. "Luna says she has seen you, and you grieve for much. Is that true, wolf-man?"

How was she able to unmoor me? I trained my eyes on her, clenched my fists, and swallowed several times. I opened my mouth, but my throat contorted my voice so I could barely speak. "Please, Suma." Do not ask why I grieve. Do not ask what I have done in my grief. I dropped my head as my skin blistered. I struggled to hold my human form.

"Grane. Stay."

What is she doing? Of course, I would stay. I would plant myself beside her forever if she wished it. I gripped my ears in my hands and panted to steady myself. I could feel my pulse hammer behind my eyes, and it ebbed as my heart clunked back into a steadier rhythm. I exhaled, wiped my face, and mined for my voice.

"Thanks for the exercise," I croaked.

She busted out laughing, slapping her thigh.

I swam in the rapids of her river-like laughter.

She chuckled to herself as she settled back down. "Grane, can I ask you a question?"

Oh, no. "Yes, Suma."

"When you had me on the end of your pole, would you have really killed me?" She searched my face with her doe brown eyes as if to draw her own conclusion.

I did not lower my gaze this time. I rose to my full height and got close enough to her so that I could feel the heat of her skin, and laid my heart open for her to flay. "You lifted me from my grief the first time I laid eyes on you, white wolf. I would not have spilled a single drop of your blood." I backed away, and did exactly what she had asked of me. I stayed. I watched her face closely for her reaction.

She strolled toward me to close the distance between us. My spine flared, but I held my ground while my heart bled all over my insides.

She reached her pale hand out and pressed the tip of her tapered finger upon my heart. "You speak with your heart Grane, even though it is broken. I forgive you." The corner of her mouth lifted into a smile that lit her eyes, rendering her more breathtaking than the first day I saw her.

I closed my eyes and inhaled her spice. I was impaled and hers forever to do with as she chose. I could not help it. I nearly buckled with the weight of the one splinter of my heart she fixed into its true place. My spine finally ignited, and my human form went with it. I stood before Suma as wolf.

She looked down at me and shook her head. "Gray wolf, I am going for a drink. Would you like to come?"

My tail swished back and forth to reveal my pleasure. She headed for the woods, and I could do nothing but follow her.

* * * *

Armand and Eaen were sitting outside of the den when we returned. They were panting and cooling off in the drizzle. As soon as we saw them, the white wolf and I trotted right up to greet them. Suma nuzzled Eaen, but when I pushed my nose under Armand's, he lifted his lip off one fang as he fell back. I stopped cold.

Then tried to greet him again.

My little brother lay rigid on his side and bared his incisors, and without thinking, I reacted to put him in his place. I straddled him, reaching for his throat with my long teeth. Armand snapped his jaws, flipped to his feet, tipping me off balance. I readjusted in time to flash a snarl at his retreating tail. He bolted for the woods, and I readied to chase him. Yet, before I could spring, Eaen interfered by striding up to me, strutting confident in his status as my superior.

I wanted nothing more than to go to my little brother, yet Eaen pushed his shoulder into mine until I lowered my stomach to the ground and lay on my side, exposing myself. It was all I could do to keep my lip on my teeth. I wanted him to leave me be, to let me go.

Suma did not leave her brother alone with me, but stood a few feet away with her hackles raised, waiting for whatever I would do. I, a well-seasoned wolf, had been checked by a pup, and though at a time like this it stung like a swarm of bees, I had freely ceded my place above him. I clenched my jaw and rattled my spine to send flares through my bones. I lay, without my fur, heaving on the wet ground.

"Eaen," I barked, but I did not rise and trained my eyes on the woods where Armand fled. "What is going on?" I gripped my head in my hands to control myself. "Let me go to him, please!"

From my position on the ground, I could see Alec rush out of the den, his muscles taut as he cast his eyes around. He halted next to Suma and gave her a questioning look. She kept her wolf form, and did not respond to him.

"Please," I whined. "Let me go to Armand." I stretched my arms away from my sides and draped them on the ground, laying myself out on my sweating back. I was in complete submission, and Eaen finally stepped away enough for me to get up. I stood up and started after Armand, but Eaen blocked me again.

"Pup! What is going on?" I dropped down onto one knee and clenched my jaw and fists. What was he doing? My stomach twisted into knots when Eaen pressed his chest onto my back. *Enough, pup!* Something was wrong with my little brother, and he was getting in my way.

Alec and Suma stood ready, but did not interfere. If I did not give in to Eaen? Then I would ruin everything. My chance at redemption, and perhaps Armand's future. I keened, and threw myself back down onto the ground and swallowed my frustration like poisonous berries. I rolled my eyes and offered the young wolf my bare throat. I lay utterly prostrate, and utterly humiliated.

Eaen pulled back again, but this time I did not rise and let what had happened with Armand worm into my heart to eat at it. I could not challenge Eaen's position. I had made a promise. I inhaled and held my breath until I thought my lungs would burst, then let my air out slow, and concentrated on the burning of my lungs. My muscles softened, and I inhaled again to repeat the process. I kept my bare back on the ground and my stomach and throat exposed to the rain. And to the black wolf, who finally sat back on his haunches to let me roll onto my side. I did not get on my knees until he looked away at his brother and sister.

"Eaen?" I breathed. "Please tell me?" I did not look directly at him when I spoke. It was not my place. Nor did he have to answer me. I could only hope that he would take pity on me and respond to my question. I kept my voice soft and supplicating. "Please."

The black wolf yawned, then rippled into his human form, and I waited for him to recover his voice. "Grane, you have insulted your brother."

I had gone to the stream with Suma. I had gone off alone with the wolf-woman he wanted to mate. I put my arms over my head and groaned as my heart split in two. Armand wanted Suma, and what I wanted could not matter. For my little brother's sake.

"Eaen, may I rise?" I kept my head bowed in submission. "I will not go after Armand." My promise thickened in my throat, yet I would honor it.

The young wolf-man stepped back, and let me straighten up. I dropped my arms to my sides and forced my shoulders to be soft. "May I leave?" My ears burned with humiliation, but I still did not lift my chin.

His voice came deep and authoritative. "Yes, Grane. But do not go back on your promise."

As if I would. I said nothing, however, and turned in the opposite direction that I had seen Armand leave. I did not look back over my shoulder, but strove deeper into the woods and let my thoughts rave. How could I have forgotten that Armand had shown an interest in Suma? Yet, I knew the answer, although it hurt no less. I wanted her, too. Needed her. With my entire being.

But Armand? And Misha? My heart constricted and I sobbed as I slumped to my knees. In my selfishness, I had forgotten them. It was not for me to find happiness. This was Armand's time. His chance at discovering a whole new part of life. I had done enough damage to him already. I could not cause more. I buried my face into my hands and yelled away my frustration into my stifling palms.

Then I swallowed my grief, and put it back where it had always been. At the center of my heart so I would not forget my atrocities. I had been a thief to have stolen those moments of happiness within my new pack. As Eaen's display proved, I was the subordinate, beneath even Armand now. I had no right to anything unless given, and the taste of dirt in my mouth was warranted. My deeds defined me, and I was no better than human. I howled into my hands and curled myself into the fetal position.

I lay in the rain until I was chilled to my bones, and then crouched and stoked my inner furnace so that my body trembled and my bones shifted. I padded back toward the den to pay my debt.

When I got there, I could smell that everyone had gone inside, including Armand. I stood at the entrance, but my feet would carry me no farther. I turned away, and curled up under one of the trees near the mouth of the cave so I would be fairly protected from the falling rain. I listened as the drops pattered on the leaves above.

Ane's voice startled me, but I flipped to my paws to greet her. Her face creased into a gentle smile and she knelt to put her arms around me.

"Grane, little son," she whispered. "Your burden is heavy, but we will lift it on occasion to make it bearable." Her strong arms pulled me into her, and I yielded and let my flank rest against her chest. Then she took my position at the tree, and asked me with her body to curl up with her. I accepted her offer of comfort and snuggled myself between her legs, resting my muzzle on her thigh. She stroked my ears and sang.

I coalesced into my human form, but remained with the old woman. I wanted to talk.

"Ane, I did not think and I hurt my brother."

The silver wolf-woman continued humming for a moment longer, and then her words took shape. "Little son, you were happy and forgot your penance. It will happen again as you heal." She picked up the thread of her song.

I stiffened. "No, Ane. I cannot allow that. I have done too much already, and forgetting what I have done in my happiness is not fair to those I have harmed."

The old woman's body shook beneath me as she chortled. "Someday your debt will be paid. Not all at once, wolf, and those will be the hardest times. The times you forget are inevitable and are a sign your heart is mending." She pulled gently at tufts of my hair, then released to tug again. She lulled my nerves and I grew sleepy.

"Ane, you are getting wet and should be inside where it is warm and dry."

She wove her response to my concern into her song. "No wolf, I am warm when I am with you. I feel no rain when I am with you."

Her words salvaged my courage, and I rose and took her hand. "We will go in together, old mother. I will not have you suffer because I am stubborn."

She raised her face to me and winked a green eye. What would I do without her and her clever sister? I smiled down at the woman who held my hand as I lifted her to her feet.

I let her lead me into the den. It took some time for my eyes to adjust to the darkness, but I could smell where everyone lay sleeping. Ane kept her hand in mine and pulled me toward her and Elga's spot in the cave. I nestled in with them, and fell asleep to the cadence of the breathing that filled the den.

Chapter Eight

The next morning, I awakened before the dawn and slipped outside. The rain had ceased and the nuances of the forest's odors had been stirred into a heady concoction of earth and tree sap. I closed my eyes, and inhaled to isolate the hidden aromas.

"Good morning, Grane." Beth's voice nearly sent me singeing into wolf. I spun around to my left to face her.

"What are you doing out here, Luna," I panted.

She chuckled. "Perhaps I am here for the same reason you are here."

I held my tongue, and let her answer for me. Who knew what this wolf-woman gleaned.

"The forest beckons." She said with a shrug, and we sat in silence for a time, watching the fading stars. A heavy, black cloud rolled easterly and away. The coming day would be clear.

"What will I do, Beth? I cannot hide from this," I asked, and tried to mask my desperation. A futile attempt, of course, given who I asked.

"You will face it as you have already. It is not for you or for Armand to decide. It is up to Suma, so you are doing well to mind yourself."

Her words were stern, but her message was kind and sincere in its honest appeal.

"It will not be easy, Luna. She cuts me to ribbons and then pulls me back together. If she chooses Armand…"

The wolf-woman beside me did not interrupt my rave of fears.

I continued to fill her silence. "Armand should have her. He

S. C. Dane

deserves the happiness of having a mate. I will just have to—"

She clamped onto my wrist with a grip of ice, and cut my breath. Luna turned to look at me, her eyes reflecting the sparkling stars. "You are doing well to mind yourself, gray wolf," she repeated. "Do not dwell on what has not happened." She unfurled her fingers from my wrist, and the skin in that one circular patch caught fire. Then she stood up and retreated into the den without another word.

I sat outside in stunned silence. My thoughts no longer raced around in disarrayed logic. Luna had been right. I had let my fear best me. Nothing had come to pass, except an insult that could be smoothed over with a little more swallowing of my pride. It was Armand I was dealing with. My little brother, who was just a wolf-pup despite what he had been exposed to in his life. As his elder, and Eaen's elder, I admitted, it was up to me to keep my emotions reined in. The young wolves would learn soon enough, and I was not the one to deliver the lesson.

I closed my eyes to give a silent thanks to the women of my wolf pack. I sat humbled in the face of their wisdom, and grateful they were willing to ease my burden in my moments of uncertainty and self-indulgence. No matter that my heart was currently being shredded. I was a lucky wolf, and I would do well not to forget it.

I remained seated and turned my face back up to the lightening sky. Armand would be out before too long and I owed him an apology. The sooner we could put this behind us the better.

I rose and jogged to the stream for a drink. When I returned, the young wolf-men were outside stretching. But so were Suma and the entire pack. I took a deep breath, and approached with my head and shoulders low. My heart quickened and my spine tingled. I had to apologize to a pup in front of the entire pack, who until yesterday had been my subordinate. The pain of humiliation crept back into my stomach, and I shot quick glances around at the members of my pack. They all watched with expectation, but without excitement. A serious situation had developed that could have a bad outcome. I knew they all awaited what I would do. Suma, I checked, was as tense as she had been yesterday. She did not trust me, that much seemed clear.

I sighed, then took Armand's strong, young hand in my own and knelt before him. "Armand," I breathed. My voice ground too thick with

56

my emotions, yet, I pushed through to say what I knew I must. "I am sorry for overstepping. I have no excuse. Please, forgive me."

Neither of the two young wolves made a move. I continued to rest my weight on my knee with my head bowed. Armand's hand heated in my mine, and I squeezed him for reassurance. This could not be easy on him, either. His older brother knelt in submission before him. If he was going to act like a full adult in search of a mate, then our altercation was necessary. I was a rival wolf, and the sooner he put me in my place the better his chances were of impressing his future mate. I could not make this easier. "Armand," I repeated. "I have no excuse."

I tilted my chin to the side to offer him my bare throat. His hand trembled in mine, yet, I could not look at him if I were to be his subordinate. He had to do this alone.

"Armand," Eaen encouraged, "he asks your forgiveness."

If Armand did not step up soon, his chances with Suma would be lost. My heart broke for my little brother in spite of my predicament. He deserved every chance for happiness. This was his time.

I could stand his hesitancy no longer, and forced his hand by getting up off from my knee, pulling my lip from my teeth, and lunging for my little brother. He reacted with swift perfection, and his hands clamped around my windpipe in a heartbeat. I did not yield, but grabbed at his arm to pull his hand from my throat. He exploded into wolf, and I followed suit, and he went for my neck again. This time, I fell back and submitted as his sharp teeth pressed through my thick ruff. I flattened out and relaxed every muscle in my body. I would not fight him beyond what I had just done. He had proven he would not take getting pushed around.

I quivered my body to adopt my human form and gargled an apology to the wolf who straddled me. Armand relinquished his grip on my throat, and I lay as still as a puddle in the deep woods. He crept backward, but I felt his eyes on me as he waited for my next move.

I eased onto my side and pulled my knees to my chest so I could rise. My little brother struck once more, sending me rolling and finishing his body check with his fangs in my bare throat again. My human skin succumbed to the sharp pressure, and I felt my blood slide to the back of my neck. I closed my eyes and slipped into my wolf form to protect myself.

I did not counter his aggression. I revealed my entire underside, and Armand relented. He moved away, presenting his back to me. I crawled to him, licked at his chin, and wagged just the tip of my tail while tucking the rest of it to my haunches.

My little brother walked away, feigning disinterest, and I skulked off to recover myself, but did not leave the pack. My subjection was entire. I was now the lowest member within our group. My age and strength in this case made no difference. I had chosen this weeks ago when I agreed to accept Luna's protection, and shoveled my pride away, as there was no place for it here. I was to pay my due, and I would do it without remorse.

I lay down to wait for what the pack would do next and was ignored by everyone, as was proper. I did not move until spoken to. It was the highest ranking member who addressed me first.

"Grane, we are going hunting. You stay here with the pups," he ordered. My heart surged with his kindness, and his understanding. I had just been relegated to the bottom rung as the pup sitter for Terra and Gor, but I could not have been happier. Alec placed me in a position of trust. His swift reaction to keep his pack in harmony shined like a great star illuminating his leadership skills, and I acquiesced without complaint or second thought.

The rest of the pack donned their fur coats and lit out with their excitement filling the air. They would flush deer and it always stirred a thrill. My body ticked in sympathy, but I looked down at the babes beside me. Gor and Terra were exploring each other's faces, causing me to smile from the inside out. I could pass my day with contentment in my heart. Armand was elevated in status, and I had shown I could be trusted. My day turned out far better than I had foreseen.

The differences in Meron's pack and Alec's pack still floored me, however. With the silver wolf, I had been second only to him but had been miserable. Under Alec's fair paw, I was the lowest ranking member, yet felt like a vital link in the family's chain. Except for the feelings I harbored and struggled with for Suma, my life would be quite acceptable.

I turned my focus to the babes so that I would not dwell on Suma.

My fate was not mine to ponder, and I would do whatever I had to for Armand's sake. I hoped the altercations with my little brothers proved I could, and decided I would do well to distance myself from the wolf-woman who drove me to distraction. I would start that as soon as they returned.

* * * *

Gor, Terra, and I waited for most of the day for our loved ones. Beth returned first to the den, and I brought Gor and Terra with me to greet her. She carried a piece of the deer's shoulder in her jaws, and dropped it as the pups and I kissed her chin. The pups wrestled with the shank until their mother vomited a good portion of her meal for them. I took the gift of meat she offered without complaint, and smiled my gratitude.

"Thank you," I held up the venison and lowered my head. She had lugged my dinner for quite a distance, and her gesture went beyond what I deserved. I sat humbled before her, and averted my eyes while her body contorted into its human shape.

Her voice scraped like gravel when she spoke, and I felt her heat in the waning sun. "Grane, rise."

I turned to look at her, and she smiled beautifully as she lifted her palm up and down to encourage me to my feet. I stood up, but moved a polite distance from her and started to eat. It was a bit more difficult chewing without my sharp molars, but I managed. I enjoyed her company too much to lose the chance to talk. "Was anyone harmed in the hunt, Beth?"

"No. It was a good hunt. But, you were missed." She peered over at me, then made herself comfortable in the shade of a young birch. I sat near her.

"I enjoyed my day. Terra was a pest to Gor, but he took care of her eventually," I reported with a light heart.

The wolf-woman smiled, her magnificent teeth gleaming. "Ah, yes. Little Terror," she chuckled.

I laughed at her joke, too, even though she spoke the truth. Terra instigated much, but Gor usually settled it. He held his own against the torments of his sister.

"They will learn to hunt soon?" I asked.

Beth nodded her red head. "Yes. You will teach them?"

"Of course, I would be greatly honored."

She laughed at how quick I accepted her offer. "Grane, you have just lost your status and yet you seem happy. It warms my heart."

"Luna, only a short while ago I had no hope, but you and Alec have opened your hearts to me in spite of who I am, what I have done. Being entrusted to teach your pups to hunt is an honor I never would have expected." My throat tightened around my last words.

She ignored my rising emotions and pressed on. "But Grane, you are a grown wolf who is in his prime. Surely, this rankles a bit?"

I could not lie to the sorceress beside me. "You know full well it does, Luna, only because of how I feel about Suma. But this is Armand's chance, and I will not take any more from him than I already have."

She reached out and took my wrist, gently this time, and rested her blue-green eyes on my face. My body hummed with pleasure and stilled.

"Continue on this path, Grane, and your heart will surely mend." Then she added, "I am sure your mate would have been proud?"

I nodded and bowed my head. "Yes. I do this for her, too."

Beth's laughter twinkled in the warm autumn air. "Gray wolf, your heart is very big and you feel so much. You are certainly interesting. And well worth the risk." She winked then, and I instantly recalled my comment to her when she had been my captive.

I quit chewing and stared at her. "Luna." My atrocities crashed cold upon my heart.

"Don't look so mortified, Grane. Someday, you will see what I mean. And you will see I speak truth."

My spine rattled to life, and I swear she looked through me. Into me. Her next words confirmed my suspicions, and my stomach lurched. "The loss of your mate was utterly devastating to you. I see, wolf, and I am not so quick to judge your offenses. Come here." She reached her arms out, and then patted her palms on the ground in front of her.

I could not refuse her, and lay down at her feet. She remained seated and lengthened her arm out to caress my face.

"Grane, we saw one another when I healed you, and there is nothing to hide between us. I know how your heart reacts to my sister, and I am pleased."

That heart she referred to constricted as I lay myself open to Luna.

"Stay your course, gray wolf. Be prepared to divulge all you have done in the name of your grief. Own it, and then release it." She pulled me into her, and I yielded as I had done with Ane. Terra and Gor tripped their way to us and plunked their fat bodies into my waiting arms.

"Luna, you strip me, too." I confessed.

Her body shook beneath me, just as Ane's had done. "That is my intent, my brother," she chuckled. "Bear with me?"

"Whatever you ask." Would Luna's forgiveness go so far? I dared believe it to be true, and let our new relationship pass across my lips. "Sister?"

"Yes. I am yours, Grane, as you are mine." She continued to pull caresses through my hair, and as she did so I stroked the sleepy pups.

"My niece and nephew will be the greatest hunters around," I promised.

I felt Beth's body warm against my skin. "That, too, is my intent. Teach them well, gray wolf."

"Yes, Luna." My eyelids dropped beneath her spell and I slept soundly with Terra and Gor wrapped in my arms.

* * * *

I woke to the voices of the hunting party, with only Gor and Terra in my company. The red wolf returned with the others. I glanced around for proof our meeting had been no dream. She padded right over to us, and vomited for the pups, offering up only a small portion. I kissed her under her furry chin, and then cocked my head. She flashed me a quick wink, then bent to lick and fuss over her pups as they ate.

She had been here.

Sister.

The red wolf glanced up from her ministrations, her ears resting back on her head as she wore a contented wolf grin. Then she jutted her muzzle toward the rest of the pack, recalling me to myself. I had not greeted the others in my new status, yet.

I shambled over to them without rising onto my two feet, and kissed everyone under the chin, dropping my shoulders repeatedly in deference to each of them. I steeled myself to kiss Suma, but my skin burned anyway, and I knew I gave myself away to her. I retreated after that until my body cooled. I did not want Armand or Eaen to know how I felt about the white wolf. She was for my little brother, not me.

Once the hunting party settled down and our reunion finished, I asked for my leave. Alec released me without hesitation, and I slipped onto my paws and into the forest. I put my nose down to follow Beth's trail, and picked up on both of them, which confirmed everything. Her earlier visit had not been a dream.

I continued on, making my way to the deer carcass. The ravens were picking at what little remained on the bones. They fluttered off in a great torrent of screams, and I froze to pinpoint what startled them. The stench of bear filled my nose and stilled my heart. I turned to face the marauder. A seasoned female and her cubs were advancing on the carcass. The black mother shuffled up behind her twins, and stood on her hind legs, warning me away. I dashed to her left, the same side as her cubs. She bellowed her warning, and I leapt in to taunt her.

She was only a black bear, not one of the giant grizzlies I had been raised with. I viewed her as great sport, and if I could snag one of her cubs? That would be one less bear to deal with in the future. I cuffed at the nearest twin with my paw, and its mother dropped to all fours and plunged her bulky frame at me.

I skipped away from her and circled. She growled her fury. I ticked her off, but that had been my aim. Risky, since I would need to make sure I stayed beyond the reach of one of her talonned paws. She may not be grizzly, but she was still bear. And a mother. I kept a wary eye on her as I darted back in to snatch the hind leg of the other twin. I pulled it a few feet before I had to release him to save my own hide.

The she-bear swiped lightning quick. She may have been smaller than her cousin the grizzly, but I took too great a risk in trying to kill one of her offspring. If I had someone with me, we would have had better odds. As it stood, I could not kill the cub before its mother reached us. I gave one last sniff at the trio, then turned my attentions north.

* * * *

By nightfall, I had arced around half of Alec's territory and had left my mark to reinforce our line. I was not lulled into thinking Meron's large pack would remain united after his death. They would disband and most would return to their old territories in the west. There would be some who would probably strike out east or north. I was not willing to chance anything, even if we did have a Luna and five healthy adults in peak shape, and did what I could to protect my new pack from intruders.

It had been dark for some time before I made it back to the den. Suma lounged outside. I could see her white coat in the darkness. I had almost turned back when she sat up on her haunches. She had either smelled me or heard me coming, and it was too late to retreat. My avoidance would be viewed as an affront. I trotted up to her and roached my back as I dropped to the ground. She stood and accepted my greeting, then shook herself into her human form.

Her bare skin glowed like fresh snow in the darkness, and I caught my breath as my groin pulsed. I could smell her in the heat of her transformation.

Suma. So beautiful.

The pale wolf-woman who stood before me lowered her dark eyes.

She said only, "Gray wolf."

I squirmed away from her before I imploded, but she stepped after me. I whined my protest. She halted and tilted her chin, then squatted and came no closer. My heart scraped raw against my rib cage.

Armand!

The white haired woman tilted her chin again and spoke. "Armand is inside with Eaen."

She had heard my silent protest. I had to get a grip on myself. Surely, she already knew how I felt.

I tried to shake myself into my human form, and it took several tries before I could. Suma watched me the entire time with an amused smile on her face, and once I could speak, I called her on it.

"You grin at my misfortune, white wolf?" Her amusement did not please me, but I kept my tone of supplication. I could not forget my place with her, which strangled me all the more.

Her smile evaporated.

Her reaction filled me with shame, and I hung my head. "Suma, I am sorry. I just—"

"You are *just* in quite a predicament," she snapped.

I flinched as if she had whipped me. Yet, I did not respond, and she did not speak again either. We sat in the darkness, stalemated. After a while, my heart found a bit of skin and I could settle once the scab secured itself.

Suma spoke the moment my shoulders softened.

"Grane, I do not take pleasure in your sacrifice."

I looked straight at her, and did not lower my eyes. "What did you say?" Her comment could have meant a number of things, and I could not understand it.

She rose to her feet and I followed her, our eyes locking. Then she trumped me with a single, withering stare. I had forgotten my place. I fell to the ground, rounded my bare back, and clamped down on my roar of frustration. My groin taunted me, and I grasped the cool earth in my long hands. Suma would be my ruin. I stole a glance at her, caught her assessing me. I looked away before she saw me.

"Suma, please," I begged. For deliverance, release, relief. I wanted to beg for her.

"You may go, gray wolf," she said, her voice soft as honey.

I understood that without an explanation, and I bolted for the woods, away from that seductress. What was I going to do? I had to figure this problem out in a hurry. Too much depended on my control, and the wolf-woman boiled my blood. I wondered if Alec and Beth would release me from my promise to them. Armand would be fine now without me. So would Ane and Elga.

I banished the thought of my leaving. I would be running away from a pack who needed me, no matter what my reasons for going were.

I slumped onto the ground, and stared up at the stars. I could not leave these northern woods. My heart had bonded to this pack, whether I liked it or not. Beth had taken the final step in her forgiveness and accepted me as her brother. I could not betray that. Not after all I had put her through.

I raked my fingers into my hair to clutch at the roots. To be honest, I could not deny the moments of true happiness I had been enjoying, despite my lack of status. I would get to teach Terra and Gor how to hunt, how to fight. I had a future here, and wolves who liked me in spite of what I had done. My future, my new life, was here.

Grane

I got to my feet and returned to the den. I crept inside, taking up my station by the entrance, and fell asleep with the scents of my loved ones on my tongue.

Chapter Nine

The next day we lazed about in the heat, and sought the cool shade at the tree line. Suma, I noticed, did not pay much attention to Armand, which was not unusual in the first days of courtship, and no one commented. My heart broke to watch his advances rebuffed time after time, but that was the way. Suma was no simple wolf-woman who would swoon from a little attention. I had seen enough of her to know that. The she-wolf had backbone and spunk.

My muscles heated from more than the sun, and I clipped off my thoughts about Suma. I spoke to my pack leader instead.

"I saw a black bear with cubs at the carcass yesterday, Alec."

He rolled his eyes in my direction without lifting his head. "Just after we left?"

"Not long after. I teased her some, but she was adamant about protecting her cubs and her spoils. I left her."

He turned his face back to the sky, and closed his eyes as he spoke to me. "I am glad to hear you did not attempt to take a cub by yourself."

I cleared my throat, and he rolled his eyes at me again. I glanced at the ground and picked at a dried leaf. "I did try. For the fun of it, I admit." I smiled at the memory. It had been a great game and no one had been hurt. My pack leader smiled in sympathy.

"I remember when my cousin and I took a bear cub," he reminisced, but then stopped when he noticed everyone gathering to hear one of his stories. He pulled himself upright, and Beth handed him Gor to hold. He nestled his son in his strong arms, and we waited for our story-teller to continue.

"We were not very old at the time. Twelve summers, maybe." He digressed some to introduce his cousin Rion to the rest of us, who was now leader of their old pack, along with their sister Fay. "It was summer, and hot just like today, so we were in our human forms to stay cool." His smile stretched across his face as he remembered. "Rion distracted the she-bear while I snatched her cub and ran. When she came after me, he grabbed the other one and ran in the opposite direction. That poor bear!" he cried in mock sympathy, and we laughed as we imagined her confusion. And her anger.

"How did you ever escape it?" Armand was all eyes, and seemed so young to me just then.

Alec winked at him. "We dropped the cubs, of course, and ran for our lives. We were lucky that the day was too hot for a fully furred bear to run far."

Eaen and Armand put their heads together, plotting for their next adventure.

"Don't you—" I started, then clamped my mouth shut. He had grown beyond my needing to be his caretaker, and I could order him around no more. I dropped my head as my body warmed. It would take some time to get used to being my little brother's subordinate.

Armand did not correct my transgression, but allayed my fears instead. "I will not go chasing bears and their cubs for the fun of it, Grane. It is dangerous business, even if the bears here are smaller than the ones farther west."

His comment piqued the interest of the pack.

"Bigger bears?" Eaen's brown eyes widened with the possibility of it.

"Oh, yes," Armand latched onto his friend's excitement. "Much bigger. And I bet faster. There are all sorts of creatures out there that you do not have here."

Eaen's face flushed and Suma interfered. "Little brother of mine, you may as well forget about it. And you, Armand, should quit putting ideas in his head." Her tone had been stern, and dare I think it? Matronly. I looked to Armand to catch his reaction. His ears turned red and he shuddered as he fought to keep his human form.

S. C. Dane

I dug my hands into the dirt to keep myself from running to him and comforting him. And from chastising Suma, who had made her suitor feel like a wolf-pup.

She caught my glance in her direction and narrowed her brown eyes. I lifted my head to challenge her, and then promptly dropped it and my torso to the ground. What was I thinking? I dug my fingers deeper into the earth to control my urge to speak up for my little brother.

"Armand and Eaen, perhaps you could do us all the favor by using your energy to catch us dinner? Gor and Terra are hungry and they could eat." Beth interfered, and I hoped the young wolf-men would not protest. Eaen rose and grabbed his friend, who went without hesitation. He seemed eager to save face, and the hunt would give him a good excuse to give in to his wolf.

As predicted, he did slip into his fur, and the rest of us watched as two tails disappeared into the thick green leaves of the forest.

I relaxed my grip on the planet, but did not look up. I could feel Suma's eyes boring into my back, and my muscles rippled along my spine.

"Cut it out," I growled at her.

"I am doing nothing, gray wolf," she sneered.

I reclaimed my grip on the earth before looking up at her. As I figured, she was staring right at me.

"You—"

For the second time that day, I clamped my jaw tight to prevent my words from escaping.

"Suma, leave him alone." Alec came to my rescue. "Grane, take the pups and go with Ane and Elga for a swim."

I jumped to my feet to gather my swimming group before anything else could happen. It was all I could do to keep from running in the opposite direction, and I left Suma, and her tormenting, with Beth and Alec.

By the time we reached the stream, I had settled for the pups and we romped and cooled off in the flowing water. Ane and Elga splashed and laughed. The boisterous group lifted my dark mood.

After a time, we just sat in the water with the babes between us.

"She is taunting you, Grane," Elga said, after we had lavished our

68

praise on the pups. The stream bubbled merrily past our bodies.

I looked at the old wolf-woman and shook my head. "She is going to succeed if she keeps it up, Elga," I admitted without bothering to hide my feelings from these wise ladies.

"Yes, she will. And she will be mortified that you challenged her." Ane and Elga laughed hysterically, and I could not help but smile at them.

"What is so funny about that?" I did not get the joke. The situation was very serious. If I upset Suma then I could jeopardize my home with the pack.

Ane and Elga laughed harder. In spite of my fears, I caught their mirthful bug, and my smile turned into a toothy grin.

"Grane, you men can be very dense sometimes!" That sent the old women into hysterics, with Gor and Terra chortling because their grandmothers did. I could contain my fear and anger no longer, and laughed with them, even knowing I had been the reason for it. Their laughter eased my heart, and I latched onto it like lichen to a rock. We passed the rest of the afternoon at the stream until we remembered Armand and Eaen were supposed to bring the pups their dinners.

As we gathered Terra and Gor from the stream bank, a shimmer to the right of me caught my eye. I tensed, recalling a time when I often saw such a reflection. Nothing in this natural forest would have made it. A low snarl escaped my throat and I positioned myself between the old women and the pups.

"Ane. Elga. Return to the den with the pups and tell everyone to get inside. I will be right along. Hurry!"

They grasped the seriousness of my tone, and swooped up the pups. Usually I asked them to do things, but not this time. Not when I stared at a human-made object that did not belong this far in the woods. I waited for my loved ones to retreat before I crept over to the rocks where the object had lodged itself during its trip downstream.

I waved my face across the air currents, but picked up no stronger human scent. This piece of debris had floated down the river far ahead of the humans, but it most likely meant they were coming behind it. The hair on my nape prickled, and I glanced around one more time before reaching for the plastic bottle. I plucked it, and raced toward the safety of the trees.

My chest heaved as my heart flung mad in my chest.

Humans.

The memories of my Misha and Meron flooded into my head, and I squeezed my eyes shut tight against them as my fingers curled around the bottle. I inhaled to center my thoughts. This discovery had nothing to do with my old life. It was my new pack who was in danger, and I could not afford to muddy my thoughts with vengeful wishes. I clutched the bottle and bolted for the den.

As soon as I burst through the entrance I could see the worried faces of my beloved pack. Eaen and Armand had returned, and I heaved a relieved sigh at the sight of them. The entire family huddled safe inside the den.

"What is it?" Alec gave me no time to recover, and his brow furrowed deep. He suspected.

I held out the plastic bottle for everyone to see, and Beth gasped. Armand paled, and Alec clenched his jaw.

"Humans," Luna snarled. She stood up, snatched the object from my hand and sniffed it with her nose curled in disgust. Alec stepped close to her, and she lifted her eyes to him. They were wide with fear and pain and I understood. Her mate. She was concerned for her mate, and Alec's brief mention of his captivity rose ominously in my mind.

"I found it by the stream bed," I informed them. My voice tightened as I suppressed my growling.

"Which means that they are not far behind, or too far away." Alec's assumption hit dead on.

"Yes," I agreed, and waited for his decision.

"Beth?" There was the sliver of pleading in Alec's deep voice. She had her hand on his arm before he finished speaking.

"We both go." She would accept no alternative, and her mate nodded his head, then turned toward the rest of us.

"Beth and I will go upriver to scope things out. You must stay here, Grane."

I caught the implications and bit down on my tongue. He had made a wise decision and I would not argue it, even though my heart cried against the unfairness of it. The pack needed my protection if the humans

70

should get by them undetected. I nodded my abeyance.

"Everyone must stay inside until we return. We will be back by tomorrow night, whether we find anything or not."

Then he pointed a stern finger at Eaen and Armand. "I mean it. This is no adventure. Stay."

The young wolf-men glowered and pouted.

"Uncle," Luna spoke softly to Eaen, "you are needed here to protect Gor and Terra."

He lowered his black head, then raised his brown eyes to her. She laid her hand on his cheek, and then kissed him under the chin. His muscles visibly eased, and Armand responded to his calm. Then she kissed her pups, and squared herself to her full height.

I drew in a sharp breath. Beth had disappeared, and the formidable creature who stood before me burned all Luna. The blue-green of her eyes stormed and eddied in a swirl of color, and then she slipped into the red wolf. Her mate smiled his appreciation. No fear clouded his countenance, only adoration shined forth.

"Come, Luna-Beth, let us go hunt." He crouched and then shook into the brown wolf. They moved together like liquid, as if one wolf had become the extension of the other, and my heart quit in my chest as I watched them. They sailed out of the entrance with all eyes following their departure.

I settled my frame at the doorway once my heart resumed its normal staccato, and assessed those left behind. Beth's request to Eaen that he protect her pups was working well on the young wolf-man. He and Armand were kneeling down to play with their niece and nephew, which gave Ane and Elga a chance to get some rest away from the frolicking pups. Thinking of the little imps reminded me of the young wolves' earlier job of hunting for them. "Did the pups eat, Armand?"

"Yes. We killed a grouse, so Luna fed, too," he answered.

His response pleased me. Even in the turmoil of my discovery, Beth managed to feed her babes. We would not need to worry about their hungry bellies while their mother went questing after danger. I cast an appraising glance at Suma, who said nothing during the entire meeting. Unlike her brothers, she had not relaxed, and she sat rigid with her eyes burning into the floor.

I inhaled to steady myself. I was stuck in the den with the woman who controlled every cell in my body, and I could guess at the reasons why she seemed so upset. I was certainly one of them, and indirectly related to the other, as most likely this situation reminded the white wolf of Beth's vulnerability and, therefore, her abduction. I lowered my head and kept myself small, and did not speak as I kept watch at the mouth of our den.

A while later Suma's scent strengthened in my nose, and I looked up and across at her. She situated herself by the opposite side of the entrance. It was her place, really, more than mine, since she would be the one in charge of our group should anything happen. We would all have to await her directions. The idea of it rankled, but I swallowed.

Beth had been right. I was a strong, seasoned wolf in my prime and to play the role as the lowest subordinate was just that. Acting. I did so for Armand's sake, and for everyone else. Harmony within the pack meant far more to me than my ego.

But in a situation as serious as this? I could not be sure I would wait to receive instructions before I reacted. Fighting for me had become instinctual and ingrained. I had seen much, and had learned to predict the moves of most of my opponents. I had not been Meron's second because of our family connection.

Could I sit back and wait if I saw something before Suma or the others did? I crossed my arms over my chest and pulled my knees in tighter to steady myself. It did no good to think along those lines. Already I had enough to worry me with Suma's mossy scent tickling my nose.

I closed my eyes and tried to doze.

"Grane?" Suma's low voice trebled like a mountain stream.

I opened one eye.

"What is that you found today?" She seemed genuine in her curiosity, without the tension that I usually heard in her voice. I inhaled out of habit to steady myself, but was relieved to see that her tone did not instigate the trembling of my nerves.

I answered her in a quiet voice. "It is a bottle that the humans carry their water in." I stole a glance in her direction so I could read her reaction.

She pinched her brow in thought, and her white hair fell across her cheek. Great suffering, I thought her so beautiful. I inhaled again for good measure.

"Why do they carry water?"

I knew then she had no experience with humans. At all. How fortunate she had been. I smiled at her innocence. That she never had seemed a pleasant concept, and it soothed me.

I answered her with a peaceful heart.

"They are out of their natural world, and so need to bring their own supplies."

"Absurd," she giggled.

I grinned to the twinkle of her laughter. "Yes. Absurd. But they are dangerous anyway." I stole another glance at her just in time to catch her smile slipping from her pale face. Damn my serious nature for ruining her humor. Except that her brown eyes softened and deepened into brackish forest pools, where the layers of earth and water were revealed the longer one stared.

"They shot my mate." I bit my tongue too late, and heard Suma gasp. My heart tripped and thumped like a wounded bird in a cage. Why did I just say that? I clenched my fists, ripped my eyes from those sylvan puddles and turned my back to her.

Her fingers against the skin of my back convulsed my body and my core temperature flared.

"Grane?"

Oh, but her voice was the liquid buzz of bees. I shivered, and my muscles contorted. I pressed my fists to my ears to control myself but she hovered too close, and her scent beckoned.

Oh no. No. Please no, Suma.

I felt the removal of her body from mine. She had heard my thoughts. I rippled and my bones swam beneath my burning skin, turning me into wolf. I shot her a look of regret as she retreated to her spot next to the den entrance.

I stepped toward the door for my escape and halted. I could not flee, and darted glances around the room while my crackling heart still thumped hard in my chest. I could not tell if it fell or flew, and a whine escaped my throat.

Everyone looked. Including Armand.

That jolted me. I had to get a grip for his sake and not show my torment. I circled a few times around my paws and thumped my body into a tight ball on the floor. I remained right there, even when Armand rose and sat next to Suma to talk with her. He knew about humans, too, and could answer her questions. I closed my eyes against the sight of them together and listened instead to the hum of their voices. Eaen did not join in with them. Pretty telling. He was giving the couple their space.

I unfurled my body and went over to him and situated myself so that I could still watch the entrance, and create some much needed distance. My body cooled, and Eaen and I were able to pass the time with our talk of what humans did and could do.

Everyone eventually drifted off to sleep. Armand came back to Eaen to rest, and Suma positioned herself with the pups and Ane and Elga. I returned to my post by the door and listened to everyone sleeping.

I had been gazing into the darkness of the den when I heard Suma in my head.

Sleep.

I pressed my nose into the air to assess her. I could smell her arousal, her wakefulness.

I am fine, white wolf.

I heard her stir, and her scent strengthened as she approached.

No, Suma.

She halted. The white wolf read my thoughts without trouble. Had my intent been so strong? Her scent lingered and then ebbed as she returned to her spot with the pups and the old women. I heard no more from her for the rest of the night.

Chapter Ten

Beth and Alec came back by the following evening just as they had promised, and shifted from their wolf forms as soon as they entered the cave. We collected as a group around them, anxious for news.

"The humans are here," Alec said, his voice scratching across his throat, and I wondered how much of the raw scrape had come from his change, and how much from his worry. I cast my glance between him and his mate.

"They are at the mouth of the river, where it drains from the pond," Beth added, her lip curling back from her luminous teeth. "They will be staying awhile by the looks of things."

A growl escaped my throat and I clenched my fists. Humans here. I assessed the rest of our pack for their reactions. Eaen paled, and I remembered the scar on his lower leg. Armand looked as frightened as his friend, and so did Ane and Elga. Besides Beth, only Suma seemed to match my anger at the humans' trespass.

I turned back to Alec. "What do we do?" I asked him, hoping that he would let us slaughter them in their little tents. My spine tingled with anticipation.

"Judging by the amount of equipment they have, they plan to stay a while, as Beth has said. She thinks they are biologists searching for something." His face grew dark, and I knew what that something was.

Us.

"Then we give them what they came after and kill them," I snarled.

"No." Beth stood adamant, her jaw set. "If anything, we encourage them to leave. Unmolested." She looked directly at me with her blue-green eyes, and I dropped my gaze. I would not argue against her decision.

Suma grasped the implications of her sister's suggestion. "You mean to approach them?"

Luna nodded, and her mate bristled.

"No," he seethed, and Alec glared hard at her. "It is too dangerous. Do not forget that you no longer look like them."

Beth softened as she rested her hand on his elbow. "I have not forgotten, brown wolf." Her proud smile radiated across her face and she winked at him. Alec grinned back at her in spite of his temper, and his golden eyes shimmered when she planted a kiss on his chin.

I looked away as the muscles in my heart contracted. That had been the extent of their argument? Beth's cool voice floated on the air.

"We can't afford to be seen, and we certainly can't hide in the cave waiting for them to leave. We'll starve."

"I know, Luna-Beth," our pack leader agreed, then countered, "but I will not let you risk your life, and—" Alec stopped short and inhaled to steady his trembling muscles. His mate's face hardened, even as tears welled in her blue-green eyes. She finished his sentence for him.

"And you cannot come with me to protect me." She slid her body against his, and pulled him to her. He did not resist, but squeezed her body tight while he pushed his face into her neck.

His fear of humans would not let him get too close to them without his changing into wolf.

I swallowed and inhaled my own steadying breath. This was no time for my own revenge. My new pack needed me here, and my heart and its wishes belonged to them. "I will go with her," I offered, and did not lower my gaze from Alec's face.

Beth turned to look at me. "Absolutely not. No one risks it but me. I will not have any of you getting hurt."

"It is a good idea, Luna-Beth."

Beth pulled away from her wolf-man and shook her head.

Alec would not be deterred. "If you insist on approaching them, then Grane will go, too." He looked at me then. "You have been in the presence of humans?"

"Close enough," I admitted. "I can walk upright among them."

Alec did not drop his gaze from mine. "Then he goes, Beth, whether you like it or not."

I could see her tense and her eyes burn, but she inhaled and flexed her fists to control herself. "Fine," she whispered, and then went to her pups as if to soothe herself.

The rest of us waited to hear more of the plan, and to get a review of what the couple had seen during their foray.

"They are biologists, then."

Beth re-joined us with Terra in her arms. "Yes, I suspect so, which means they won't shoot us, at least. But their curiosity will be just as dangerous."

"True enough," I agreed. If they ever discovered what we were there would be no end to their probing until every one of our species was either dead or incarcerated. Approaching them would be an extreme risk.

"Is there another solution?" Suma asked, her brown eyes shining. I admired her care and thoroughness, and had to lower my gaze from her face as my heart thumped its appreciation.

"We cannot leave the area without endangering the pups," Alec stated.

"But there are four more of us now," she countered. "We would be better protected than when we journeyed here."

"Your brother is right, Suma." I softened my voice and shoulders so that she would not think I meant to be hostile toward her. I looked at Armand while I spoke to her. "We have lived exposed, white wolf, and the pups are always the first to suffer. They are safer at the den."

Armand did not deny my experience, and his voice heaved with the sadness of his memories when he addressed his prospective mate. "It is true, Suma. We not only lost them at the hands of the humans, but also to bear and cougar."

Suma dropped her head in sympathy. "I am sorry for your loss, wolves. Your advice is well taken." She raised her brown eyes to me and I glanced away before I betrayed myself.

"Thank you, Suma," I managed to gruff, and then shifted my attention back to Alec and Beth. I could not afford to speak any more with the white wolf. My skin had heated and I felt a single bead of sweat trickle down my spine.

"How do you plan to approach them? We are going to look out of place without clothing."

Beth's face fell, and Alec burst out with a quick, chortling laugh. "Luna-Beth, you have done it again. You have adapted so seamlessly you forgot this is not normal in the eyes of humans." His gold eyes shined with merriment as he ran a pointing finger along his bare body, his laughter echoing throughout the cave. Beth succumbed to it, entwining her husband's laughter with her own.

None of us were immune, and smiles erased the worry from our faces. The dire atmosphere in the den dissipated, and we settled down to a quiet night underground. We would discuss the situation the next day, once we had all had some time to think about it.

I took up my usual station next to the entrance while everyone else settled into theirs. Suma resumed her post at the mouth of the den, as well. I stole a look in Armand's direction, but he and Eaen were too busy talking about the humans and what we should do about them to notice the white wolf's position. I stayed where I was this time, since I had chosen the area first, and it was Suma who was moving in. If Armand had problems with that, he would have to take it up with Suma. I was not going to compromise our safety.

We both kept our human forms all night, but did not speak. Instead, we spelled one another so that we could both catch some sleep. Who knew how long we would have to keep vigil against the interference of humans. We would all be better off if we were well rested.

* * * *

The airy breath of Suma's sleeping body filled my ears and caressed my heart. The sun had not quite tipped over the lip of the earth and the songbirds had not yet awakened, so the landscape lay in pre-shadowed stillness. I had the last watch before the others would stir, so I let Suma sleep.

Alec tiptoed from the back of the cave and motioned for me to follow him outside. We exited in silence and eased our way toward the western tree line so we could catch the first rays of the rising sun as they spilled over the tree tops. The temperature during the night had dipped so a heavy dew saturated everything. The moisture plopped in sporadic droplets to the damp ground.

"I assume all was quiet, Grane," Alec spoke in a hushed tone, as if in reverence to the quietude of early morning. He looked as though he had not slept all night.

"Yes, and you should not have worried and gotten some rest," I admonished him as lightly as I could. "Suma and I both kept watch."

He turned his chagrined face toward me and offered up a tight smile. "I knew you would watch, Grane, but I could not help myself. I am worried about Beth approaching the humans. I hope the fact that we have no clothes prevents her," he admitted.

I nodded. Going to speak with the humans was the last thing I wanted to do, especially since they were biologists and tended to have curious natures. They would pick up on our physical anomalies as soon as we neared.

"I think we should stay put and remain human as much as we can." Alec searched my face for my reaction.

"It is a fine idea, and it would be wise to pair up, as well."

Alec winked. "You are reading my mind, gray wolf. You, Armand, or Beth should always be with one of us. As a precaution. Suma has never seen people in her life, and I am not certain how Eaen will react. Any idea about Ane and Elga?"

"No, but I get the feeling they would be just fine. They are very wise wolves. I am not so certain about Armand," I confessed. "He has seen many of his friends and family die because of humans."

"Good to know, friend, and I am sorry." Alec rested his warm hand on my shoulder and squeezed. He read my pain with ease, perhaps because he bore his own. Whatever happened with these humans, we would slog through the mess together. As a pack. But at the moment we had more pressing needs.

"We will have to hunt today, brown wolf."

He shook his head, but agreed with reluctance. We would starve if we did not hunt. "I know. And I think for now we should stick to small game so that only two of us has to go at a time. No big hunts until the humans leave the area."

It was a wise choice considering the evidence that one of our carcasses would leave. Which reminded me of our moose. "We should pull that into the water and sink it," I proposed.

"Not a bad idea," Alec agreed, then stood up to stretch. "I will go back in and tell the others what we are going to do so they will not worry when they wake to find us gone." He trotted up to the den and disappeared inside. He came back in no time.

"Suma knows," he informed me, and we walked side by side until the forest grew too dense to do so. We fell into a comfortable jog and were at the pond by late morning.

Not much of the moose carcass remained, and enough rain had fallen since we had been there that our tracks were obscured. Lucky for us, since the stench of the humans lingered around the bones. We both crouched and caught ourselves. Alec laughed in spite of the seriousness of the situation and wagged his long, tapered finger back and forth.

"Caught you," he teased.

Indeed he had. I had been ready to transform into my wolf self so that I could scope out the area. I smiled, and pointed an accusatory finger at him, too.

"Guilty," he readily admitted, and stood up on his two feet. "Let us try this again." This time he stuck his face into the air and snuffled while I scanned the area for tracks. Human evidence lingered everywhere. What a sloppy species. Their presence here eliminated the need to dispatch with the moose carcass, but now we had to assess where the biologists had been.

We worked our way north and west until a whir and click froze my heart. I stopped dead and ducked onto my hands and knees. I knew that sound, and I knew what I needed to look for. Alec dropped down behind me.

Camera.

He darted his widened eyes around and sniffed.

I held my hand about two feet off the ground to indicate the height we should scan, and we pored over every square inch of area at that level. I finally found the damned motion-sensory camera strapped to a small birch. My stomach knotted at the sight of it, and I ripped it off the thin trunk. Sure enough, it framed my image, frozen in time. I showed the device to Alec and raised my eyebrow.

"Trouble," was all that I said.

Alec's friendly face grew fierce and darkened. He understood the full implications. There were probably more of those things around. "Keep it," he growled. "To show the others."

We retraced our tracks back to the den with our ears and eyes sharpened even though we had left the scent of the humans back at the moose carcass. The presence of the camera sat like a rock in my gut. The humans knew for certain some large canines were in the area. We could only hope that they had not noticed our human footprints down by the pond.

When we arrived back at the den, we were greeted by anxious eyes and faces. Alec held the camera with my likeness out for the family to see. Everyone marveled but Beth and Armand. Luna scowled and flashed her eyes at her mate.

"I am going," she seethed. "I don't care if I have to demolish their camp to convince them to leave, either." She paced with Gor straddled on her hip. He whimpered, and she relinquished him to the waiting arms of Elga. "I don't care if I am naked. Let them stare."

Armand backed away as her fury filled her, and Alec moved in to settle her. The rest of us dispersed to the walls of the cave while she ranted. Alec moved lithely alongside of his mate, letting her pace through her anger. He absorbed her energy like the great mosses of the deep forests during the rainy season, and she quieted beside him. Luna reached for him and he pulled her back into his stomach while he gripped her nape with his teeth. She drew her knees up to her chest, and Alec lowered them to the floor where she straddled to accept him.

I held my breath, but could not look away. Luna's entire body hummed and she trembled as her muscles corded and rippled under her skin. My hair stood on end as she threw her head back to release her song. Her mate clamped his hand like a vice at the back of her neck, causing her to bite down on her howl before it escaped her throat. He convulsed, and as his arm withdrew from her nape he fell forward, pulling his mate's furring skin between her buckling shoulder blades with his sharp teeth.

He penetrated her, and Suma gasped beside me. The white wolf's breath pulled my attention away from the Luna and her mate like an irresistible magnet. She was trembling too, and her brown eyes darkened like the deep waters of the forest's oldest ponds.

An electric current shot through me like a bullet, and I crouched in readiness as my muscles did their own rippling. *Great suffering.* I could not control my shift. I scanned for Armand, but he still had his attention riveted on Luna; and then I felt Suma's eyes searing into my back, and I threw a tortured glance in her direction. She stared back, and my heart tore with the truth upon her face. She did not want Armand, and my membership within the pack went from strenuous to tenuous in the length of that one stare.

I would have to leave for Armand's sake just when I would be needed the most.

Chapter Eleven

The next morning, I hid along the eastern side of the tree line and waited for Alec to emerge. Beth came out instead, and she located me as if she had an extra sense from the rest of us. With several quick strides she stood in front of me. I dipped my head in greeting.

"Good morning, Luna."

"Good morning, Grane. You are out early." She smirked amiably, and wasted no time with stating her business. "I need you tonight."

I inhaled and let it out on a slow exhale. "Yes?" I did not reveal my plan to leave.

"Since I can't very well go strolling up to these humans and talk with them," she wrinkled her nose, "I'm going to sabotage their equipment. Are you in?"

I grinned wide at the prospect. Nothing would give me greater pleasure, and I stated as much.

"Good. You know what to look for, gray wolf?"

"Yes. I have made raids like this one before. Only we were searching for weapons, not surveillance equipment."

She quirked a questioning eyebrow.

"It was before we were finally driven from our territory in the west. Meron bid us to steal the ammunition that the humans used against us. It is very dangerous business, Beth," I warned her. "Wolves are killed doing it."

She placed her long hands over mine. "Well, let's hope that the biologists will ask questions first and shoot later." She smiled, then winked one of her blue-green eyes. She enchanted me and I would not have cared if I ran across an open hillside full of avid hunters, so long as she asked me to. Which only made my decision to leave that much harder. But I had to tell her, talk to her about it. She beat me to it in her eerie way.

"This little expedition should keep us away for a couple of days, Grane. We will worry about Suma and Armand when the humans are gone."

I gaped at her, and she poked my nose with her tapered finger to break my stare.

"How did you know?"

She chuckled. "Gray wolf, you hide things in your heart and head worse than I do. You are very obvious."

I groaned. "Does everyone else know, then?"

"No, just me. And Alec, of course. You know we will both do everything in our power to discourage you from leaving, right? I won't play fair, either." She said the last part in jest, but the truth still reverberated. My scarred arm bore the testament to that. She could be very cunning when she needed to be, and I knew that she would stop at nothing to make me stay. It was enough to make me re-think my decision. For one second.

"I have to leave," I argued. "For Armand."

"Well," she sighed, although I knew she did not do so with resignation, "we will worry about this later. In the meantime, we will do our work and perhaps we'll be pleased with how things play out under their own motion."

"Fair enough, Luna," I ceded. "We leave soon?"

She nodded. "As soon as I see my babes for kisses. I will tell Armand where we are going so that he doesn't worry."

"Thank you, sister."

She smiled, and the day seemed brighter because of it. Then she turned on her toes and headed back to the den to say her good-byes. We lit out as soon as she re-appeared.

* * * *

We traveled fast in spite of retaining our human shapes, but kept our ears alert for the whir and click of the motion-sensory cameras. By mid-morning of the second day my nose picked up the undeniable stink of humans. At least this group seemed conscientious about how and where they urinated. The entire perimeter of their campsite had been pissed on. They had marked their territory. Too bad they had not stayed in it.

Beth and I hovered in a dense thicket and chuckled amongst ourselves. At least they acknowledge they had moved into a new area, and claimed their campsite as inviolable. Which was more than could be said for hunters. Except that we would not honor the biologists' claim, regardless of how often they urinated around their tents. We would trespass into their campsite, just as they violated our territory. These forests harbored no room for us and the humans. We would drive them away like we did with the coyotes.

But, we needed to wait for complete darkness to descend before we stole our way toward the tents, so we took turns dozing. I watched the humans as Beth slept, and marveled at how these creatures managed to best our species.

Their bodies were pathetically soft and they had no fur to protect them from the elements. Nor did they have intrinsic weapons like fangs and claws. They could not run fast either, and had dull senses. Yet, for all their frailty, they were diabolically ingenious in their tool making. I detested them for that, too, since all they managed to do with it was further remove themselves from the natural world. To our detriment. My lip involuntarily curled up over my teeth.

Sorry.

I glanced over at Beth, the sender of the mental message, and her blue-green eyes were sad and moist with tears. I offered her a pursed smile and closed my own eyes. I had been showing my heart again, and she had picked right up on it. Yet, I was glad she did. Her observation checked me. No human was to be injured during our foray. Only equipment. Tonight there would be no avenging Misha's death, and I had already begun reconciling my heart to the fact there never would be. The time for that had passed, no matter how much I hated the humans for what they had done.

I resettled myself, and watched as the biologists went about their last activities for the day. The moon sat fairly high in the sky by the time the last flashlight in the tent had been extinguished. I cast an excited glance to my fellow thief, and she grinned. Her teeth glowed in the dim light of the stars and my heart warmed with the comforting sight of them. A wolf's smile.

She unfolded her lithe frame and stole toward the campsite. I swept away from her and approached from another angle.

Their myriad scents tickled my nose and I crinkled it to suppress a sneeze. The humans had so much, and everything had its own stink. The combination nearly overwhelmed my sense of smell. I sharpened my eyes and breathed through my mouth instead.

Here.

I straightened up and looked in Luna's direction. Her slender figure was silhouetted against the dark of the night sky and the shadow of the tree line. She must have found what we were after. I skulked toward her, and as soon as I got within touching distance, she placed two small, hefty objects in the palm of my hand for me to inspect.

Batteries.

She proceeded to show me how to look for them inside of the equipment. Her idea to steal their power source reigned diabolical in its own right.

Once she had a handful, she carried them to the pond and slipped her stolen cache beneath the black water, releasing it into the murky depths. The heavier cameras she sunk right along with the batteries. She crept silent and lethal in her mission, but as we closed in on the end of it, Luna's graceful frame stiffened, then froze altogether.

My own body reacted to hers, and my breath stuck in my lungs. Even in the dark I could see her eyes illuminate with an inner fury, and her skin quickened to roasting. She sent no mental thought or image. Only her rage blasted apparent, and my muscles quivered in response.

Luna.

Her upper lip curled away from her brilliant teeth. I followed the path of her murderous glare, and the hair on my nape sizzled upward.

Collars with antennas and tracking equipment.

The biologists meant to trap us, then follow our movements, and my heart tightened with dread and hatred. Luna's low growl turned my attention away from the gear and onto her, and the sight of her swept my mind clear of the evidence she had revealed.

The wolf-woman beside me shivered and trembled like a bonfire. I stepped away instinctively, as her wrath crept upward into a pique I had witnessed only once before, and my stomach clenched in preparation for her onslaught.

Luna meant to protect her pack.

The humans slept like newborn fawns in their tents, unaware of the murderous storm that swelled and gathered above them. The red wolf meant to decimate them all.

And I could not let her.

Sweat prickled across my shoulders as my spine vibrated. Confront Luna? Was I mad? Did I have a death wish? But Alec's image rose forefront in my mind, and I knew that I had to step into the path of this tornado for him. He entrusted me with the safety of his mate, with the safety of his entire family. I could not stand back and allow Luna her justified fury. I had to interfere before she shifted into wolf form.

If we left any sign of wolf right there in the camp? I shoved the thought of that terrible scenario aside and squared my shoulders. I needed to deal with this tempest in front of me now, before she could shred me with her resistance.

I stepped into her space and the brush of our skin quivered electrically across my nerve endings. My hair stood on end, but I did not retreat.

Luna.

She latched onto my face with her flashing blue-green eyes and the distance between us, great suffering, was not enough. My stomach clenched in retaliation. Gently, slowly, I coiled my fingers around her scorching wrist and shook my head from side to side.

Those stormy eyes narrowed and my spine thrummed.

I clenched my jaw and inhaled a huge lungful of air. Now was not the time to succumb to my own wolf. Luna must be settled. I pressed my fingers into the flesh of her arm and her upper lip curled back from her teeth in a menacing snarl.

I dared to breathe one word: "Please."

She tilted her chin and sheathed her lethal teeth. My heart bounced around in my ribcage like a red squirrel as her lids lowered across her mercurial eyes, then lifted. For self-preservation, I descended onto one knee and laid my throat bare, but did not release my grip. Luna's muscles twitched beneath my fingers.

With my own muscles screaming in protest, I forced my other arm to reach for the firm leg in front of me and cupped the back of Luna's thigh in my palm. Tentatively, I pulled her toward me until her burning body pressed into mine. My pulse throbbed against my skull, and I shut my eyes against the pressure as each heart beat recorded the seconds that elapsed, as if they were suspended in cobwebs.

The wolf-woman's body softened as she yielded to my embrace. She lowered herself, and I released my hold upon her forearm to reach across her back. Her skin felt cool against my own, and she rested her chin upon my shoulder. Her mouth sat mere inches from my ear.

Luna's breath stilled my body, and it seemed as if I were a deer in a forest of predators. Nothing within me moved or made sound.

She murmured my name.

Then pulled her face from my neck to rest her gaze upon me. A chagrined smile curled one corner of her lip, and then she winked.

Beth.

The wolf-woman in my arms nodded. There had been no urgency in my thought and yet she heard me. Was she still preternaturally intuitive? Could she see into my heart even now?

A wondrous, understanding grin spread across her face and warmed her friendly eyes.

She could, or at least definitely, had.

I dropped my face and blushed. I had given her eerie intuition no thought when I had confronted her, and my interference had left me exposed to her. Her body slid along mine and Beth stood on her feet above me.

I reached for her outstretched hand and she pulled me upright. Still, I did not look into her face, but averted my eyes. She did not release her hold on my hand but turned my palm up to the night sky. She placed one of the collars into my hand and rolled my fingers around its hard, thick edge. She turned and gathered up the rest of the surveillance equipment and tip-toed toward the pond. I followed on her heels and hurled the damned thing toward the center of the pond. I did not care if it splashed loud or not. The relief of seeing it dip below the surface was worth the risk of waking the humans.

I cast a quick glance toward the tents, but no sounds emanated from the thin skins, save the steady gush of slumbered breathing.

Our task was completed and no humans were harmed. As we retreated back toward the forest, I halted beside the tree where the biologists had strung their food supply out of the reach of hungry bandits. I placed my mouth over the taut rope and sawed at it with my molars. It frayed easily, and the bundle dropped into my outstretched arms.

We wove our path deeper into the protection of the trees, where we opened the food pack and strewed the contents across the forest floor. As I rose to my feet after scattering the last of the humans' food supply I stiffened and thrust my nose into the air.

Suma.

She emerged from behind a heavily boughed spruce and went right to Luna, where she smothered her sister with kisses and hugged her. Beth smiled and kissed her sister, too, while I stood there seething with my fists clenched.

What was she doing here? My heart flittered around in my ribcage like a distressed fledgling. I still had not recovered from my inadvertent exposure to Luna, and now I had to greet the white wolf no matter how I felt. I dropped my shoulders and crouched.

"Hello, Suma," I gruffed past the knot that tightened across my chest to cinch my throat.

She reached her hand down to touch my shoulder, and my stomach twisted. Why did she have to show up?

"Hello, Grane," she acknowledged my greeting with her bubbling voice. I gripped a straggly alder in my hands and twisted it as the truth of why she had come wrapped its cold fingers around my beating heart.

She did not trust me out alone with Beth. A frustrated snarl rose in my throat and I swallowed to quell it. When would that wolf understand that I meant her family no harm? And did she think I could hurt Beth? Suma needed to see her sister in action. The red wolf was no fawn who required protection. My body and mind still burned from the shock of being in such intimate contact with Luna.

All Suma succeeded in doing by following us here was endanger herself, and disrespect her pack leader's wishes. I wondered how severe her lashing would be and I cringed for her, even though I thanked the stars in the sky it was not Meron who would deliver the blow.

Beth whispered to her sister. "Suma, you should not have come. Alec will be furious."

The white wolf-woman hung her head for a brief moment, but then raised her face to her sister. "I know, but I was going crazy waiting for your return." I felt her gaze rest on my lowered head as I concentrated on my twisted alder.

"We should get back," I suggested through my clenched teeth. The sooner Beth, and now Suma, returned to the den the better for all of their loved ones. I stood up and snuffled to find our trail and blazed our way homeward. Our scents were now blended with the mossy spice of Suma's. It would be a long, tortuous hike toward home.

Chapter Twelve

We were back at our own den by the following night, but I did not go near. Instead, I volunteered to backtrack and trail the humans to make sure they left. Beth did not answer right away, but she squeezed her warm hand over mine. Every fiber of my being was transported to our foray into the biologists' campsite. My stomach flipped.

Luna's blue-green eyes swirled, and she offered me a consoling smile before releasing my hand. "Be careful, gray wolf, and hurry back with the news."

I nodded. She understood my heart better than I did, and knew I would not abandon my new family, in spite of my earlier determination. I muttered quick good-byes to her and Suma as I tucked my burning hand against my stomach. Then I dashed back through the woods in the direction we had just come.

The increasing distance eased my muscles and I walked through the trees until my legs tired. My nerves had not settled since the white wolf had joined us, and they savored the relief to finally let go. I walked a little farther, and then snuggled myself in at the base of a birch tree for some rest.

I dozed fitfully as visions of Suma bubbled into my subconscious and her smile spread across my sleeping brain. I curled my body into a tight ball and fought against her image until dawn, when I finally succumbed to my exhaustion and slept.

* * * *

By the time I woke, the air around me had grown unseasonably warm in spite of being deep in the woods. I had slept for longer than I wanted. I unfurled my limbs, stretched and yawned, and then tuned my ears to the sounds around me. All carried on in their natural rhythms, so I rested the back of my head against the birch trunk. I was in no particular hurry. The longer I could drag this mission out the better, as it would give Armand time to win over Suma's heart. Seeing the hunger revealed in Suma's eyes strengthened my resolve to stay away from her as best I could.

I inhaled to erase the image of it, situated my two feet under me, and jutted my nose around to pick up our trail. Thankfully the humans had no sense of smell, as this would be the third pass on this trail, and our wolf scent accumulated.

At least I whiffed nothing human until I reached the area where we had spread out their food supply. I crouched low behind the spruce that Suma had used to hide behind and assessed the area. Her spice lingered upon the boughs.

I could not escape her. The only way to do so had me concentrating like a fiend on the task before me. I stepped out from the spruce to check out the area.

The biologists had been there to recoup some of their provisions, which could not have amounted to much. I grinned as I pictured them picking over the few remains strewn around. The raccoons had done their rascally damage just as I had anticipated.

I crept along toward the campsite. All the while I kept my senses honed for anything that might be tracking me, or recording my movements. I picked up nothing, and hope swelled in my chest, then rested comfortably in my heart. The humans were gone, and their campsite spread out before me as an empty expanse of trampled grass.

I skirted the area to pick up their departure trail, and found it easily enough, and followed it to another big pond. They were gathered at the southeastern bank, and it looked as though they were awaiting something. They were slumped in various poses upon their colorful bags. The drone of a plane behind me slaked my curiosity, and I pulled myself deeper into the protection of the tree cover as I watched the giant, gray bird descend and skid across the water.

Grane

The biologists loaded their gear and the plane skipped across the expanse of water, then heaved itself into the air. The menace had gone. I would have excellent news to report, but I was not so naïve to think that they would not return. Our sabotage only delayed the biologists. I shivered my spine into flames and coalesced into my wolf form. I had missed it, and I raced through the forest, yet made sure I took the long way toward home. My anxiety about Suma and Armand had not been forgotten, but I wanted to share the news with my family.

Chapter Thirteen

The following days were scorchers and the pack languished along the tree line or spent hours in the cool atmosphere of the den. Despite the news the humans had left the area, the heat prevented us from donning our fur selves, and we stretched out and sweated in our human skin.

Like the wise wolf-women they were, Ane and Elga spent most of their time under the earth of the den, as did Beth and the pups. Alec eventually left us to retreat to his wife. The rest of us lazed beneath the shading canopy of the trees.

Suma did not sit with Armand, or Eaen for that matter, but she positioned herself a ways behind me. If I had to endure her proximity, I hoped it offered her a better view of Armand.

"Grane," said Eaen, breaking the heat-stifled silence, "is it true that there are deer out west who have rounded horns and climb cliffs?"

I laughed at his description, but shook my head. "No, little brother."

He dropped his eyes, disappointed.

"They are not deer, but sheep. If you tasted one, you would know the difference."

Eaen's face brightened. "So, it is true."

Armand's countenance mirrored that of his comrade, and a shadow crossed my heart. They were still pups who still hungered for adventure, for excitement. I turned to look at Suma, and she arched one eyebrow above a liquid brown eye. I looked away, and focused on the two young wolves in front of me.

I changed the subject. "Eaen, Armand. I know I am below you, but if I could still show you some fighting tricks?"

Eaen jumped at the chance. Armand stood up and went to sit next to Suma, who promptly moved away from him.

I kept my attention focused on Eaen, who squared himself in preparation for our mock battle. Armand soon joined us since he had been rebuffed again, and I noticed Suma did not retreat into the den, but sat at its entrance to watch us.

I demonstrated a few moves on the young wolf-men, and then let them practice on me. They got very good as they practiced, and I no longer needed to pretend their techniques were working, especially when they ganged up on me. I made use of my position as the subordinate and pleaded for their mercy. They had no choice but to ease off. The evening passed in laughter and roughness, and when we tired we rested on the ground in the setting sun.

"I could use a swim. Would anyone like to join me?" Suma offered as she strolled over to us. Eaen jumped at his sister's idea, but Armand hesitated. I stood up and accepted too, which forced Armand to do the same, unless he wanted to be left out.

We picked our way toward the stream. Three of us were sweaty and dirty from our wrestling and bounded right in, but Suma waded along the shore, then changed her mind. She headed back toward the den and left us in the water.

"What is up with her?" Eaen asked in general.

I kept my mouth shut and made myself comfortable on the bank.

"I do not think your sister is interested in my advances," Armand admitted with petulance.

I closed my eyes and listened to them rationalize a wolf-woman's motives, until they ultimately dismissed her and carried on with their own fun. I was not amused. Armand was not ready for a mate, and Suma had been right to rebuke his advances. I did not look forward to the outcome of this. I got up and asked for my leave, and barely received their attention as they practiced their new fighting skills in the water. I rose and strolled back to the den.

Suma, of course, was waiting there. I would get no reprieve from her. I sighed and lowered myself to the ground beside her.

"You did not stay long at the stream," she observed.

"No, Suma, I was refreshed." I did not lie, but I did not divulge the real reason for my leaving.

"He is just a pup," she said, her tone soft with a sister's affection.

I turned to look at her, and then lay back with my face to the sky. "Yes, I know. But his intentions are good."

She did not comment on that, and we sat in silence as the sun dropped below the tree line.

"Suma, you must give me my leave. It is getting late, and Armand will return soon." I offered no more of an explanation, but she nodded her understanding. I did not want to be reprimanded for invading my little brother's space again. I got up and went into the den. It had been a long day even if we had lazed around for most of it. I closed my eyes and tried to sleep, but the scent of moss kept tickling my nostrils. She had remained sitting outside of the entrance. I hoped she waited for Armand, but I knew better. Suma had an old soul, in spite of her youth, and I was fairly certain she would never accept Armand.

* * * *

Although the threat the humans would return hovered, the early autumn days stretched out in an endless fashion. I figured out how to be less available to Armand and Suma, and spent many hours in the woods with Gor and Terra teaching them how to hunt and how to fight. They were quick learners, but they were often distracted by butterflies, or snakes, or skunks, or any other creature that tickled and tempted their attention. I laughed endlessly on those days, and my heart mended and grew strong in my love for them, while I grew accustomed to and enjoyed my status as the lowest pack member. The twins grew fast as wolf pups, but I still had to watch close for when they shifted into their human shapes. They could crawl around, but not anywhere near as well as they could when they had their four paws beneath them.

Terra squawked whenever she was prevented from doing what she wanted because of her human shape, but Gor often laughed and his round belly jiggled with his merriment. Terra always succumbed to his humor, and many times I left the two of them to figure their bodies out. They almost always triumphed, and I smothered them with kisses and bubbles on their bellies when they did. Their delighted screams filled me till I dripped my happiness onto those around me.

"The pups are very fond of their Uncle Grane," Beth commented one rainy morning when we were left behind at the den with the babes.

I smiled at her and shrugged. "Perhaps," I allowed.

The red haired mother laughed. "Perhaps." She lifted Terra into the air and blew kisses upon her creased neck. The babe squealed her delight, and Gor begged for his turn. We both broke out into hearty laughter.

Suma came in during the middle of it, smiling amidst our mirth. I settled down and lowered my head.

"What has the two of you so happy?" she asked as she hefted Gor to her hip. I raised my eyes because her sister had not answered her. And learned why. Suma was looking at me, not her sister.

"The pups, Suma." I answered without embellishment. I had learned to keep my answers short and to the point, and then ask for my leave. It was the only way I could cope with my affections for Suma, and it seemed to work. I could now keep my human shape when I was around the white haired wolf-woman, and my heart did not cartwheel all around my ribcage.

"This little pup right here?" she gurgled at Gor and twirled him. Her beautiful white hair swirled as she spun and her muscles flexed with the weight of the babe lifted in her pale arms.

My stomach flipped and my groin made a singular throb at the sight of her. "Suma, Beth, may I go now?"

"Go? You always leave whenever I come around, Grane. Please stay."

Suma had not released me. I turned an imploring look to Beth, but she shrugged as if she were unable to help. I hunkered back down onto the floor of the den and waited to see what Suma was up to. At least we were not alone, so Armand could not get upset if he saw us together, even though Suma still had not returned him any affection. I would just have to deal with our lengthened visit.

"Are the pups making progress with their hunting, Uncle?" A flush of pink rose in her pale cheeks.

"Yes, Suma. They do well." A grin tugged at the corner of my lips in spite of my best efforts to remain neutral.

She nodded, wanting to hear more, and I fell for her trap like a near-sighted bear.

"Except when they spy something more interesting than what they had been trailing. Just the other day, Terra roamed completely off track and found a mud slide into the stream instead. Gor and I could not resist the fun either, and we missed our hunt." I grinned with the memory of it, and Suma's laughter thrilled my heart.

"I suppose Terra is always our troublemaker?" she cooed at the babe in her sister's arms.

"Not always," I volunteered like an ass. I stood up and sauntered over to Suma while I gushed about Gor. "He sometimes—" I stopped cold as I caught my hand reaching for Suma's elbow.

"I am sorry," I breathed and folded onto the floor. "Suma, I forgot," I whispered. Her scent drifted through my body as she bent down to lift my chin in her hand. I gazed into those doe eyes of hers, which were only inches from my mouth. It burned, as did the rest of me.

"Grane, it is fine," she smiled and her brown eyes were the stones from the stream.

"Suma, you must not," I croaked, and pulled my face from her grasp as I turned my back to her. So much for neutral.

"I must not what? Speak to you? Visit with you?" Her voice grew edgy.

"Yes, all of those things. Armand—"

Suma cut me off, her temper strident. "Armand is a wolf-pup and I will never mate with him. Nor will I mate with anyone else!"

"You are saying this now?" I bellowed, and stepped right back up to her. She squared herself to me and the heat from our bodies collided as my skin scorched to life. I glared straight at the face that glared at me, and my heart pounded in my throat as my stomach flipped inside out. I grabbed her head with both of my hands, pressed my mouth onto hers, and she responded with gripping force. Sparks shot through me, and I convulsed as I released her.

"May I go?" I barked, and did not wait for her permission. I fled away from the woman who drove me mad, who buckled me with her scent. Who goaded me on purpose! And I had just kissed her. Sweet suffering, I was in for it now. I could taste her on my tongue.

I ran and did not stop until my breath left me. I lay my body onto the wet ground to cool myself and recover. I shut my eyes against the world, and the image of the white wolf floated into my head. I could recall her flavor. She tasted as she smelled, and my groin pulsed with my need for her. I thought then of Armand, who did not know yet that she had no intentions of mating with him or any other wolf.

I sat up, then heaved myself to my feet. He would need to know, or perhaps he had found out already. I turned back toward home, and contorted effortlessly into wolf. I would make better time, and I grew anxious to be near Armand.

I arrived back by twilight. Everyone had already gone inside, except for Beth and Alec, who cradled his mate in his arms as I had seen him do many times before. They were very beautiful together.

"Welcome back, Grane," she whispered when I neared.

I crouched and adopted my human form so that I could address them, and kept my body lowered when I spoke. "I am glad to be back," I admitted, and went right into my apology for my earlier outburst with their sister.

"There is no need for you to apologize for that, gray wolf, she had it coming."

They were both chuckling, and I raised my eyes to them. "What is so funny?"

"Grane, you are so serious sometimes," my sister admonished. "*You* are funny. And so is Suma."

Alec agreed with his wife. "It is true, friend. You were both so opposed to one another you attracted yourselves like bears to honey." The couple burst out with more peals of laughter, but then shushed themselves. Yet, they giggled harder the more they grasped for restraint.

I smiled in spite of being the reason for their laughter. "That is very funny," I whispered. "But you have it all wrong. I am sure after today Suma will have nothing to do with me."

That sent them into convulsions.

I asked for my leave, but they did not grant it, and my baffled look seemed to sober them.

"Grane, we are sorry. The situation, for you and Suma, is not very funny." Beth did not hide her smile very well, and she nearly busted with her stifled giggles.

"Yes," said Alec, but then they broke into guffaws. I sat down and waited while I enjoyed their good humor. Obviously, they were not doing it to harm me or their sister, so I stared up into the sky and bided my time. It was a beautiful night anyway and I did not mind sitting out beneath the blinking stars.

"Sorry about that, brother," Beth tried again. This time she seemed to have herself tightly wrapped, and so did her mate.

"The reason we did not release you is we need to talk with you. Let us move away a bit so we can have some privacy." The two of them rose and Alec gently lowered his wife to the ground. Suma emerged behind them.

I scurried backwards at the sight of the pale woman who had come from the den. "Suma," I breathed, and then chastised myself for letting her catch me off guard so that I reacted like a startled fox. I nodded a polite greeting and then lowered myself for her onslaught. She came toward me, then stopped a couple of feet away.

"Grane," she whispered with her bird song voice. "There is no need for you to bow. Please rise." She held out her exquisite hand but I could not take it. I shook my head, but she did not pull her hand away.

Alec came to my rescue. "Suma, leave him be for now and come sit by us."

She smiled down on me before she stepped toward her siblings.

I straightened up and walked over to the trio. "What does Suma mean *there is no need for me to bow*?" I searched their faces and found the worry I knew would be there. "Suma, you have told Armand."

She nodded her white head, but did not lower her eyes.

"How did he take it?" My heart hammered in my chest. "He is all right?" I looked right at Beth, who would know better than anyone. Myself included.

She sat upright, and held none of the merriment of moments before. "He is fine, Grane. He and Eaen have gone out for the night to talk things over."

I could not keep myself from looking into the trees and casting my face about for their scent, even though I knew Eaen would be the one to

100

help Armand through his first refusal. They had become even closer since my removal as my little brother's rival.

I looked helplessly at Suma. "You were gentle with him?"

"I think of him as my little brother. I would not purposefully harm him."

I kept my eyes on hers. She did not lower her gaze, but added "I am sorry, Grane. I know you wanted it very much."

I hung my head then as my mind went spinning into the future. If Armand did not mate with Suma, would he be content to stay? I did not know, and my chest constricted with the possibility of his leaving.

I raised my frightened look to Beth and voiced my concern. She rose to swallow me in her embrace. Her scent filled me and her heart beat strong and hard in my ear. She knew my fear, and I felt her voice as it resonated through her chest and out of her throat. Her words were my undoing.

"He and Eaen both wish to leave," she sighed.

I pulled myself away. "I cannot." I shook my head and shot a beseeching look at the sorceress in front me. Who knew. Who had experienced it. "We cannot let them go. There are wolf-men out there who are like Meron. They have no honor. They will kill our boys for the sake of doing it."

Alec's voice reigned calm as the surface of a pond at dawn. "Grane, they wish to go, and if we have the chance to re-build the population of our species we should take it. You yourself noticed how our numbers had dwindled the farther east you came."

His words slid into my heart. I dropped to my knees and curled my body in tight before I exploded. Here had come my penance for all that I had done with Meron. I was expected to lay my beloved boys out for slaughter. This I could not stand, and I coiled my body tighter and snarled against the fire raging inside of me. This was the one time when I could not run or lash out. I had to face this horror for the sake of Armand. For Eaen. This family meant too much to release them to the horrors of the outside world.

"No," I growled, protesting. "You are all too precious." I pushed the words past my clenched jaw. My back muscles contorted and pulled my bones. Luna dropped down beside me and gripped my wrists in her ice cold hands. I flinched and raised my face in surprise.

"Gray wolf," she whispered like the breeze through tall grass. "See." She latched her blue-green eyes onto mine and my body froze in her grasp. There was no heat in my spine, no struggle against contortion. I settled and crystallized. And saw. The earth in its cycles. Living things in death. Living things in birth. I saw. And my arms thrummed beneath her steady hands and the vibration coursed into my shoulders, across my chest and into my groin and legs. I saw the life beyond the death and then the inevitable death before the life. Everything cyclical.

Luna.

She released me and backed away. I curled into the fetal position, my spirit exposed like a seed without its husk. The scent of moss filled my head and I felt Suma's warm arms surround my body. She pulled me close and sang her song. I had never heard this melody from her before and I lay spellbound. I did not shake or tremble or burn, and I pushed myself in tight to her so I could feel her singing. She did not stop until my eyes beheld the starlit sky and the moon teetered at its apex.

"Suma," I whispered, and sat up to look at her. Beth and Alec had left us alone. "I hoped you would love him and then he would stay."

She lowered her face. "I am sorry for it, gray wolf."

I sighed and stared back up at the night sky. "I once thought the stars were like the fishes in the lakes. We could see them but could not touch them. I think now a heart is like a fish in the lake, too, and will not be touched if it does not wish it."

I unfolded myself from Suma's embrace and smiled down at the wolf-woman at my feet. "Thank you for your song, Suma. I will keep it in my heart always." I held my hand out for her and she clasped it so I could pull her to her feet. "Good night, white wolf," I pressed my lips to her pale cheek and pulled away before I forgot the path she had chosen. I would not dishonor it.

I turned my back on her and strolled into the forest. I had no desire to sleep underground this night.

* * * *

I crouched in the forest for the remainder of the night, absorbing the sounds around me. My ears rotated and snagged every sound, but I did not hunt because my stomach did not cramp with hunger. My thoughts instead were turned to my little brothers, who were planning to do what wolves their ages did. They left in search of mates and joined other packs or claimed their own territories. The mating ritual was an accepted necessity for the well-being of all wolf-people. Or the young wolves simply strayed in their quest for freedom and adventure.

But leaving one's family was never as fraught with danger as when Meron's pack was around. The wolf-people to the west had learned that at the cost of their lives. We had brought our pestilence east, and now Armand no longer had that one benefit of belonging to such a gruesome pack. They would kill him and Eaen on sight if they did not yield in submission.

I shuddered as the image rose in my mind. I could not imagine either one doing so. Armand had lived that life and was glad to be rid of it. Eaen had been raised under the privilege of pack leader status. Neither wolf-man would submit.

But what could I do? I could leave with them, which meant strapping Alec with the burden of Ane and Elga to care for, plus his sister, wife, and pups. I would not do that. The other option would be to teach the wolves how to fight properly before they left on their journey. I could reconcile myself to that. I hoped they would accept my offer, and spend the coming winter learning before they struck out on their own. I would present the idea when I returned in the morning.

The buzz of an airplane overhead disintegrated my musings and raked the skin from my heart.

Humans.

I watched it cross low over the trees and did not doubt where the giant bird would land. I shivered my spine to hide my fur. I would progress on two feet in case they spotted me, and set my determined course west. I picked up a slow run and settled into the mile consuming pace of a steady lope. I arrived by late afternoon, well after the plane landed, and aimed for the eastern edge of the large pond where the biologists first departed.

I kept myself close enough to the shore to grab their scent, but far enough back so I would not be seen. I still did not know if the original group returned or not, and I was not taking chances.

S. C. Dane

I crouched and cast my face side to side to better catch their scent. It flitted in wisps, but I recognized it. The team had returned with more gear, but were, at least, fewer in number. There were only three of them.

Still, the hair on my nape prickled to attention and my stomach tightened. They would be on high alert this time. I slunk deeper into the forest and cut toward the south and west. At least from that direction I had the wind advantage, even though their disgusting smell hovered and rankled. They were easy to detect.

I could kill every one of them, but I knew I would not. My experiences with humans taught me one thing, at least. Killing one brought the curse of many. Killing many brought the dogs, and I would not jeopardize the pack like Meron had done.

The truth of it lifted my heart, and I knew in that instant I had truly grown beyond avenging Misha. My muscles tremored, and I hid myself in a thicket and put my hands over my face to silence my cries. I hiccupped once, but the sobs did not come as I had expected them to. Tears dropped down my face, but my heart beat steady.

Luna and her pack had worked on my ailing heart without my even knowing it. Those days of laughter and fellowship had incrementally resealed my shredded faith. I trembled with the power of my revelation and clamped my teeth on my tongue before my exultant howl escaped my throat. I leapt to my feet, but could not decide whether to remain, or rush back and rejoice with my loved ones.

I opted for rushing back. My relief crackled my skin and if I did not move to expel the heat rising in my spine I would put us all at risk by turning into wolf. I turned my smiling face south and raced back to the den.

Chapter Fourteen

I ran all through the night and arrived just as the sun began to peak over the tree tops. No one stirred or sat outside. I dashed through the den entrance and tripped over Suma, who had obviously crouched to attack whatever it was running toward the den. Her fangs were embedded in my arm before we stopped tumbling.

"Suma!"

She released, and yelped as she thrust her furred frame backward, then lowered her belly to the floor of the cave and slid into her human form. Our cries awakened the pack and everyone gathered within seconds. My chest heaved from my running and my near miss. It could have easily been my throat in the white wolf's crushing jaws.

"Grane! I am so sorry. I did not know what to think. I could not smell you, I thought you might be the humans, I thought you were a threat." She rambled in her regret and fell onto her knees.

The sight of her in such a shameful state wrenched my thumping heart. "It is all right, Suma. No harm is done." I steadied my breaths and crouched down to hold her face in my hands. Tears wetted her cheeks and I brushed a crystal droplet with my thumb. Her anxiety caused me more hurt than her bite, which proved how deep in trouble I was when it came to Suma. I swallowed, winked, and then backed away to take in the faces of the rest of the pack. They had all witnessed my compassionate gesture, and I lowered my head, abashed by my untoward display.

"I am sorry. I overstepped." My excuse fell lame. Without thinking,

I had revealed my tenderness toward Suma. Armand said nothing and neither did any of the others, but Beth took me in her arms and put her lips to my ear.

"You have been bitten, Grane. You are bleeding a lot," she observed in a hushed whisper so that Suma could not hear.

"It is a scrape, Luna, nothing more," I protested.

"No, it is not. Come outside." She would hear no argument and gripped my hand to pull me away from the others. I could not resist her. I felt Suma run up behind me, and I knew Beth could feel my hand heating as she closed in on us. Luna turned to face her sister and whatever she had meant to say, she did not. She clamped down on her tongue and her blue-green eyes softened with sympathy.

I imagined Suma's stricken face silenced her. The red-haired woman's next words rattled my nerves and transported me to early summer. She invited her sister to help with my healing.

I planted my feet as my stomach rolled. "Oh. No. Er." I stammered like a coward. I did not want a repeat of my last healing, and I told her so without shame. I did not care if I was not being very brave, and Luna's laughter tickled the fine hairs on my skin.

She smiled up at me, and her blue-green eyes were the delightful lakes of summer. "Grane, it will not be as last time. Trust me?"

I started to shake my head, but she raised her eyebrow and then lifted her chin to remind me that Suma stood at my back. In my dread toward the healing that would come, I had forgotten about her spicy scent in my nose. I closed my eyes and inhaled before speaking. If I resisted the healing I would only distress Suma further. I would have to undergo Luna's scrutiny for the white wolf's sake.

"I trust you, sister." Surprisingly, my breath came easier just saying those words, encouraging me. Enough to add in jest, "But do not harm me, Sorceress."

Suma gasped behind me, but Luna threw her head back and laughed from her belly. She lit back quick with her retort. "Do not harm me, gray wolf."

We chuckled in our shared memory of my last healing, and my heart threatened to burst from my chest. My healer stopped our progress toward the tree line and eyed me.

Grane

"You are full, brother," she remarked.

I nodded and grinned.

"Come then. I am anxious to see. And to feel." With that, she tugged on my hand again, and I followed like one of the pups. I felt Suma's heat on my bare back, and the blood run down my arm. My wound was worse than I had thought, but for Suma's sake I did not look at it, making as little of it as possible. It was bad enough to warrant Luna's interference, I did not need to see it.

We knelt together, and then Beth looked beyond my shoulder, toward the den. I turned my head to see what had captured her attention. The rest of the pack hovered close.

"Would you mind, Grane?"

I knew what she asked, and shook my head. "Not at all. I welcome them, Luna." My body quivered with excitement, with my love for every one of them.

She waved them over and they circled us. Suma wrapped her long fingers around my arm and then reached for Eaen. He in turn put his hand over Armand's, and then each member of the pack entwined with his sister or her brother, and we fused into a continuous entity when Alec took Beth's hand in his.

Elga and Ane hummed, and Suma threaded her voice into the harmony of theirs. I twisted my head around to catch the faces of the men folk, yet Luna bolted me into immobility with her swirling blue-green eyes. We were every one of us attached and were going on this adventure as a unit.

The unified energy swarmed around my bones, and I panted from the heat of it. The humming grew and rasped discordant and beautiful as the deep voices of the males' and the softer pitches of the women's songs plaited into a supple rope. The underdeveloped yowls of the pups were sunny strands.

My eyelids dropped and I felt my body fall back, but many hands received it, and the song of my pack saturated my brain, my brawn, my being. My arm ignited while my heart throbbed a steady rhythm.

The singing ebbed as my eyes fluttered open, and I gazed into the beatific eyes of my Luna. She lowered her lids and then raised them as her grin spread across her shining face. Armand's handsome voice

107

ruffled my ear.

"Brother," He was breathless.

I was speechless.

I turned my gaze to every set of eyes that surrounded me, and saw myself reflected in the deep pools of them all. I was overcome and my body too small for my spirit, so I threw my head to the morning sky and bayed. The deafening chorus of my family's howls rose in raucous joy around me.

* * * *

Luna had been right. That healing far outstripped my first healing by her hands. I stared up into the canopy above me, mesmerized by the bubbles of blue sky that popped forth as the dried leaves swayed and scratched in the warm breeze.

Armand settled himself in beside me but did not speak for some time. After a while, he cleared his throat, and I turned my face to look at him. He offered me a shy grin, his shoulders were soft and a little bent. His countenance revealed what he wanted.

"My little brother, you tried." I smiled for him and opened my arms. He scooted closer so that I could embrace him, then turned his head to expose his throat.

"No, Armand," I murmured. "There is no need. We both tried and failed. It is not time, yet, that is all."

His expression remained pained despite my reassurances. I lifted his chin with my knuckles and held his eyes with mine.

"Little brother, if you had not tried you would not be wolf. It was the right thing to do. I hold no ill will." I let my smile stretch across my face. "I am honored that it was me you challenged."

"Grane, I thought perhaps I was ready. But I am still enjoying my time with Eaen," he confessed, but a smile lighted his handsome face.

"As you should. You are young, and too long you were denied a true friend. Enjoy this time while it lasts. All too soon you might find that Eaen has become your rival." I softened my warning, but it still needed saying.

"I hope it never comes to that," he admitted.

"Me, too, little brother." I stared back up into the branches and wondered aloud of the others.

"They are waiting for you. Luna told them you had something to say," Armand answered.

I sat up and swiped my hands along my thighs. I had yet to report what I had seen at the pond. Armand helped me to stand, but I did not feel nauseous like I had with the first healing. Nor did my entire body feel as if it rebelled against itself. My arm felt a bit stiff, and very warm, but that was all. I glanced at my wound, which was already covered in shiny, pink flesh.

"Some healing, eh Armand?"

His face beamed with the memory of it, and it pleased me to no end. My little brother. Happy still. Luna had healed more than my arm, and I draped that arm around him and walked toward the den where the others were waiting.

I sat down among them, but I could not help smiling. Grandly. Idiotically, really. Every face reflected mine, so I felt no shame. When I glanced at Alec he shrugged and winked. The Women, indeed.

Beth spoke first. "Well, Grane, you have something to tell us?"

"Yes, Luna." I had planned to thank every wolf in my pack, but I could see there was no need. We had transcended words, and they were unnecessary. I went right to the news about the airplane.

"Yes, we all heard it or saw it," Alec confirmed. "What did you see?"

"The biologists are back." I addressed my pack leader, but glanced around to read the reactions of the faces that surrounded me. Alec's snarl pulled my attention back to him.

"Damn their rotten hides. They should leave well enough alone."

I knew by the faces around me, too, that we had erred.

We had howled. Very loudly.

And most likely, because of it, we were in a lot of trouble.

I hung my head. If it had not been for my hasty entrance into the den our celebration would never have happened. "I am sorry." I made eye contact with every member of my pack, especially Suma, my smile disintegrating with the revelation.

"We all knew, Grane. The responsibility belongs to the pack. To me." Alec stepped up to keep his family united, humbling me with his sincere artfulness for pack politics. "Our bonding was too valuable to set aside because of human interference. We will figure out what to do about the biologists." His voice rang clear and his almond eyes shimmered. I hoped our healing had had some effect on him, too. We would need his courage to face our enemy if it came to that. Beth rested her hand on his thigh as if she shared my thoughts. I took heart she knew more about it than I did.

"It is time for us to do our own spying, husband," she declared.

Alec narrowed his eyes at his mate, but waited for her to speak further.

"If we can find out our voices were not heard, there is no reason why we can't repeat our first raid." She raised her eyebrow for Alec only and he pursed his lips.

I voiced the question that was most likely on all of our minds. "How do we find out what they know?"

Suma answered for our pack leaders. "We go ask them."

Beth nodded and Alec tensed.

"I will go," I volunteered, yet Alec did not relax as I had hoped.

"Wait. No one goes," he dictated. "We spy first, as Beth suggested."

"But..." Luna looked into the face of her mate and bit her tongue. He trembled and she softened to soothe him. He inhaled automatically when she coaxed him to breathe.

"I will go first," I volunteered again.

Alec nodded his acceptance of my proposal. "You would be my first choice, brother. You have had the most experience of all of us, and I trust your stealth. I have watched you hunt," he added. He tacked on the last part to ease me. He knew I would be thinking of my days with Meron. I lowered my lids in silent thanks.

"I will go right away. The sooner I can get to the humans' camp, the more likely they will be talking about our howl."

Everyone nodded, and Suma squared her shoulders.

I cut her off before she uttered a single word. "I go alone." I showed no remorse for my tone. We were in danger, and I would not risk the life of a single pack member.

Alec was quick to side with me. "Grane goes alone for this one. We will decide what to do when he returns."

110

Not even Beth argued with him. He was our pack leader and his decision-making sound. I rose to my feet and kissed them all beneath their chins, including Suma, even though my heart skittered around in its bony cage as I got closer to her.

Alec's deep voice steadied me. "If you do not return in four days, I am coming after you."

I nodded, muttered a quick farewell, and jogged out of the den. I had no time to waste.

* * * *

I resumed the same pace toward the biologists' camp that I had used to leave it. By the time I reached where their skin-like tents were huddled, darkness had long ago descended. I hid in the thickets for a while until I got my breath back, then crept near. My nose picked up the funk of a raccoon and I halted. It had probably figured out where the food had come from before and returned for its own raid. I followed it into the camp.

The creature did not bother being quiet, and I welcomed its nosing interference, figuring the coon's noisome rummaging would wake the occupants of the campsite. I retreated a bit and lay down in the tall grass while the coon foraged without concern. I kept my head low and my ears honed, and did not wait long before I heard the unmistakable rip of a tent opening. The beam of a light flashed around in a search pattern and then clicked off. The murmur of human voices strummed my heart into a rapping rhythm, and I held my breath to steady it, and to better hear the voices.

The scrape and flare of a match cut through the darkness and the unmistakable pungency of tobacco smoke coiled through the air. I lifted my chin enough to see two humans sitting on a log. They were sharing their smoke, and talking about the raccoon, which still rummaged blithely through the heavy bags brought by the biologists. Who apparently gleaned great fun from watching because they chuckled and joked about the futility of its foraging. Good. I now knew they had not changed where they kept their surveillance equipment.

Eventually the coon waddled away, its stomach dissatisfied, but the men stayed up and continued talking. The word wolf stopped my heart, and I held my breath. The biologists had heard our howling. My heart eased only a bit when they mentioned the likelihood of it being coyotes, but their sense of direction hit too close. They would come our way with their tools, and my thoughts raced backward toward the image of the moose carcass.

I listened with sharp attention as I retreated in calculated steps, moving only when the men on the log shifted their positions. My retreat went painstakingly slow and my nerves flared my skin, but I swallowed deep, long breaths to keep myself steady. If I changed into wolf and left sign of my presence we were all surely done for.

Once I reached the trees, I got back onto my two feet and tiptoed until I felt I had slipped far enough away. Then I broke into a fast run. I could not get my message back to my family soon enough.

* * * *

I reached the den by late afternoon, and my lungs burned as if on fire. As did every muscle in my body, but I kept my wits about me and halted at the entrance this time. Alec strode to the doorway to greet me, and he bid me to enter without haste. I gladly obliged his order, then dropped to my knees while I sucked down the cool air of the den in great gulps.

My pack leader gave me time to recover while everyone gathered to hear my news. All wore anxious expressions, except for Terra and Gor, who kept trying to taunt Ane by snapping their sharp teeth onto her elbows. Beth and Suma rescued her, but the pups were finding it difficult to remain confined. They squeaked and whined with their pent up energy.

I got enough breath back to speak and looked around at the pinched faces of my audience. "They heard us," I panted.

All pairs of eyes widened, and I held up my hand for them to wait before they said anything. I inhaled and spoke again. "They suspect coyotes, but are coming this way."

Beth jumped to her feet and marched back and forth across the room with Gor in her arms, who smiled grandly with the fun of striding around the den at his mother's fearsome pace.

Finally, she planted her feet. "We sabotage their efforts, then, like we did before."

I shook my head. "Luna, they are suspicious this time and awaken at the slightest noise."

Her eyes narrowed as her anger rose. Her compulsion to protect welled too strong and Alec finally went to her. He lowered his head to kiss Gor, his paternal care settling his mate. She inhaled, held her breath for a few moments, then looked at him with an imploring expression that would have sent a lesser wolf off to kill every human walking the planet. I itched to erase that look by doing just that, and noticed I was not the only one. Jaws and fists were clenched in sympathy.

Alec spoke to diffuse us all. "Our anger will do nothing to help us. Everyone breathe." His order was not to be disobeyed and we relaxed our tightened muscles. "There will be no killing. That is probably what has brought them here in the first place." He faltered for a brief second, but regained his composure, and I wondered about his confession to his being in captivity. Had he already killed humans in order to escape? Is that why they were here? The scenario loomed possible. Anything concerning humans threatened with the possible.

"We stay and let them come to us." Our pack leader gave us all time to mull over his edict. He turned to Luna and wrapped his arm around her narrow waist. She snuggled herself in close to him and my blood warmed at the sight of them. They were unified in their respect for one another, and I trusted the decision because of it. I glanced around the room and saw my feelings expressed on the faces of our devoted pack.

But had I just witnessed a conspiratorial glance between the young wolf-men, before they adopted their dutiful expressions? The electric flash passing between them had been too brief for me to be sure of what I saw, so I attributed the exchange to fatigued misconception on my part.

Beth transferred Gor into his father's arms, kissed her mate on the throat, and announced her intention to hunt.

"I will take Armand," she said. "We need food, but we also need to be able to retain our human forms if we encounter the humans." She steadied her gaze on the young wolf-man, who stood up bravely. Had she seen something pass between the young wolves, too? I shook my head to dispel my worried thoughts, and concentrated instead on Armand. I still had my doubts about his abilities to remain upright in the presence of humans, but Luna seemed utterly confident in him. I did not argue her decision. I bowed my head as she made her way toward the entrance with my little brother, even though I desperately wanted to go.

The red wolf-woman turned her attention to me before exiting. "Grane, you have served us well. Rest for now. I will keep our little brother safe."

"I know," I whispered, and knelt before her. She would without doubt. Armand resided in the Luna's heart, and the certainty of that eased me. I kept my posture low until they left, and then assumed my position at the entrance.

Eaen squatted in front of me and I opened my eyes. "Big brother," he said, "let me take your place by the door this day, while you go deeper into the cave to rest."

I started to protest, but his friendly smile stopped me.

"Our sister spoke truth, Grane. You have served us well. Let us return the favor."

He held out his strong hand to help me to my feet and I grasped it willingly enough, as I stifled a yawn. I had not slept for days, a feat I had accomplished numerous times while I was with Meron. Eaen's relief of my watch presented a luxury I wholly welcomed and I returned his encouraging smile with gratitude in my heart.

"I would be utterly happy for you to do so, little brother," I admitted, and dragged my tired body toward the back of the cave. Ane and Elga adjusted their bodies to make space for me, and I snuggled in with them without haste. My fatigued muscles would appreciate the softness of their arms. I fell into a deep sleep as soon as my eyes closed.

* * * *

I awakened with a start and bolted upright with my heart hammering against my breastbone. The den was steeped in utter blackness against the glare of the moon, and I had to take a moment for my eyes to adjust to the contrast. I pushed my face into the air and sniffed. Everyone had returned and slept inside, except for Suma. Ane and Elga dozed soundly and did not move as I pulled myself from between them. I picked my way toward the entrance and gazed out.

The moon glowed bright, casting a blue pall on the landscape.

Unlucky for us. We could be seen if the biologists decided to observe us at night. I crouched just outside of the den and surveyed the tree line. I could now smell the spicy moss of Suma, but I could not see her.

She approached from behind me, yet I did not turn to look at her.

"Grane," she said in greeting, and sat down opposite me, at the other side of the entrance.

"Suma," I responded past my tightened throat. In spite of what we had recently shared through my healing, she still unsettled me. I dropped my shoulder, and hoped she could not hear my nervousness.

"The humans will come?" She kept her gaze forward so I could not read her face.

"Yes, I believe so." I saw no point in softening the probability of it. If we were prepared for them they could not surprise us. The last thing I wanted was for this pack to be caught unaware by the humans. Especially Suma, who had shown no fear when faced with the prospect of defending her family against them. The new scar on my arm boasted the evidence of that.

I ran my finger across the pink welt of the scar. "White wolf, can I ask you something?" I stole a look her way. Her face glowed beautifully pale in the moonlight, and she nodded.

"When you thought the humans were coming and you attacked me, could you control your wolf?"

"No," she clipped, then stood up and strode into the den without even looking my way. She gave me no chance to respond or defend my question, and my lower status did not allow me to pester her about it. I had to let her go.

I flexed my fists to relax my nerves. My question had been necessary, and I had meant no insult. I did not seek to taunt her, but she seemed to think I did. I tightened both fists and suppressed a frustrated growl. We had just bonded. Did that not count for something?

I peered into the black abyss behind me and Suma's scent lingered in my nose. My body trembled, and I headed into the moon-mottled woods to ease its shake. I had not eaten for several days and needed to hunt, and to work off my frustration with the white wolf. I disappeared into the serenity of the night forest.

Chapter Fifteen

The den seemed strangely quiet when I returned at first light. I circled warily and sniffed, but found nothing human around. Still, I approached with caution, then slid inside. Suma, Ane, and Elga were there with Gor and Terra, but everyone else was gone.

"What the..." I scanned, even as my nerves scratched. Beth and Armand hunted last night, where were they now? And Alec and Eaen? Suma rose to her feet and strode toward me. I dropped to my knee and turned my face up to her. My spine tingled and then scorched.

Suma's white hair fell upon her cheek as she looked down at me. "Eaen and Armand are gone, and—"

I sprang to my feet. "What?"

Suma flinched, and then squared her shoulders. "They left some time in the night. Alec and Beth went looking for them." Her eyes were wide with worry.

"How?" I snarled. How could Armand do this? He had witnessed firsthand the risks of human encroachment. Apparently, I had caught a glimpse of their true intentions the previous day and had let it slide because of my fatigue. Anger at myself and at the young wolf men quickened my pulse. My skin caught fire, rendering it hard to speak. "Why?" I gargled.

Suma braced herself. "For the adventure, I would guess."

"Adventure," I growled, but it was all I could say. I dropped to my knees as burning embers popped throughout my body. I looked up at Suma as wolf, and in my outrage at both Eaen and Armand I could not stop my lip from lifting into an ugly snarl.

The earth eyes in the pale face staring at me blazed, and Suma shivered, twisted, and crushed her sharp teeth onto my throat before I realized she meant to cower me into my rightful place.

I yelped and stumbled backward.

Suma?

The white wolf pressed her teeth deeper into my flesh and straddled me. I did not resist, but flipped to my back and tucked my tail tight against my stomach.

"Suma." Elga's sharp voice cut across the den. I rolled my eyes to her and watched as she placed Terra in Ane's arms and dashed toward us.

"Off, Suma," she scolded again, and the white wolf's jaw relaxed, but did not release. I did not move a single muscle. Nor did I breathe. What was the matter with her? Did she not see my snarl was not meant for her?

Please.

I begged. A whine squished passed my clenched throat, and Suma removed her fangs from my neck. I pressed my back to the dirt floor and made myself as unthreatening as possible. Did she still not trust me?

"Little sister," soothed Elga, "he meant no harm. He was upset about Armand and Eaen that is all."

Suma shook her great furred body and sat on her haunches. She licked her lips and released her own whine to the old wolf-woman, then retreated toward the back of the cave. She could not leave without exposing us all.

Neither could I. We would have to settle down in each other's presence. I rolled onto my stomach and pulled my body with my front legs toward the white wolf, but did not rise off the floor. She ignored me, even though I roached my back and exposed my bruised throat again. I lifted my head and licked her chin. She allowed an instant of acknowledgement in the flick of her pink tongue, righting my world with that single gesture.

I curled up close to her, yet she did not move away. She stayed put for my sake, and the truth of that assuaged some of the hurt of her attack. I dared press her no farther. I had apologized for my own unseemly behavior, and she had granted her forgiveness. I would have to accept that as enough for the time being.

Elga returned to her duties with the pups, and she and Ane stole glances at the two of us while they hid their laughter in the fattened bellies of the babes. Their antics soothed me even though I knew we were the reason for their mirth, and my body cooled.

I yawned and my muscles quivered across my yielding bones. I remained prostrate on the floor and turned my face to Suma, who remained wolf.

I whispered a scratchy apology, and explained myself past my rough vocal chords. "Elga spoke truth. I am angry with Armand. And with Eaen." I dropped my gaze, as was proper.

The only response I received from Suma came in the form of three bumps from the tip of her bushy tail. Then she went still. She wanted to be left alone.

I rose and positioned myself at the entrance of the den. I would have to wait for her explanation, and I could not leave to go looking for my little brothers. I was the only one whom I knew for certain could keep his human form if the biologists showed up.

I heaved a sigh and tried to catch a nap while Suma collected herself.

* * * *

I smelled my pack leaders before I heard them. They skirted the den as I had learned to do and moved in with just as much caution. They were alone. I knelt at the entrance and waited for them to come in. Suma glided into her human form and rushed to greet them.

They exchanged embraces and then Beth rested her eyes on my face as she pulled me to my feet and hugged me, too. The pressure of her arms revealed her sympathy and she murmured against my shoulder. "Grane, I am sorry."

I slid to the ground in front of her and pressed my hands to my ears. I could not speak while the questions swirled rampant in my head.

Ane's raspy voice drifted from far away. "You did not find them?"

I raised my face to Luna, to Alec. They shook their heads, and their voices blended as they both uttered *No*.

"We followed their trail to the west for some distance, but dared go no farther." Alec moved his gold eyes between me and Suma, who glowed paler than usual. "We do not know if they continued west, or if they turned north to spy on the humans." His deep voice tightened, and he clenched his fists in anger. Beth wrapped her hand around his elbow, and they breathed in concert.

"I am going after them." Suma's heated voice startled me, and I twisted on my knees to square my look at her, the memory of our recent skirmish flying out of my ears so that I forgot my place.

"No," I blustered.

She spun to face me, and I dipped my head and softened my shoulders, then let my arms drop to my sides, correcting myself.

"No," I whispered. "Please, no."

Her silence delivered my answer, and I dared to lift my eyes. "I will go, Suma. It is too dangerous. You are too—" I bit down on my tongue and could not finish. How could I tell her I thought her much too precious to risk such a dangerous mission? If something happened to Suma? My world would crumble along with my heart. It hurt enough that Armand and Eaen were out there.

I studied the floor for fear she would see my heart in my eyes. Precious or not, she wanted nothing to do with my love for her, and I had to honor that. "I will go," I restated instead.

Beth squatted in front of me. "No. You will stay here where you are safe. I cannot protect you if you go to the west."

"I know, Luna, but there will be no one to protect Eaen and Armand, either, if I do not go." I searched her face in the hope that my argument resonated.

She narrowed her eyes and my heart tripped. I had not seen that leer since her days of captivity. I steeled myself. These were far different circumstances now, and I trusted her. And tested her. "My sister, you know my words are true."

"Grane, your old pack will kill you if they see you," she argued.

"Yes, but it is likely they will also try to harm Armand, which Eaen will not tolerate. He would be slaughtered as well."

Suma gasped. "What is this talk of killing, of slaughtering?" She stood adamant, yet suddenly very worried. She looked at all of us, including the old women, who shook their heads and kept the pups entertained while we discussed my leaving. "What have you not told me?"

Oh no. "Just let me go, please," I begged my pack leaders. "It is possible their trail heads north toward the humans, and not toward Meron's pack."

"Meron's pack?" Suma's brown eyes widened and were like wet stones against the snow.

Alec spoke to us all, but he meant his words for his little sister. "I agree with Grane. The young wolves most likely went to rescue us, and are right now sneaking into the biologists' camp."

I sighed my gratitude and closed my eyes.

"I will leave right away." I raised my lids and offered Luna a shy smile. "I will be very careful, I swear. I am as fond of my new skin as you are." I winked at her, and she grinned back.

"You are something else, gray wolf." But then her eyes swirled and her heat radiated from her bare skin. She could not hide her innate worry. "Stay safe. I mean it. And bring our wolves home."

"I will do all that I can, I promise every one of you." I bowed my head and stood up to go. But when I raised my foot to take my first step Suma's voice broke like the ice on a river behind me.

"I am going with him."

I shut my eyes against the turmoil roiling through my stomach and my heart. Come with me? I would want nothing more in the world than to spend the rest of my days with the white wolf! But, to come with me now? I groaned.

Suma persisted. "I am going after Eaen, Alec. You cannot stop me from that."

Alec bristled, but Beth gripped his elbow again. He inhaled and held his breath before he spoke. "All right, but do as Grane tells you. And please do not be as foolish as your brother."

My heart fell into my feet, and Suma bounced around on hers and smothered her older brother and sister with kisses. Her relief beamed profound and I warmed to it. I knew exactly how she felt, and I could not begrudge her going.

"Come on, then, if you are going with me. We are wasting time." I headed out before anyone could see my smile. Before Suma caught up with me I had it masked as we set out to find the trail of our young, heroic wolf-men.

* * * *

We took off toward the west by following Beth's and Alec's return trail, and could just catch light wisps of Armand's and Eaen's scents. We would have to hurry if we did not want to lose their essence. I could also smell the rain in the air, and I worried that it would erase what little we had to go on. Heavy, gray clouds already smothered the setting sun, and the woods darkened sooner because of them.

I picked up our pace, and Suma followed with graceful ease. She was breathtakingly agile, and my chest tightened each time I stole glimpses of her. I was glad to be running.

By the time we reached the end of our pack leaders' uniquely mingled scent, it had grown fully dark and a cool rain had already been falling for some time. We circled around the area with our faces close to the ground. It would have been so much easier to find the scent path in our wolf forms, but we could not afford it. Suma's lilt chimed through the rain after several minutes of scouting close.

"Here, Grane. I found the trail."

It led north. The wolf-men did head toward the humans' camp. Suddenly, a faint howl dragged across the soaked air and into our ears. Suma and I turned to each other, her fallen face a mirror of mine.

Eaen. Armand.

The howl came from the northwest. I bolted toward it with Suma on my heels, and my heart clogged my throat. I could barely breathe as I ran. The young wolves were luring the biologists away from our den. My muscles trembled and I pushed faster to avoid my transformation. I turned my head to see how Suma fared.

Her breaths were fast, but even. She was holding up well and it gave me courage. Another howl burst across the sky, and it was joined by another, and then another, and still another. I stopped in my tracks and tilted my head to hear better. Suma nearly ran into me, but she recovered fast and emulated my posture for listening.

"They are changing pitch to sound like more wolves." She turned her astonished face toward mine.

I nodded. It was an old trick we had used many times to confuse our enemies. Armand had learned well. The cacophony of a large wolf pack would certainly divert the attention of the biologists toward them. It would have been a clever scheme in any other circumstance, and if I were not so angry with them I would be very proud. But I could not help but wonder if either inexperienced wolf-man understood the danger of it.

Suma read my mutable expressions. "They have endangered themselves," she whined.

"Yes," I answered frankly. Then the rain dropped in a deluge, and I could hear nothing except the roar of falling water through the trees. I grabbed Suma's arm and pulled her with me as I retreated to the protection of a copse of mature birch trees. Their leaves were thick, and we huddled close under the branches. Suma's spice rose off her heated body to tease my nose. I talked to divert my attention from my heating spine.

"Suma, I am sure they have attracted the full attention of the humans. It was a clever thing to do, for the sake of the pack, but it puts them in jeopardy."

She nodded, but said nothing.

I continued, and made direct eye contact with her. Why not? I had already grabbed her and dragged her out of the rain. What was one more transgression? Her deep brown eyes were nearly black in the darkness, but she stared directly back at me, without a hint of anger.

I had her full attention, which I would need if she were to grasp the full weight of what I needed to say. "If we follow Armand and Eaen, we will no doubt come in direct contact with the humans. They are biologists, and will not shoot to kill, but they have other ways of harming us, Suma. You should go back to the safety of the den."

Suma shook her head. "No, Grane. I am going after Eaen and Armand. I am responsible for Eaen, at least. You do not know our history, but I am one of the reasons he is here in this forest in the first place." She said no more, and I did not know if she would ever tell me her life story. I hungered for it really. I wanted to know it all, to know everything about her.

"White wolf, it is very risky. And if they continue in the direction they are going, they could very easily encounter more wolves. They could meet up with Meron's pack."

She did not falter in the face of that seed of truth. "I do not care. I must do this."

I inhaled, and held the air in my lungs as my stomach twisted into a knot. For all her courage, Suma did not realize what she traveled toward, and I covered my face with my hands. Suffer it all. I would have to tell her, and I could not do so without revealing who I was. Who I had been. What I had done.

No, no, no. Just go back.

Her dark eyes narrowed. She had heard me.

"Suma, please. It is safer for you," I begged. The sky released another roaring cascade onto us, and it may as well have been my blood pounding in my ears. Suma shook her head *no* again.

It tore at my heart to see the hurt on her face. Fine. She would come. And I would have to reveal myself to her sometime soon. Great.

"All right, you will come," I shouted over the blast of the downpour. "But you had better do as I tell you."

She nodded, and the light that glowed from her eyes sparked my spine. Sweet mercy, she was breathtaking. My groin pulsed and I pulled my knees to my chest. Suma did the same. I saw no point in moving. We knew where Eaen and Armand were, and we could light out as soon as the rain stopped. I closed my eyes for a quick nap.

I waited a few minutes before stealing a peek at the wolf-woman beside me. She had her chin on her knees, but her eyes were open and staring straight ahead. I had no doubt she mulled over her decision. Suma was no trifling wolf, and the thought of it helped to ease my heart. I closed my eyes again.

* * * *

My eyes fluttered open when I felt Suma's warm hand on my shoulder, and an involuntary smile lifted my cheeks.

"We should go," she said, and got to her feet and stretched. The rain had tapered to sprinkling, and the forest air echoed with the placking of raindrops on the broad leaves.

I inhaled the bursting aromas surrounding us. I loved the smells after a freshening rain, and I glanced over at Suma, who had her pale face held to the sky. She sniffed too, and my smile returned in full force as my heart fluttered. I cleared my throat and muttered we should go.

I led us in the direction we heard Eaen and Armand the night before. Suma followed close and we jogged along in comfort. The earth felt cool and rain-softened beneath our bare feet, and the sun emerged in snatches from behind the storm clouds as they rolled across the bluing sky. The forest steamed around us while the day grew hotter as the day progressed.

We were getting closer and would have to slow down to pay closer attention to our surroundings. I had not forgotten about the surveillance cameras. As we walked I described them to Suma. Her voice filled with wonderment and dread. She understood their power fully.

"They can see us without being near us."

"Yes. It is why it is so essential that we retain our human forms," I explained. "Of course, once we get farther from the den and find out where Armand and Eaen revealed themselves as wolves, it will not matter if we shift. Providing it is not caught on camera."

Suma grasped my warning. "I will do my best to control myself, Grane." Her voice lilted sincere.

"I know you will." I did not dare to look at her just then. Her voice, her presence, her earnestness were going to convulse me into my wolf form in spite of my warnings about the humans. A look at her would surely tip the precarious balance I was barely maintaining.

I changed the subject. "Are you hungry, Suma? We could hunt."

"No. I am fine for now. I would rather wait until we pick up the new trail."

Her decision to go hungry was an admirable one, and pride for the wolf-woman swelled my heart. If we were seen as wolves, at least we would be in the area the biologists were expecting to see us. We walked on until the sun lowered in the western sky.

I caught a whiff of Eaen, just as I heard the whir and click of a camera in the same instant. I crouched instinctively and Suma dropped to the ground behind me. I pointed toward a skinny birch tree and Suma's brown eyes widened when she saw the device. I stood up and walked right over to it as it snapped several pictures in rapid succession before I ripped it from the tree. Suma stepped in timidly behind me, her skin burning. I could feel her heat on my bare back.

I turned and showed her the pictures, which had captured my progression toward the camera. Suma's brow pinched as she studied it, she looked at me then back at my picture.

"It makes you look funny," she replied.

I blushed. "Thanks, Suma." I flipped the batteries out of it and smashed the camera against a rock. My images were destroyed, and I flung the batteries away. I stole a glance at the white wolf-woman. She stood staring at the mangled box.

"Come on," I coaxed. "It can do nothing now. Let us follow our brothers."

We picked up a steady jog, but Suma still carried that studious look, her mind drawn back to the place where we had found the camera. I wondered what else she could be thinking. Perhaps seeing the box had made the other weapons the humans wielded seem more real.

"Are you all right, Suma?" I asked, but did not break our pace.

She nodded, and I saw her set her chin. I stopped and confronted her.

"Are you all right, Suma?" I asked again, only this time I searched her brown eyes, but made sure I lowered my frame so that I looked up at her. "It is not too late to turn around," I offered.

"No, Grane. I am fine. It is just that I knew I had seen the camera before when you and Alec brought one back to the den, but seeing it out in the woods—seeing it work? It is…unsettling. I worry very much for Eaen and Armand." Her cheeks flushed, and I watched anger creep into her countenance.

"They never should have gone," she snarled, baring her teeth. The instant she did it she clapped her hand to her mouth, and her cheeks reddened more.

I stifled my chuckle. There was no need for me to nip where she had just been bitten. She knew now why I had reacted the way I did back at the den.

"I am sorry, Grane," she whispered.

"It is fine, white wolf," I assured her. "Our boys are too full of themselves, and it leaves the more responsible ones to deal with it."

She let go a small, knowing grin and nodded her head. "Very true, gray wolf. Very true."

"So. Let us go find them before they cause more trouble." I jutted my chin toward the northwest and smiled, then stretched back up to my full height and set our course. Suma again settled right in behind me and easily kept pace. Her presence felt like paradise, and I wallowed in it as we moved along.

* * * *

We quit running when the moon emerged above the tree tops. Suma's belly growled behind me. We needed to rest, and to eat, but the wolf-woman waited for my go-ahead, keeping to her promise to listen to my instructions. I turned to her and shivered into wolf. Suma did the same.

We separated to increase our chances of finding a small meal, and not much time passed when I had the firm body of a partridge in my jaws. I returned with it to the place where we departed from each other. The white wolf was already there, waiting with the body of a rabbit laying crumpled between her front paws.

She had not eaten her kill, either. My heart stretched and filled, and I could not help showing my sharp molars in a wide wolf smile. My tongue lolled, and I crawled up to Suma with my tail tucked low in greeting. She stood and waved her tail then snatched up her rabbit and commenced to devouring it.

I fell on my bird and gobbled it, bones and all, then kindled the fire in my core so that I could change into my human form. Suma mimicked me, and fired off questions as soon as she could.

"Grane, do you think we will see other wolves?" Her brown eyes were wide with anxious curiosity. "How many wolves were in your old pack?"

I clenched my jaw and inhaled. I knew where my answers would lead. "We had around twenty, Suma." I replied, then cast my eyes to the ground as if to study the grass. "And I hope we never see a single one of them," I spat.

Without even having to look at her I could feel Suma tense. I regretted my tone, and tried to ease the edge that I had created between

126

us. "I was glad to leave them, white wolf. I was not happy." I hoped my explanation would be enough for her. Of course, it was not.

"Yet you traveled all this way with them?"

I nodded at the half-truth, but would not look at her. She would learn soon enough that most of the wolves in Meron's pack were picked up as we had steam-rolled our deadly way east, and we left more bodies than we salvaged. The thought of it sickened me so I changed the subject, and asked her what she knew of biologists, of humans.

"Not a thing, really," she was forthcoming and I felt her relax. "Only bits from the stories Alec and my father have told me. And Fay, too. They are not pleasant."

"The stories or the people?" I fished.

"Both. My brother was in captivity for three years, Grane. He will not reveal all of what happened to him, but I know the humans tortured him. For three years."

I could hear the tears in her voice, and could not help but look at her then. She had hung her head, and I reached out to touch her arm. My heart fluttered wildly as the heat of her skin warmed my fingertips.

"I am very sorry," I gruffed, and pulled my hand away before I overstepped my bounds. I wanted to comfort her, but did not trust myself. I kept the topic on her brother. "He is too great a wolf to have had that happen. I am honored to be his subordinate." I was wholly sincere and hid nothing of it from the wolf-woman before me.

"Then things really have changed," she allowed.

Oh no. We were headed back toward my life with Meron.

"We should rest, Suma," I dodged. "We will need our senses sharp for tomorrow." I pulled away from her and made myself comfortable beneath a pine tree. My heart remained on the ground beside her while I sat as an empty shell beneath the tree. I could not deny I loved the white wolf, so I closed my eyes against the vision of her sitting alone in the grass.

Eventually I dozed.

Chapter Sixteen

I opened my eyes to a blue shadowed forest. The full moon sat fat in the night sky. I sidled over to Suma to wake her. She opened her eyes as I approached, and I sucked in my breath. The glow of the blue moon on her pale skin contrasted starkly with her dark eyes.

Her name fell from my mouth.

She sat very still and I froze. Then remembered myself and ducked my shoulder and dropped my gaze. My groin lurched as my spine sizzled, and I pulled away before I revealed my excited torment.

Suffer it. I had to be more careful. Not an easy task since we would always be in each other's company. I stole a furtive glance in Suma's direction. She was awake, at least.

I sniffed the air for the scent of humans or other wolves before I spoke out loud.

"Are you ready to go, Suma?"

I turned to look down at where she had been sitting. My eyes met the white wolf, and it startled me so much I braced my feet. Then I chuckled to myself and shook my head. "You have to quit surprising me, wolf," I teased.

Suma waved her magnificent tail in response. At least she was not mad that I overstepped my bounds. I crouched and shivered into wolf, too. Why not? We would make better time, and the biologists already knew there were wolves in the area. Suma fell in behind me as we settled into a steady trot.

It was late afternoon when we sniffed out Armand's and Eaen's

128

trail. They were now going directly west. I could only assume they had every intention of leading the humans to the other wolves. Not smart. If the other wolves figured it out, the young wolf-men would surely pay for their little trick with their lives.

Their heroic caper was getting more dangerous as the days passed, and my concern eroded into tense anxiety. Suma and I needed to catch up with them soon, and just as I decided to increase our pace, something bit my shoulder. I flinched, yelped and snapped my jaws at the offender. The fluff of red feathers bounced before my frantic stare.

A dart.

My heart seized in its anguish, and I tumbled to the ground as the forest blurred, spun, and narrowed around me.

Run!

It was my last conscious thought.

* * * *

I stared up at the night sky and tried to focus my eyes on the wavering moon. I lifted my head and shoulders to stand and felt the strangling of something looped around my throat.

A collar. I had been collared.

My blood shot through my veins as my heart galloped and flip-flopped. I gathered my paws beneath me and staggered sideways until I straddled my four legs for support. My head hung heavy and thick, and I shook it vigorously until my vision cleared. I gave a quick scan of the area, and bolted. Where did not matter. I rushed away. I lost my breath in my panic.

I had been collared, and directly linked to humans, who could track me at any time. I had become a danger to any wolf-being around me.

Suma.

Had she gotten away?

Chapter Seventeen

I planted my nose to the ground and spiraled with renewed purpose. I had to know. I needed to find her. My heart raced, and my lungs burned as they tried to force air past the constricting knot in my throat. Please let Suma be all right. My spiral widened, until finally I picked up her sweet, spicy, mossy scent.

I chased her smell, and it grew stronger and stronger in my nose, on my tongue. Then I stopped and would go no farther. She was close, but I dared not approach her. I could not endanger her. I peered hard toward the spot where her scent lingered strongest, and could just make out her form at the base of a birch tree. She had curled up in a tiny, tight ball, hiding herself very well, at least from a human's perspective.

Suma.

She lifted her furred head, and stared directly at me, then rose to her feet.

Follow.

Sweetest mercy, at least she was all right. I aimed my body west, and raced like a shadow through the trees. Suma soon caught my tail, and I raced faster to get us as far from the biologists as possible. I needed to do some fast explaining to Suma and I could not do it if the humans were around. If they witnessed me changing form one species to another we would be done for. I drove us relentlessly, and the white wolf never lagged. Her courage and trust in me stripped my tortured heart.

By dawn, we could run no more. Suma's pant rasped behind me and

I was no better. I circled to a stop at a little stream and plunged my entire body into it. Then I shook and adopted my human form to cool down faster. My hands flew to the collar at my neck. Suma whined and then shivered her body several times before she could assume her human form. My capture had her rattled, and my heart smashed around unfettered against its bony cage.

"Suma, we are in a heap of trouble," I blurted out.

She stumbled toward me, her brown eyes wide with fear. "What have they done?" Her voice had risen in pitch because of her distress. "I watched them. They did all sorts of things to your body, studied you, they took your picture."

I fell to my knees, and gripped my head in my hands. A growl rumbled in my lungs and out of my throat as I ripped at my hair. I could not control my heaving breaths, yet I dared not let loose the howl that grew inside me. I clamped my jaws and roared at the ground.

Suma hovered over me, then wrapped her arms around my back. She pulled me against her birch tree body and I succumbed, and turned myself so I could bury my head against her abdomen. Her song vibrated in her body, soothing me. I inhaled and held my breath, over and over, until my heart stopped careening in my chest. Many moments passed before I could speak.

"Suma, the humans can track me at all times now. It is the collar they follow."

Her body stiffened beneath me and she pulled me away from her. Her hands remained on my shoulders as she peered closer at the band around my neck.

"It sends signals to the humans." I could not look at her, and hung my head as I clipped out my explanation. My greatest fear of the biologists had been realized, and it squeezed my neck like death itself.

"We will take it off then," she replied. She reached for the collar and I did not move away, even when the thick, hard fibers abraded the skin on my neck as she turned it to find some kind of buckle or hasp. "How does it come off?"

I raised my eyes and stared into her bewildered face. I shook my head in resignation. "I do not know. But, Suma, you have to go back. The humans will stay out here following me now. You have to return to the den where it is safe."

She resisted, rose to her feet and stared down on me. "No, Grane. I will not go back. We came out here to find Eaen and Armand and that is what we will do. In the meantime, we will figure out how to get that collar off." She stood glorious in her determination, and the sight of her filled my frightened heart with hope.

But, I could not allow her to make that choice without her understanding who she risked herself for. I took a deep breath and exhaled. "Suma," I sighed and I held her eyes with mine while I remained on the forest floor. "What you wish to do is very noble." My heart lurched. "But you are risking too much for someone like me." My pulse pounded in my ears. She had the right to know. She needed to be aware of the things I had done. To stay with me when the humans could find us at any time jeopardized her freedom. I could not let the white wolf do that for me, especially since she did not know who I really was, did not know the full scope of the crimes I had committed. I inhaled again, and prepared to strip myself bare before the wolf who owned my heart.

"There is a reason why your brother trusted I could protect Armand and Eaen. Alec knows me, Suma. He knows what I have done." I delved into her brown eyes without flinching, and added, "What I can do."

I dropped my eyes to the ground for her sake, sat back and fingered the collar on my neck. "Is this justice, or what?" I scoffed and shook my head. Life could be very ironic in its cruel mockery of compensation. I never suspected I would pay for my deeds at the hands of the humans.

Suma sat down beside me, her gesture an invitation to speak.

To tell her all.

"You really want to know me, white wolf?" Please say no. Just go back and I will figure out how to bring our young wolf-men home.

"Yes," she warbled.

Of course. I was not going to get off so easily. I would rather endure being tied to the humans for the rest of my life than confess myself to the wolf-woman I loved, but it was not to be. I sighed and closed my eyes. When I opened them, Suma had her brown eyes pinned on me.

"Suma, be careful. I know you are the keeper of your heart, but even friends can get hurt."

The stream gurgled beside us.

"Grane, I will move away before you eat me." She giggled and smiled, and my heart swelled in spite of our predicament. She was no foolish wolf-woman. She understood. She was a courageous wolf. I cleared my throat to begin my story.

"I was mated once, Suma, and I loved her very much. Her name was Misha, and she was Armand's full sister. We found happiness with each other, and we raised Armand as if he had been birthed from our loins. We were very loving amongst ourselves, and we were very adept at gleaning that happiness in spite of our pack leader."

"Meron?"

I nodded and inhaled. "Yes. Meron. He was a hard leader and took too many chances with us. We stole from the humans often and it filled our bellies, but endangered our lives. Meron had no regard, and the humans stepped up their efforts to protect what was theirs. Our territory was no longer safe, and the more Meron took from the humans, the more they reaped from us. We lost several of our pack mates, and more of our hunting ground.

"Misha and I decided to flee with Armand to keep him safe." I stopped my telling as I thought about my beloved mate. My throat constricted and my breaths would not come. I forced a deep breath so that I could keep talking.

"We did not make it." I stood up and waded into the stream, where the water bubbled by without concern. Suma's hand slid into mine, and she squeezed it to give me courage. I looked down at her. "The humans shot Misha the morning we planned to leave."

Suma did not release my hand when she knelt with me in the stream bed. Even though my heart bled through its cracks, I continued. The wolf-woman had yet to hear the worst of my story.

"I was outraged, and begged Meron to let me attack the humans. He would not release me to do so, and my vengeance stewed in my heart like poison. Not long after, he gathered what remained of his pack and we left the area to move north and east, away from the humans and their weapons. I was not happy to be leaving un-avenged. Neither was my pack leader. The poison in my heart spilled throughout me and I hated everything, was angry at everything, at everyone. Except Armand. Who was the last untainted sliver of my wrecked heart. He was all that was left of my Misha, and I protected him with a savagery I never before thought myself capable of.

"I gladly slaughtered those who wished to harm us, even though we were the aggressors and they were only defending their own territories. I did not care. For every life I took, my heart felt pain again, and I welcomed it, sought it out. The pain I felt meant somewhere in my blackened heart the old me still resided. The self who once loved, who had laughed.

"But the farther we traveled, the more we killed and the less pain I felt. I murdered our fellow wolf-men because I had already done so, not because I grieved. Armand bore witness to my disintegration."

I turned to the wolf-woman beside me and she pulled away as I knew she would. There was no honor in my grief, in my keeping Armand safe. There was no honor in me. I would kill my fellow wolf-man again if I had to, even if I knew the cost to my own heart. I saw myself through Suma's eyes, and I hung my head. "I am very much like a human, Suma. And now you know."

She sat silent for a moment and I left her to it. She had her own thoughts to sort, and I studied the water as it slipped by.

"Ane and Elga? You killed members of their pack?"

"Every one."

"But them."

"But not them, Suma. I do not know why, even to this day."

"Nor did you kill our pack."

I turned to look at the white haired wolf-woman, who seemed so exquisite sitting there in the late summer sun. But her face did not reflect the horror I expected it to. She looked perplexed, and my heart fluttered nervously.

"Nor did I kill your pack," I repeated. "I did not lie when I answered your question to me. You were like a lightning strike to my heart when I saw you, Suma. You were life. When you showed your courage for Luna, I witnessed hope in the face of despair. So I did the one thing I had not done since my Misha had died. I allowed no bloodshed on that raid. I let you go."

It sounded so simple to my ears now. But my actions that day set off a chain of events I had not foreseen, but for which I was now entirely grateful. My heart whispered tentatively then, and because of the white wolf I had listened. I owed her my life.

I rose and stepped farther into the stream to immerse my entire body in its cooling waters. I felt light in its depths, and my heart did, too. Luna had been right, of course. Telling my story was surprisingly helpful, but I was sorry it was my white wolf who had to hear it.

Yet, she had proven her strength to me before when she had been on the end of my pole. Perhaps she would prove it again, and already she appeared to be taking things better than I thought she would. She was, at least, still sitting at the streambed with me.

I strode back to the bank, knelt in front of her, and lowered my head. "I am always yours, Suma, even if you do not want me. You saved my life, and you saved Armand's as well. I owe you everything I have to give, for what that is worth."

The weight of her hand on my shoulder rippled through my body like a shockwave. I tensed to control myself.

"I want you, Grane. Still."

Her words fell upon my head like flower petals, and I lifted my face in surprise. Those were not the words I had expected to hear, and my stomach tightened and rolled.

"Suma," I breathed as I searched her doe eyes. They were liquid with her tears, and I pulled her to me. Then I remembered the contraption encircling my neck, and I started to push away.

"No, wolf," Suma corrected, and she stepped into me so that our bodies were tight once more.

The curve of her supple body against my bare skin rippled like rapture, and I took her mouth with mine. She responded with surprising ferocity, and I crushed our bodies together, then lifted her away from the riverbed.

Her spicy scent swirled in my mouth, my head, and I collapsed with her onto the earth, my mouth seeking the soft flesh of her neck. She moaned as I smothered her nipples with my tongue, tugged them with my sharp teeth, and she arched herself into me, the length of her supple body branding my every cell.

I circled my arm beneath her and flipped her to her stomach, swept

S. C. Dane

up by this wolf-woman. She backed herself into me, splitting herself across my hips, and I gripped her nape in my hand. The taut skin of her back glistened like the snow of the mountains, yet it burned like the sun, and I snarled with my need for her.

She straddled, and I could hold myself no more. I submerged myself into my salvation, the liquid heat of her engulfing me. Her body around mine milked as she rocked, and I cupped her hip bones in my scorching hands.

I cried her name into the sky, as my tears fell in my abandon, then lay myself across her back, held her breasts, felt her heart crash against my palm. I lifted her to me and breathed her name into her neck, tattooing my need for her onto her skin, as our joining etched itself to my spirit.

She raised her arms to clasp my neck, and twisted herself to take my ear with her mouth. The brush of her breath seared a path straight to my heart, striking it so it fluttered madly.

I collapsed beneath her, and she ignited me with the lick of her tongue to mine, and sat herself down on me. She moved fluidly, undulating like the leaves upon the branches above us, and my hips pumped beneath her, driving my body deeper into her hot sheathe as she consumed me.

She locked her eyes on mine while she swayed like the treetops, and I lost myself to her as she pulsed and burned me with liquid fire, yelping on the verge of her howls, and I stood no more.

I rolled us both, Suma coiled tight in my arms, and when we faced our earth she yielded, and straddled for me again. I took her mercilessly, yet she bucked back, matching my urgency with her own. I fell across her, and bit onto her neck as I spilled my seed, and she howled my name.

We dropped in our exhaustion, but did not separate. Neither of us moved from the other as I pulled her with me, mindful that I not crush her with my weight, preferring hers upon my chest and stomach, and my heart. Her scent smothered me, and I wanted more as I breathed her in.

"White wolf," I could barely whisper. "You own me."

She giggled and my heart kicked around in my breast.

"Then we are even, gray wolf."

We said no more, but dozed by the bank of the stream under the

136

watchful eye of the sun. I held on tight to my heart and did not let her go.

I awoke to Suma studying me and my many scars. The sun had barely begun its descent, so we had not slept long, and my wolf-woman still lay in my arms. I could not shade my shy smile, and dropped my eyes.

She giggled again, and I pulled her close.

She had given herself to me!

"I know what I do," she replied, having heard my thought.

"Then you do not regret what we have done? That you bond yourself to me?" I searched her eyes for any sign of remorse.

She bolted me to the earth with them. "I regret nothing except not killing Meron myself," she admitted. "I find your heart to be lacking nothing, gray wolf, and am honored you give it to me so willingly."

"I thought you wanted no mate, Suma," I reminded her, teased her, even though the ecstatic pain of our coupling gripped my heart.

"That was before I got to know you. Then I tried showing my affection for you, but you kept pushing me away, especially after you yielded to our little brother. You broke my heart the day you lay yourself down in front of him."

"I am sorry. I did not know. I never thought you would see me as more than I saw in myself. I never thought you would give yourself to me. I still cannot believe it. Why did you not say something sooner?" My heart flipped around in joyous spasms, and my body warmed with my pulsing blood.

"I figured you wanted nothing to do with me," she lamented. "The more time you spent with us, Grane, the more I saw of your heart, and the more I wanted you. I kept trying because I could not give you up so easily."

We laughed in triumph at our misconceptions because they were behind us. I tried to pull her closer to me, but she was already as close as a body could get.

"We are mated, Suma." I could not get enough of it, and I squirmed like the pups. Her giggles sent me into convulsions.

Her lithe body stretched along mine, and we basked in the early autumn sun as we watched puffy, white clouds glide across the blue of the sky. Her mossy scent blended with the pungency of the dark earth, intoxicating me. I closed my eyes against a reeling sky.

"Grane," her breath tickled my ear and my heart trotted.

I did not answer and waited impatiently for her to breathe into my head again. She did not disappoint.

"Grane, we have to figure out how to get that collar off from you."

"I know." A shadow smothered my sun, and I sat up. "But we should go. The more distance we can put between us and the biologists, the safer you will be."

"Then we go together?"

I gazed down on her. "No, my beautiful white wolf. You should go home and be safe with Luna," I implored her.

She shook her head, but giggled. "Not a chance. I will go with the wolf who has my heart."

I shivered, and fell upon her to sink my teeth into the yielding flesh of her neck. Her giggles reverberated across my lips and I gasped. She was the brook I could not hold, and I coveted her all the more for it.

"Suma." Her name slipped across my tongue.

"Quiet, gray wolf. It is not open to discussion. I go where you go."

"Loyal wolf, you could find yourself wearing your own collar," I warned. "You see now what the humans can do."

She nodded and planted her fathomless brown eyes on my face. "I have witnessed. Now I am aware. I go with you to find our brothers."

I ceded. She had also learned about the humans from her brothers' troubles, and came this far. I held her pale face in my hands and touched my lips to hers. The caress of her tongue jolted me.

"Really, Suma, quit surprising me," I breathed as my smile spread across my face. It kindled her and her earth eyes crinkled at the corners.

"You are sure about staying?" My tenor remained light in spite of the fact I was still flabbergasted by this turn in my life. Not only had Suma chosen to mate with me, but I discovered a playful side to her I had not known existed.

"Absolutely sure, Grane. I finally have you and will not let you go so easily." She adopted a wicked grin, as if daring me to try, and I crushed her to me. My chest tightened, and I could utter nothing. I finally willed myself to peel away from her, and crouched to the forest floor.

With a final, frustrated tug on my collar, I revved the heat that resided in my body and convulsed into wolf. I set my eyes on Suma.

She knelt, tucked her arms to her chest, and coalesced as if made of fluid. My white wolf stood in front of me, and my tail waved strident above my back. I could have taken her again right then. Instead, I sidled up to her to rub my body against hers. I smothered my fur with her scent as she did the same. My heart pounded, then expanded to overwhelm me.

I turned toward the west so I could refocus and regain some composure, and moving would be the best remedy for that. I picked up a trot with the white wolf falling in beside me.

I soared. Then admonished myself. My paws pressing the ground centered me so my thoughts ran lucid through my mind. I sharpened my nose and my ears. It would be one thing for the biologists to track me, but now I had Suma to worry about, as well. The best thing for us was to do what Eaen and Armand had done. I had to lead the humans away from the east and our den, and toward the other wolves. I could only hope that we found our wolf-men before Meron's pack did.

At least then, the young wolves' mission would be completed and they could return home. It would be Suma and I who would remain on the run, unless we figured out how to get that suffering collar off.

* * * *

Mercifully, we encountered no human interference as we traveled, but the scent of wolf tickled my muzzle the farther west we went. It was not just the familiar odor of my little brothers, either. I stopped short and lifted my tail in warning. We were on claimed ground, but could not move off, as Eaen and Armand were somewhere in the area.

Suma stood rigid with anticipation, having also scented the other wolves. She followed without question when I diverted our direction slightly north to skim the edge of this forest. I knew this area well enough, as I had hunted it many times while still with Meron.

My hackles lifted off my back as we made our way, and I refused to stop and rest until I found a protected area, which took until late into the night before I felt confident we had found a safe place. I stopped and slipped into my human form. My belly growled. Suma cocked her head and bounded away.

"No," I barked. "Do not, Suma."

She returned to my side, and I dropped to my knees to hold her. She licked at my chin and whined.

"It is all right, little wolf. I did not mean to speak so harsh. But we stick together, unless the humans come." I rubbed my face into her mane. The fur on her body singed and she shifted in my arms. I embraced her, and pulled her into me as I suckled her searing throat.

She squirmed, but then stilled when she laid her face on my neck. I removed myself from her to grip my fingers around the ever-present collar.

Suma squatted in front of me, and rested her warm fingers on mine to coax my hands away. She knelt into me, and her breath feathered my burning skin as she brushed her lips along my shoulder.

I shivered, but held as her lips pressed under my chin and followed my jaw to my ear. I rolled her nipples in my fingertips. She flinched, then groaned, and the scent of her need filled my head. I turned to catch her mouth with mine, my tongue searching, tasting her spice.

Yet, she did not yield. Instead, her fingers coiled around my collar and she shoved me to the ground. Her brown eyes danced with mischievous hunger, shuddering anticipation straight through my loins.

She meant to undo me, and I readily surrendered to her. Suma straddled her strong legs across my waist and resumed her exploration with her lips. She kissed the raised skin of my scars, the contours of my muscles, and where my bones jutted taut against my skin. My hips twitched with my ache for her. Finally, she lowered herself onto me, sliding her body up and down, milking me. I shut my eyes and lost myself to the ecstasy of her rhythm.

I writhed beneath her while she curled her fingers around the collar at my neck, holding me in place as she churned her body above me. Her heat spread through my blood.

Suma.

She maddened me, and I gripped her rocking hips to ground myself, even as I plunged relentlessly into her. I teetered on the verge of exploding with my need for her, yet still she taunted. My entire body shivered as I emptied. She lowered her torso to mine so that I could wrap my arms around her back and pull her close to me.

"You wreck me, wolf," I panted into her ear.

She pressed herself against my chest, our hearts thumping against each other. Suma's breaths evened and lengthened as she dozed right there on top of me while we were still joined. Her heat enveloped me and I grew sleepy.

Yet, I dared not sleep. Meron's pack was too crafty. I knew because I trained most of them. So I would not rest easy while we were here. I hoped Eaen and Armand continued north and away from this place before they were detected. I shut my eyes against the terrible thought someone might recognize Armand's scent and pursue him.

My mate stirred. Her pale skin slid on mine and my thoughts flashed to my white wolf. Who lay in my arms. The idea of it swamped me in happiness until I felt as though I would burst with it. I inhaled the spicy moss of her scent while my pulse resounded in my head. I loved her. Needed her. She was the reason I lived again.

"What are you thinking about, gray wolf?" Her voice wafted like the morning mist across my ear.

"You."

She squirmed her taut body against me and I hugged her closer. Our bellies growled at each other and she giggled.

"I had better turn my thoughts to hunting," I suggested.

Her head rubbed against my chin when she nodded, and I raised myself up onto my elbows. Suma sat up, but remained straddled across me. I gazed into her mellow, brown eyes and my stomach flipped. I could not get over the fact we were mated. I felt a wild desperation to protect her. Especially now. I took a deep breath before I uttered the words I knew would resurrect hurtful memories.

"Before we hunt, I need to teach you about the poles." I dropped my lids in shame as her thighs tensed against my waist. I inhaled again. "I am sorry, Suma. We are in my old territory and Meron's pack is still here. If they catch us, it is imperative you know how to escape."

I raised my eyes to her then, and she met mine with an animosity I had seen before. I cringed inwardly.

"Tell me," she snarled, and then settled my heart when she clasped her hands around mine and squeezed. "It is good you know," she said as her eyes softened. "It will help us if Eaen and Armand have been captured."

I raised my brows in surprise. She harbored an incredible aptitude to foresee problems and to adapt accordingly. I had a strong ally in this hostile place, and her courage spread through me.

"The secret," I ventured, "is to not let the pole carriers surround you. I have run with you, Suma, and your best defense lies in your paws. Run if they come after you with the poles. I mean it. You stand a better chance if you can separate the pole carriers."

"I will do it, mate. But if you are captured? What should I do then?"

The sound of the word mate rolling from Suma's tongue rippled my spine and consumed me, and I had to take a deep breath to collect myself before I answered her.

"Run, Suma. For everyone's sake, including mine. Run." My throat tightened around my words and she cocked her head.

"Grane," she murmured. "I could not."

"You can because you have done it before," I replied without hesitation, even though my words whipped our hearts. She ran before because Luna told her to do it for the sake of the pack. "White wolf, if I am captured they will kill me. There will be nothing to rescue."

Her eyes widened with her fear for me. "I have not heard all of your story, Grane."

"No, little wolf, you have not. You would have been very pleased with your sister. Her Luna is extremely powerful. It is why we escaped and the other wolves did not follow."

Gone was the fear of the red wolf I once held in my tattered heart. The last healing she performed had been done with me as a member of her pack, and I had seen her with a different eye. She was glorious in her power, and a prideful grin spread across my face. I looked up into the shining eyes of her sister.

"You are thinking of Luna, gray wolf," she observed.

"And you are as uncanny in your ability to see as the rest of your family," I retorted, but smiled with pure joy. Her pale cheeks flushed pink with my compliment and I dreaded my next words. "But, Suma, I meant what I said about running. We are in a dangerous place here, and if I tell you to run, please do."

She shook her white head in refusal.

"Suma, you must. You promised Alec and Beth that you would do as I say."

"That was before we were mated, gray wolf. I will not leave you." She set her jaw and her brown eyes hardened to stones.

I slid myself out from under her and grasped her face in my hands. "Then we are both dead, along with the pup you could be carrying in your womb." I struck her directly, but without malice. I would do anything to keep her alive. "We have mated, Suma," I reminded her, and mercilessly held her eyes in mine.

She closed hers against me, and when she lifted her lids they revealed a heart torn. Her eyes filled with tears, and I crushed her to my chest.

"Shush, my little wolf. I mean no harm," I murmured into her hair. I pulled away just enough to see her face. "But it is possible you carry the seed of our pup, and if you lived you would know one way or the other."

A tear plopped onto her bright cheek and I pressed my lips upon it, licked it from my lips. "I am sorry I have brought this violence into your life, white wolf." I lowered my head and sat back. "It is a world I wished with all my heart I did not have to return to. But it is so."

Suma's voice bubbled down to lift my spirits. "I will run if it is necessary. But perhaps it will not be?"

I raised my face to look at her and her brown eyes shined with hope. I shivered in the glow of her faith, and could not suppress my smile. "Perhaps not," I replied, and wrapped my fingers around her delicate hand. "But, you will head straight for our territory, where Luna can protect you?"

She nodded, but her brown eyes still harbored that light of hope. "Tell me about my sister, Grane. How she helped you."

I pulled my mate into my arms and snuggled her in close to me. Her warm back pressed into my stomach and the smell of her hair drifted through my head. I inhaled to gorge my senses on her.

"Your sister is the most powerful Luna I have ever seen. Meron had a Luna, but she was just a child when she was taken, and her abilities were not strong."

"You knew about the Luna, yet you were a subordinate?" Her curiosity touched me so my heart tightened.

"Only because she was very human-like, but Meron bred her anyway. She produced two humans, which Meron promptly murdered when they drew their first breaths."

Suma rasped in a sharp breath, and twisted her face around to see if I was being truthful. "He killed her babes?"

I nodded and continued. "Yes, little wolf. They were useless to our pack as far as Meron was concerned. They would have required too much care to raise, and the risk far outweighed their benefit."

"That is cruel," she whispered.

"Yes, it was very hard for Kayla, and she was a long time reconciling her heart to it. The birth of a wolf-babe eased her loss considerably, even if it was taken from her and given to my sister to raise."

"She did not raise her own pups?"

I chuckled, though with a heavy heart, and nestled my nose into Suma's hair. "Of course not. That was for the lead female to do."

"Then your sister is Meron's mate?" The white wolf, of course, cleverly pieced the information together.

"*Was*," I hissed. "He is dead now, thanks to our Luna. She bit him when he tried to rape her. Twice. They were wounds he never recovered from because of her poison." I paused to let my words resonate. Suma dipped her chin as she grasped the scenario in her head. My spine ignited as shame crept through my heart. My wolf-woman's hands gripped my wrists and she squeezed tight.

"You reassure me, mate?" I breathed.

"Yes," she whispered. "I have been on the end of your pole and I know your strength. You must not have been holding tight."

I shook my head and inhaled. "You are oddly accurate in your assessments, white wolf. I did not hold her well, you are right. And she was able to protect herself from Meron's advances. But that came at a very high cost, and it nearly ended her life. My pack leader injured her, too, when they fought, and then he forced her to heal him."

Suma spun back around to face me again. Her brown eyes were wide with concern. "Luna should never heal when she is not strong herself."

"I know this now, but I did not know then. There was much I did not know about the abilities of the Luna, since I was only second and not allowed to breed." I kept talking. My tongue it seemed, had been loosed by my heart. "Your sister knew, of course, but she had no choice. Meron and his men held your brother hostage to force Beth to behave. She was very uncooperative." I chuckled at her ferocity now that she was safe. At the time, however, it endangered her and it had taken every bit of influence I had to convince Meron and my sister to let her live. I had yet to reveal to Luna how close the silver wolf had come to having her killed.

Rather than that truth, I told Suma another version. "Everyone wanted her dead because of her refusal to bow to Meron's rule. She was dangerous to have around. I saw her heart when she had healed me the first time. I knew she would never give in. She could not conform to Meron's will. It was not in her nature to do so."

Suma surprised me with her own chuckle and admission. "Yes, gray wolf. I know all about Beth's inability to conform. She challenged my father, who is," she paused and corrected herself, "who *was* our pack leader, in defense of Alec. She was dreadful in her wrath, and it was very obvious if it had not been for my brother, she would have attacked her pack leader. She obeys only her heart, Grane, and I count myself as fortunate to be hers."

"All the more reason for you to run to her if we get in trouble with other wolves here. They have seen Luna, and they are very afraid of her. They will not bother you as long as they know you are under her protection."

"But you cannot run back to her," she whispered, and she dropped her chin low enough so that her hair fell forward to expose the knobs of her spine. I sucked in my breath. She harbored such an exquisite blend of strength and vulnerability that my heart bucked around in protective confusion.

"No, I cannot run back toward our territory. The humans will follow, and they do not care about Luna's power. If anything, it will only pique their interest and they will examine her more tortuously. I have brought you and your family enough pain, Suma, I will not do that." I tightened my arms around her in my remorse for the things I had done to them. Being this close to my old territory bombarded me with memories.

145

The white wolf's forgiveness resonated all the more poignant because of it.

"Little wolf, you save me," I whispered hoarsely. "I will release you any time the truth of what I have done becomes too much for you to bear. I will not abuse your compassion."

"Abuse my compassion? You would abuse my heart if you let me go, I know that much. I did not mate easily, gray wolf, so please banish any thought of our parting."

I crushed her to me and inhaled her scent, while my stomach lurched and my skin ignited. "Suma," I breathed. "I am always—" But those were the only words I could say around my contorting vocal chords. My mate fell from my arms as my bones shifted and my muscles buckled. I sat beside my mate as wolf, and a satisfied grin flushed her pale cheeks.

So much for talking.

Suma, on the other hand, was in complete control of herself and she laughed merrily. "I hope I rock you like this until the end of your days. I love you, too, gray wolf." She twined her fingers into my ruff and pressed her forehead to mine.

My tail swung like a maddened pendulum behind me, and my heart thumped hard and rhythmically. I licked her chin and whined as I rolled to my back. Suma bent over on her knees and buried her face in my belly. Oh, the thrill of her breath upon me. I squirmed but remained on my back for her. She slid her bare body along my underside and burrowed herself into my fur.

Her breaths evened and soon she dozed. I did not budge for fear of disturbing her, and remained wolf even when I calmed. The white wolf-woman needed her rest, and I would give her anything it was in my power to give.

Chapter Eighteen

Later that night, Suma woke refreshed and starving. We needed to hunt. She shivered into the white wolf, and I rubbed my body all over hers in welcome. I hoped with all of my heart she would heed my warning if the need arose. We had enemies on both sides, and the humans were most likely decreasing the distance between the signal from my radio collar and themselves.

Suma's proximity to me set me on edge as we hunted. I had too many scents to pay attention to, but it was not long before the white wolf's tail stiffened with anticipation. I poked my nose into the air to catch the odor of our dinner, and then flanked Suma as she darted after it. She snatched a rabbit in her jaws expertly and the spry little beast had no time to scream.

I trotted away in search of another trail before Suma could offer any of her meal. She needed to eat, and I did not want her sharing.

I managed to snuff out a skunk and back-pedaled to a safe distance. Suma trotted up behind me and her triangular ears were laid back soft upon her head. She did not need to vocalize her laughter. I nudged her chin with my nose and resumed my hunt. Eventually, I unearthed a mouse nest and gobbled the unsuspecting tribe in quick bites. It was not a big meal, but it was something.

But we were losing ground in our search for Armand and Eaen.

Their trail continued north, and Armand seemed to be doing his best to keep them at the edge of Meron's territory. At least he seemed to comprehend the danger they were in. We followed our little brothers' scents until dawn, but by the time the sun squeezed itself up past the tree tops their trail cut back toward the west. They were headed in.

I planted my feet and glanced back at Suma, who stopped and issued a low growl. She was mad that the young wolf-men's trail wound back into Meron's territory. I understood her ire completely.

Suddenly, she flattened her ears to her head, then crouched, and I heard the ominous drone of an airplane in the same instant.

The humans.

I braced to bolt but then realized it did not matter if they saw me.

Hide.

Suma did not hesitate, and dashed into the heavier tree cover. She lay well hidden by the time the plane circled back around us. I knew for sure they homed in on the signal from my collar, and the best thing I could do was run headlong toward Meron's pack.

But Suma? I could not leave her, or ask her to run toward danger. It was one thing to follow carefully after Eaen and Armand, we could not afford to rush toward them without keeping ourselves safe.

I stayed put and waited for the biologists to get their bearings. The plane circled several more times and the longer they took the more nervous I grew. They would attract attention to this very spot. I knew it would not take the western wolves long to figure out why the plane circled.

They were very familiar with the tracking behavior of biologists, and would investigate the area as soon as the plane left. Suma and I would be found.

I whined my impatience, and finally I could wait no longer and fled north, away from our brothers' trail and the interior of Meron's territory. Suma shadowed me while remaining in the dense underbrush. I trotted slowly so she could stay within range without being seen, but sped up whenever the cover thinned. The more distance I could put between where we were and where we were going the safer for Suma. Ultimately, the plane banked toward the east and disappeared out of sight.

I halted and shook into human form. "Suma," I croaked past my burning throat. "You are all right?" My heart thudded and anger boiled in my stomach. Damn humans and their interferences! I yanked at the collar around my neck until I felt blood slide across my shoulders and trickle down my spine.

Great suffering. Humans were so inept and so damned clever they were maddening. Suma sidled up to me, her eyes shining with her alarm. I released my hold on the immovable collar and stood heaving before her.

"I am so sorry, little wolf, but we could not stay." I paced to quell my seething anger. "If the fools had not circled. If they could just not be so—" I clenched my fists and roared at the eastern sky where the humans had gone. Suma slid in next to me, and her mere presence centered me so I settled and crouched onto the ground. The white wolf-woman knelt beside me, resting her warm hand on my back. I inhaled and released it slow through my pursed lips.

"Meron's pack will come." Suma's lilt caressed my raw nerves, and her intuition of the danger we were in steadied me. I turned to gaze at her openly, and shook my head in wonder.

"Suma, for such a sheltered wolf you are strangely adept. Are you sure you have never dealt with humans or strange wolves?"

She giggled at my oddly delivered compliment, and my heart swelled in spite of my anger. My muscles relaxed as though she stroked my fur and I clasped her hand in mine.

"Grane, you are like Beth and worry too much." She lowered her lids and when she opened them her brown eyes were brackish ponds. My groin twisted as I fell into their depths, yet did not mind drowning. Her voice carried like the pleasant aroma of blackberries in the summer air. "I remember when I first met Beth," she said. "She had still not realized her full potential, and she acted as helpless as any human." Luna's little sister snickered and shook her white head. "Our knack for drawing conclusions unnerved her. But as her pups grew in her womb, her essence thickened until eventually she understood. Someday Grane, as you spend more time with us, you will hone your inborn wolf skills, and I will not seem so unusually adept." She smiled and I felt her sun radiate throughout my body.

I could say nothing, and wallowed in her knowing gaze. She had me as surely as any fly in a spider's web. I was enchanted, effectively mesmerized.

"Now, we have a good sense of which direction Armand and Eaen are in. Let us start looking. I am anxious to find them so that I can swat them into the next day." Her laughter bubbled forth despite her threat, and I bobbed like a branch upon its current, and laughed with her.

She stepped in behind me, and her tongue licked like flames upon my back. My mate cleaned the trickling blood from my skin and I moaned.

Suffering sprite. She stirred my emotions until they were so mixed together I did not know which way I felt at a given moment. She was as much a sorceress as her sister.

She pulled back as if she had heard my thought and her giggles tickled the hair on my nape. I turned to fold her into my arms and she yielded readily. I bit her ear and she squealed her delight. I lifted her with me as I stood up and set her on the ground, then held her a few seconds more before I released her.

"All right, little wolf, let us head west from here, and then south. Perhaps we will pick up Eaen's and Armand's trail then. And Suma?"

She lifted her pale face.

"Remember to run if I am captured?"

The wolf-woman nodded her head, but the pain of her decision flared in her eyes. I drew her hand to my lips and kissed her palm, then I shivered to ignite the embers smoldering in my spine and shifted into wolf. When the biologists came back I did not want to be standing on two feet with their collar around my neck.

Suma followed my lead, and we made our way west.

* * * *

We traveled cautiously since the last thing we wanted was to accidentally come across Meron's hunting party. After a full day of traipsing through the woods, we found a small hill with a sheer face that would protect our backs, at least. The air hung with the promise of rain and we knew it would erase the wolf-men's scent. It would make finding them that much harder, but we were exhausted and needed to rest.

We snuggled our bodies into the hill, and Suma promptly dozed. Her body expanded and contracted in my arms as she breathed, and my eyes grew heavy until I realized I mimicked her breathing. I yawned, and reorganized my thoughts to keep myself awake.

I thought of Armand and Eaen, and hoped we would find them soon. I knew the longer we were out here, the more likely it would be that we would be discovered. The idea no sooner entered my head when I heard a snapping branch to my left. I jutted my face into the air and sniffed.

Humans.

It was impossible. Yet, here they were, and they were close. Suma crouched to her feet in a flash. Even asleep she had heard my fierce image. I yanked her searing body into the cover of the hill and pressed my finger to my lips. I did not know how close they were, or if they could see us. If we changed in front of them? I shuddered to think it. Suma shivered and growled in spite of my warning. She could not stifle her wolf.

"Breathe, Suma," I whispered. She turned her frantic eyes to me, and I knew she would not be able to hold her human form. I bundled her into my arms and turned my bare back toward the forest, to shelter her as best I could. Her body convulsed with her effort and her skin burned like solid fire. She trembled and clamped her jaw.

I heard more snapping of branches, then the sickening whir and click of the camera. Suma's brown eyes widened.

"Do it, Suma," I muttered through my own clenched jaw. "Now!" Her body rippled fluidly once she quit fighting her shift, and I held the white wolf in a tight embrace. I turned with her in my arms and stared straight at a human being.

Suma snarled, but I held her tight. The human stood as if he had forgotten he was a physical being. He seemed utterly bewildered and did not move.

My human hair prickled upright and sweat pooled at my lower back, but I did not set the white wolf down. Her rumblings raised in pitch and her ears flattened to her skull. Her long, bared fangs were only inches from my face. They would flay human skin effortlessly, and I knew it would not be mine she would tear.

Suma's life depended on her not attacking the human. Biologist or not, he would have no alternative but to kill her if she charged. I went on the offensive in her stead.

"What do you want," I growled. My entire abdomen clenched in anticipation of an assault. I swallowed a deep breath to steady myself.

The human who stood before me found his voice, but he dropped the metal rod he had been gripping in his left hand. The tan box he carried fell to the ground, as well. His tone mewled pathetic, and I resisted the urge to release Suma.

"I—our group is following a w-wolf," he stammered, but said no more and instead gaped at Suma.

"She is not wolf," I snarled my lie. "Leave us!" I lunged at him, and he flinched, but he did not move his feet. He was rooted to the ground, and his camera dangled like bait from his neck. The idiot. Suma squirmed to remove herself from my grasp and her growls escalated into frustrated screams.

No Suma. Stay.

Her snarling ceased, but her body pressed rigid into mine. I squatted to set the white wolf onto the forest floor, and commanded aloud for her to stay put. I had to get that camera, and I could not do it with her in my arms. But I could not have her attacking the human, either. I lowered my voice, but kept my eyes on the trespasser, who gawped at my neck.

"White wolf, I beg you. Stay. No matter what."

Suma whined and minced her paws, but she did not move forward. I straightened my knees and squared my shoulders, then stepped forward. Suma moved with me. Her breath fanned against the backs of my legs, and I halted.

"Little wolf," I whispered, "please stay put."

I did not look back when I stepped forward again, but I did not feel her behind me. I took calculated steps toward the man and homed in on every signal he unintentionally revealed. His fright rankled my nose, and I resisted the urge to sneeze the rancid stench of urine and cold sweat from my nostrils.

I held my breath and stepped closer. He was now within ten feet of me, and I knew I could easily close that gap if I rushed him. The human seemed too petrified to move, and I cocked my head. What was the matter with him?

He was just a boy. No more than Armand's or Eaen's age. But, he was human, and he was not alone in these woods. Other humans, I knew from experience, would be nearby. So, why did he not act more aggressively? I halted and braced for an attack from him that I suspected would not come.

I held out my hand. "Give me your camera."

He lowered his eyes from my neck and gaped at my hand. As if he thought he dreamed, he held up his own hand in front of his face to marvel at it. Then he looked back at mine, his brain methodically calculating the differences.

I swallowed my snarl, and repeated my demand. "Give me the camera, boy."

He raised his eyes slowly to my face, but then they flickered to my neck.

"You—," he licked his lips and spoke again. "You wear a collar?"

He was an ass. I could snap his fragile neck if he provoked me.

"But—," he continued.

I shook my head in warning. "Close your mouth and give me that camera." I advanced so there remained only five feet that separated us.

The human trembled and quaked, but shook his head no, and as if in dumb reflex, he reached for the camera strap.

I inhaled to steady myself. The boy was simply in survival mode and not using his brain. It occurred to me if he felt like talking, I might learn something. I did not have to guess he would not know enough to withhold information.

I glanced back at Suma, who stayed back by the hill, waiting. I breathed a sigh of relief and rubbed my hand across my face, then leveled my gaze on the human. "Okay, boy. If you will not give me your camera, what do you need it for?"

He dropped his eyes to his chest as if remembering for the first time he carried the mechanical device.

"What is that?" I fired my questions at him. He followed the line of my pointing finger, and his eyes widened.

"It's an antenna. To follow the wo..." His eyes grew impossibly larger. What a pathetic example of his species. He stared at the collar around my neck again.

"To follow the wolf," I finished for him.

He nodded as he lifted his own finger and pointed at me.

I cleared my throat before I spoke again. "What have you found so far?" I prodded.

"A gray wolf."

I was going to have to kill him.

Because he was as stupid as a porcupine, he said, still pointing, "We put *that* collar on it."

I shook my head in amazement.

"How many are here in this forest with you?" I continued undeterred, but my skin warmed. Suma whined behind me.

The boy looked past me as he answered, and stared at the white wolf.

I snapped my fingers to get his attention back on me. I did not need him provoking Suma. This human had to die at a human's hand, not by the fang of a wolf.

"Just me. The others are back at—"

My gratified smile stuck his words in his throat. He realized too late he had given himself away, that his life would end.

I squared my shoulders, and he hiccupped as tears dropped to his cheeks. That checked me, and my head cocked to the side again.

"Suma," I addressed the white wolf without turning around. "Come and see this human up close." Before I killed him, I could at least put him to some use. The white wolf approached with caution. Her triangular ears twitched and she sniffed the air around us. The tip of her beautiful white tail wiggled uncertainly.

"It is all right, little wolf. Come and meet your first human." I glued my eyes on my toy in case he tried something foolish. With my mate this close I was not going to take chances. He stood silent and let his tears drop unnoticed. The stench of his fear unfolded fully, and I felt a pang of sympathy for the porcupine.

"Suma, practice. If you can, reveal yourself."

The white wolf whined as she pressed her flank against my leg. I lowered my hand to caress her back to comfort her.

"Try it," I coaxed, and her body shivered and erupted with heat. She shivered once more, and I kept my eyes on the human before me. His face blanched and he wobbled, then crumpled in a dead faint when Suma unfolded before him.

I looked down at her crouched upon the forest floor. Her cheeks were pale, too, but not nearly as ashen as our victim's. I chuckled and extended my hand to help her to her two feet. The boy remained passed out.

Suma furrowed her brow and wrinkled her nose with disgust.

I laughed outright.

"What do you think, my mate?"

She tip-toed closer to the boy and tentatively reached out to run a tapered finger across his leg. "Are these clothes?" She looked up at me with curiosity rounding her beautiful brown eyes.

I grinned and nodded. "Yes, Suma. Those are clothes. Humans are shy about their bodies," I explained.

The wolf-woman shook her head in wonderment, and I knelt down beside her. "They are so fragile," she whispered.

"Physically, yes. But do not be fooled. They are more dangerous than bear or a pack of coyotes," I warned her. "Look him over, but do not lower your guard. And listen for others. Always. Humans are like coyotes and do not often travel alone."

She examined him closer, and I pulled the camera strap from behind his head, then tossed the incriminating device beyond the human's reach so I could destroy it later. The human stirred, and Suma growled her warning.

"Step away, little wolf." I held her hand as we backed up a few paces, and then I offered her an impish grin. "Want to say something to him?"

The young man stirred and groaned as he pressed his palm to his forehead.

My mate nodded her willingness to try, her brown eyes dancing. "Can I?"

"Of course. He is to practice being human with," I encouraged her.

The porcupine sat up, but did not remove his hand from his head. He stared disbelieving at the pale woman who crouched down in front of him. She trembled and her heat radiated. She did not speak, and I wondered how close she bordered on changing again. Her back muscles expanded as she inhaled, and when she finally spoke, her voice carried very soft and scratchy. I strained to hear her.

"Hello," she said, and reached out her hand to touch the young man, halting it a few times before making contact.

He stared at her with his mouth hanging open, but reached out just the same. Suma yanked her hand away and slipped backward several paces. She clutched her fist to her stomach and looked at me for encouragement, but she still grinned.

I laughed, yet my heart tightened as I witnessed her courage. It required bravery to interact with humans, and Suma was doing just fine in spite of her trepidation.

She straightened to her full height, then approached the young man again, whose skin seemed transparent he was so pale. He curled his legs to get his feet under him.

"Careful, Suma," I snarled, and stepped sideways so I could grab him if he tried anything.

Suma halted, and asked the boy his name. "Ken," he replied, "Ken Rickey." He shot nervous glances between the both of us.

"Well, Kenrickey, what did you see today?" I arced my eyebrow. I could not resist playing with him.

His eyes drifted to Suma and he blushed, then shook his head as he dropped his incredulous stare. "I saw...I don't know what I saw," he admitted.

I laughed and cajoled him to say more. "What else have you seen today? Yesterday?"

He narrowed his eyes, his suspicion aroused by my questions. Play time was over. "Suma, is there anything else? Would you like to talk to him again, or touch him one last time?"

She nodded, and Kenrickey stood on his knees.

"Please," he begged, "don't."

Suma knelt down in front of him. "We have no choice," she said softly, and not unkindly. She reached out to touch the novelty of the scraggly beard on his face. His hand raised to cover hers, but otherwise he did not move.

"It is a pity," she said, but did not take her eyes from the human.

"The pity is what he is," I spat. "He is young like our brothers, but he is still human."

"Yes," my mate agreed. "He seems so innocent. What if we did not kill him and he helped you get that collar off?"

I sighed. "Suma, your compassion goes too far. But, you do have a point," I allowed and stepped up beside her.

She mustered full command of herself for the moment, impressing me with how readily she adapted to the situation. I crouched and assessed our porcupine.

I stared at him hard, and he dropped his eyes. A good sign, for his sake. I squared my shoulders and leaned toward him. Kenrickey trembled, and his shoulders dropped in deference. He was a subordinate to his bones.

I glanced sideways at Suma, who nodded her appreciation for his instinctive submission. She grinned at me and my heart galloped. I stole a quick kiss, and watched as her brown eyes danced. I dragged my attention from Suma to concentrate on the young man.

"Can you remove the collar, porcupine?"

"I can't," he admitted, and would not look up as he spoke. He sweated horribly in his fear of us. "I need the…I need the proper tools." He hiccupped and his cowardice in the face of his death struck me as sad, and not the least bit pathetic as I would have thought. He was just a boy.

I inhaled, looked around then rested my eyes on Suma.

She glued her eyes on the human before us. "Can you get them?"

"No," I yelped.

The young man raised a hopeful expression at the same time. Suma looked from face to face, and I curled my knuckles under her chin and shook my head. "No, little wolf. That is much too dangerous." My heart skittered around in my chest, and I inhaled to steady it. "The human does not leave."

The white wolf was not deterred. "We have to remove this thing from you, Grane. We have already been discovered by one of the biologists. What if more see us transform?"

I stood up without answering her. She had struck on the truth of it. Kenrickey stood, too, and Suma rose up and growled. The boy dropped back to his knees.

"Suma, what you wish to do is too dangerous. Humans are not to be trusted. As soon as we let him go, he is going to run to the others and tell them everything."

"I won't," the human promised, interrupting my discussion with my mate.

"Your oath means nothing, porcupine," I snapped. His time on the planet waned, and we were losing precious time in our search for Eaen and Armand.

"Take off your clothes," I ordered.

The young man obeyed without question, but he trembled with dread.

Suma stood back and waited to see what I planned.

When he stripped to stand as naked as we were, I snatched his wrist and pointed a long finger at his tracking equipment. "Make a tool from that."

He looked at his things and then at me, doubt clouding his eyes.

"Your life depends on it, Kenrickey," I warned him as I squeezed his wrist until he cringed.

"Yes," he cried. "I'll try."

"You will not try, you will *do*. Now."

He fell down in a pile to begin, but his hands shook too hard for him to work.

I heaved a heavy sigh to curb my temper. I was through playing. I wanted that suffering collar off, and I wanted to get moving. In his fear, the young human bumbled everything. I picked up his shirt and ripped it until I had a long strand of cloth.

"Come here, porcupine."

He froze, and his face fell when he saw my lash. Then he pissed himself.

I raised my eyebrow at my mate. She covered her mouth to hide her grin. We stood in the company of a pathetic example of his species, and I wondered if it was even really necessary to tie him. Amusing as my thoughts were, I could not take chances, especially when I had Suma with me. If he ever harmed her? I shuddered to think it, and spoke to cut off my morbid thoughts.

"I will not harm you, but I do not trust you. Come here." I softened my stance and dropped my arms. Even he understood then I meant him no harm for the moment. He inched toward me, and as soon as he was within reach I grabbed his wrists and tied his hands together. From his wrists I ran the cloth to his neck and fashioned a collar. The remainder I used for a leash. I handed our new pet to Suma and winked.

She grinned. In spite of our captive's vulnerability, the wolf-woman had not lost sight of the fact humans had tortured her brother and cousin, and had trapped Eaen, nearly killing him. She felt no remorse for our cautionary measures, and kept a close eye on our unexpected prize. Yet, when she spoke to him, she retained her soft tone to ease him.

"Kenrickey, no one will come after you?"

He hung his head and his body language did not lie. "No. They do not expect me back for several days."

"That is good," she replied, although our captive did not look so pleased about it.

I found the camera, smashed it against the trunk of a tree until it disintegrated into a hundred little pieces, gathered up the surveillance equipment and led the way west. The porcupine said no more as Suma pulled him along behind her.

* * * *

We traveled along for several hours and did not offer to stop until our guest began to stumble with fatigue. He splashed right into the small brook we halted by, and clouded the water.

Suma and I headed upstream of him, and pulled palmfuls of the refreshing water to our mouths. When we slaked our thirst, we splashed in too. The water running across our skin cooled and invigorated us, and I pulled Suma to me in a hug, hungry for the touch of her. I had been itching to do so for some time, and to feel her skin on mine saturated me with a heady bliss. I nuzzled her neck and chewed her ear.

She giggled, and sent my heart flapping around in my ribcage. I spun her around so her buttocks curved against my thighs, and clamped my hand to her neck. She straddled readily.

We both looked at the human and stiffened simultaneously, then broke out into a fit of laughter. Our poor porcupine sat in the water with his head hung low. We did not have him tied anywhere, nor did we hold his tether. He just did not offer to run off, and it struck us both as comically absurd.

"I told you humans were unpredictable," I reminded Suma, and we both laughed again. Kenrickey raised his head to look at us.

"You do not run, porcupine?" I asked.

He swiped at his soaked bangs to pull them out of his eyes, then shook his head no.

I stood up and offered my hand to Suma. When she rose to her feet, water cascaded from her bare skin, and I eyed her with fevered appreciation. She blushed and I stole a kiss from her lower lip.

She responded with wafting heat, and ran her tongue along my jaw. Then she emitted a frustrated moan, and pulled away.

The porcupine.

I inhaled and pushed a lock of white hair away from her reddened cheek. She cocked a rueful smile and whispered, "Wait. You are burning up, and so am I. I am afraid if we shift in front of the human he will have another spell and not be able to make his tool." She searched my expression for understanding.

My smile spread across my face. "You are incredible, little wolf, and very clever. I have to agree with you on that score. He is not the bravest human I have ever seen."

Suma giggled, and once our skin had cooled we approached the young man, who still sat, dejected, in the stream.

"Are you ready to make that tool, now?"

He glanced up with expectation, and I was pleased to see his enthusiasm for the task. "Yes. But first," he hung his head again. "First, may I look at the collar?"

I stiffened, and Suma rested her hand on my back.

"You may," I agreed. "But keep in mind I can snap your neck like a dry twig if you try anything stupid," I added as warning. I stepped back so he could get out of the brook and onto dry land, then I knelt in front of him to expose my neck. Suma sidled in next to us, growling low as she kept a close scrutiny on the human's every move.

He bent over me to inspect the contraption. "This is the collar we put on the gray wolf," he breathed. His hands trembled and he stepped away as the color drained from his face like he bled to death. He was going to swoon again.

"Kenrickey," Suma murmured. "It is all right."

The porcupine shook his head. "It's impossible," he croaked.

My mate spoke soft to keep him focused. "So then, you know how to remove it?" She reached out to touch him and he flinched as if she had stung him. "Breathe, human," she reminded him in her quiet way. He turned his face to her, and inhaled as she had instructed. "Again. Breathe," she hummed.

The porcupine breathed at her insistence until the color returned to his face. Suma took his hand in hers, the contrast striking. We definitely were not human, even if we did walk upright. I tilted my head and bared my throat as they neared.

The young man bent over me again to re-inspect his handiwork. He sighed and then said, "I need a wrench and a screwdriver."

"That is bad?" Suma was also bent over me and eyeing the collar. Her soft voice drifted down to me and my pulse quickened.

I took a very deep breath before I spoke. "Make them."

The porcupine stepped back, and looked as though he would cry again. He remembered to inhale and regained his composure. "I think I can do it, but it's going to take some time."

I shot upright, pushed him into the ground and straddled over him. "We do not have time," I snarled in his ear. "You have taken up too much of our precious time already. Get this collar off from me now." I released my hand from his neck and shoved away from him. He did not get up, but pressed his bound wrists to his face.

I had no more patience for him. Either he would help us, or I needed to kill him soon. I had enough to worry about this far into Meron's territory. We would be discovered eventually and we still had not found Armand or Eaen.

The human mumbled something from the ground. I inhaled to steady myself and walked back over to him, then crouched beside his prone body.

"I can do it, but I need my hands free."

I glanced at Suma for her approval. She nodded. Obviously she did not feel very threatened by him, either. I unleashed his hands, but kept the tether around his neck.

"Work." I turned my back to him and left him to do his thing.

Suma sauntered over and leaned herself into my opened arms. We watched the porcupine rummage and bend things. Suma's taut belly rumbled against my forearms.

"You are hungry and hunting alone is too risky," I whispered into her ear. She pulled my arms tighter around her and I obliged her mood by lifting her completely into my embrace like one of the pups. She hummed her pleasure and my anger abated.

"Hunt, Grane," she said after several moments of quiet. "I will watch the porcupine."

"Suma, we are too far into Meron's territory. It is only a matter of time until we are discovered and I do not dare leave you alone." I snuggled my face in her hair to breathe in her spice.

"We have to eat, gray wolf. If Meron's crew shows up I promise to run. I will even leave the boy behind to keep them busy." She looked up into my face and her brown eyes shimmered. I kissed her nose and she giggled. "Go, wolf, before I threaten to stay and fight. I am hungry."

I released her to the forest floor with reluctance. She was right, of course. We needed to eat. She gave me a quick hug and I shivered my spine to crackling. My muscles rippled and I stood before my mate as wolf. I stole a glance toward the human, who gaped and rocked unsteadily.

Suma noticed him and headed over to run interference before he fainted again. I hurried toward the woods in search of a meal.

Chapter Nineteen

I returned a short while later with a partridge in my jaws.

Suma sat resting beside the porcupine, who had either fallen asleep or lay unconscious. My heart tightened in my chest. My white wolf was safe and now she could eat. Plus, I had sniffed out Armand's and Eaen's trail. They had looped north again, and I hoped it meant they were leaving Meron's territory and heading east toward home.

I trotted over to Suma, who stood up when she caught my scent. The human did not move. I dropped the partridge at Suma's bare feet and she scooped it up. She shimmied her pale body and crouched so she could eat her meal with her wolf teeth. I knew she was hungry enough to crunch up the bones and all. There would be nothing wasted.

I slipped out of my fur and nudged the porcupine. He muttered until his eyes opened and bolted upright when he saw me squatting next to him. I noticed Suma retied his hands, and a flush of pride for her caution rushed to fill me.

"Wake up, porcupine." I grinned at him with my best wolf smile and made sure all of my teeth showed. I knew it was mean, but teasing him seemed better than torturing him, which I would have done less than a year ago. I followed his disbelieving eyes as he stared open-mouthed at the white wolf.

"That is my mate you are disrespecting, human. Mind your manners," I growled. He quickly averted his eyes and stared at me instead. "That is better, porcupine." I nodded my approval, and he visibly relaxed with my assurance of what his proper behavior should be.

S. C. Dane

"Are the tools finished?"

Kenrickey blinked a couple of times before he answered. I held my breath and waited with affected patience. I tugged on my collar to bring his brain back to the task.

"Yes. Almost," he stammered.

I raised an eyebrow. "Which is it? Yes or almost?"

"Almost," he answered in a hurry. "The problem with your particular, uh..."

"Just speak," I sighed. I glanced over at Suma who was just finishing up. She had made short work of the bird.

The young man continued. "The problem with your collar is that it was designed to really last."

I said nothing, and he adjusted his position, like he was squirming under the pressure.

"Since we have never seen wolves in this part of Maine, we wanted to be sure we didn't lose you, uh, I mean the wolf...who is...you."

I grinned. His brain struggled to adapt to his current situation. Suma snuggled up behind me. The smell of blood on her breath fluttered my stomach. "Go on." I encouraged the human to distract myself.

"Well, so, its removal is a bit tricky without the right tools. But I'm getting close." He sat back and watched with his breath held. He seemed to have no idea what my reaction to his news would be, and awaited it with not a little touch of fear.

"Are you hungry?"

He shook his head as if to clear his thoughts. "What?"

"Are you hungry?" Suma repeated for me. I reached back and squeezed her ankle. Her leg radiated a delicious heat from her recent change.

The porcupine nodded in the affirmative. "Yes." Then he added after looking back and forth between the two wolf-people in front of him, "But, I'm a vegetarian. I don't eat meat."

Suma's laughter burst from behind me, and I could not help but join her. This human was a prize.

Our captive did not see the amusement in his answer. He did not laugh with us, which only made him funnier.

"Then you will go hungry, porcupine," I warned once I recovered

164

enough breath to speak.

We turned our backs on him and left him to ponder his dilemma, but I kept a grip on his leash. My mate and I settled in for the night, and I would have to wait for daylight so the genius could see what he was doing, although I itched to have the damned collar off. One more day, I consoled myself, and nestled in tight to Suma.

I told her of my discovery of our brothers' trail.

"There are more of you?" The human's anxious voice disturbed the stillness of the night.

"You are being rude again, human," I growled, and he went silent. I barely heard him breathe. I felt my mate's heart flutter and her mossy scent sharpened. "We will find them soon," I offered, scraping up as much hope as I could. She nodded, and then fell right to sleep. I kept the first watch.

The human eventually fell asleep with an empty belly and unanswered questions. I stared up at the stars and thought about my new family we had left back at the den. I would have to ask Kenrickey more questions about the biologists and what they were finding. Most important, I would have to ask him how he knew about the wolves in the first place. If it did have something to do with Alec, he would want to know.

I smelled the wolf-men before I heard them, which meant they were not sure where we were positioned. I nudged Suma gently so as not to alarm her, but she needed to wake. I bent low and whispered in her ear.

"Meron's pack."

Suma froze and then sat up very slow, silent as an egret. I leaned over the human and clamped my hand across his mouth, knowing that when he startled awake his mouth would open first. It did. I kept him pinned to the ground with my palm across his mouth, and held a tapered finger to my lips and shook my head.

The porcupine nodded his understanding, and I slid my hand from his lips. He honored his word and lay still, although his scent escalated in his fear. I barely heard Suma instruct him to breathe.

What I heard finally was the airy pass of fur through leafy branches. I held my breath and counted at least three wolves. A good sign. The wolves around us were hunters, not scouts, who would be in human form because they needed to carry poles.

I leaned back over Kenrickey and put my mouth next to his ear. "Do not run. They will kill you." I pulled away and studied his reaction. His eyes widened and he stiffened, but he did not move. I turned then to Suma and nodded. We needed our fur, and she folded and shifted with ease. I followed suit, and looked over at the porcupine, who could no longer deny our existence. At least he remained conscious. I perked my ears toward the forest around us and poked my muzzle into the air.

Meron's group doubled back. They found our most recent trail, which meant a fight loomed inevitable. My hackles lifted and my lip curled off my teeth. I willed my heart to steady. This was the first time I ever had to protect the one I adored from another wolf. Luna had been different. The others were afraid of her and she was stronger than my white wolf.

I stole a quick glance at Suma. Her legs were set secure beneath her and her tail jutted out stiff behind her. My heart soared with new courage. My white wolf was not afraid.

One of Meron's wolves huffed from our left, and Suma spun around to face him. I did not budge, but waited for what I knew would come next. The ambush from the right. The wolf burst out of the thicket and careened toward Suma's back. I body-slammed him and sent him rolling, then retreated to tighten our flank. There was still a third wolf who had not shown himself.

My anger boiled and my skin crawled with the thrill of this fight. It had been too long since I fought with any honor, and my heart hammered strong against my sternum. I could not hide my wolf smile, and I felt my lips pull back from my sharp teeth.

Suma caught my tail wagging out of the corner of her eye and stole a quick glance my way. I could not deny the feeling of utter well-being growing within me. I snarled, relishing its deep rumble.

The first wolf finally lunged toward Suma, but I would have to let her handle him. I knew beyond a doubt the other two would swarm her since their first advance failed. They did not disappoint, and I barreled into them and sent one reeling, then latched onto the throat of the other and crushed with all my might.

His blood cascaded hot into my mouth and I braced my legs, locked my shoulders and wrenched my head down. Flesh ripped beneath my fangs and the wolf's blood gushed. I released him to die on his own and sought my next victim, who had recovered quickly to descend on the white wolf in order to help his pack mate.

Suma fought ferociously and my heart quickened. I dodged my head low and snapped a dark leg in my jaws and pulled. The wolf yelped and spun with his maw gaped wide. I released, hopped back and reclamped my fangs onto the leg when the surprised wolf overshot his target. I rolled with the leg still in my mouth and felt the gratifying crack of bone, and the tortured shriek.

That time, though, I did not follow through to snap the spine. Suma and her attacker were still at it. I knew in an instant it meant the white wolf merely defended herself, and did not inflict debilitating wounds on her aggressor.

My heart wrenched, and I roared toward the melee. They were fighting too fiercely for me to pick a spot to intervene, so I smashed into the both of them to separate their bodies. An instant of regret flashed into my heart, but my onslaught accomplished what I hoped. I flipped my paws beneath me and lunged for Suma's rival.

He rose onto his hind legs, but instead of rising to meet him I dropped and lurched for his hind leg. I sunk my fangs into flesh, clamped my jaw shut, and ripped him to the ground. He shrieked his surprise and agony, but I did not relent. As soon as he crashed to the ground, I drove my face into his vulnerable underbelly and gnashed with my incisors.

My opponent's teeth snapped onto my ruff and cheek but I did not falter. His bite would only wound me, but my advantage would kill him. I could not sway because of pain.

The wolf's steaming blood wetted my face and his efforts weakened as quickly as his blood flooded out of him. I had severed a main artery. It was only then that I backed away and went to Suma. I snuggled into her and licked at her chin and ran my body the length of hers. She braced her feet, but did not reciprocate, and I stepped back to gauge her. The white wolf watched me with her dark eyes, but stood rigid.

I whined my confusion and minced my paws on the forest floor.

Suma? What was wrong?

The white wolf jutted her chin to stare beyond me. I spun around to see what captured her attention. The wolf whose leg I had broken stood upright in his human form, the porcupine clutched in his hard grip.

My regret for not killing him mushroomed to weigh like a hundred stones in my gut. He threatened my future, and a low growl bubbled from my lungs. I stepped toward him on stiff legs and pricked my ears forward.

"Stop, Grane, or I will kill your pet."

I halted, and pressed my ears to my skull. He could do it even with a broken leg. The wolf-man holding the human was one of Meron's better fighters. I should have detached his spine when I had the chance. I crouched and forced myself into human form, then straightened my knees and stood before the assailant on two bare feet.

"Put him down, Lars," I growled, "or I will kill you." I did not bluff and he knew it. He had been my subordinate when I had lived with Meron's pack. My skin seared and I barely held my human form. "Drop him." I stepped forward, and Lars flinched but held his place.

"Nice mate," he sneered, and I followed his amber eyes to Suma, who was circling to my right.

My heart choked me as it leapt into my throat, and my pulse shivered my nerves. Rivulets of sweat coursed down my spine, and I shook my head.

"Finally found another, eh? Is she as feisty as your first, gray wolf?" he taunted.

I clenched my fists and swallowed to keep the roar from exploding from my itching body. "Leave her," I seethed from my contorting throat. I could hold my human form no longer, and we had talked enough.

I crouched and lunged as my blood erupted like lava, and landed on Lars' chest as wolf. We fell to the ground with the human, and I saw the instant where my opponent still gripped his quarry, which left him vulnerable for that split second. I sunk my teeth into naked flesh and crushed my molars together to lock my jaw.

Lars' scream bubbled in his crushed throat, and I rolled to my back and brought his twisting figure with me. His muscles buckled and contorted in my mouth but I did not release, and somersaulted him to his back. He thrust against me with his hind legs, slashing the thin skin of my belly, but I would not release.

168

Never would he hurt Suma, even if he wounded me mortally. I braced my front legs against his body and yanked backwards with his throat in my jaws. He mangled a final squawk from his mutilated throat and fell limp beneath my paws, dead.

I felt no exultant joy.

I pushed myself from the tangle of our bodies and shook his filth from my fur. My stomach stung from the wounds Lars' inflicted, but at the moment it did not matter. The white wolf did. I found her sitting tight with her tail curled around her paws near the base of an old pine tree. She fought with so much bravery, and I shivered into my human form so I could hold her, and check her for serious wounds. I knelt beside her and cupped her head in my hands as if she were a delicate flower.

"Little wolf, are you all right? Are you injured?" I searched her rounded brown eyes, but all I saw was confusion and fear. "Suma?"

She whined her response, then drew her tail in tighter around her white paws.

I ran my hand down her front legs and then her flank.

She growled her warning.

I pulled away and caught her eyes in mine. "Are you injured, little wolf?" Panic pushed bile up my throat, and I ran my hand down the white wolf's flank again. Her snarl sliced my heart; Suma had to be injured.

"Let me see, mate." I was on my knees but my stomach had fallen somewhere on the ground. "Shift so that I can see better," I pleaded.

The white wolf whimpered, but refused.

"Suma, if you are hurt I must know." The panic wended its gritty fingers into my bowels. Suma pulled her lips from her incisors. I leaned back and removed my hands from her.

I heard the human's footsteps behind me and then his shaky voice asking if the white wolf was okay. I snarled for him to keep his distance, and he withdrew.

"Suma, please," I begged, and barely choked my words past the lump in my throat.

"If she is hurt I can help," the porcupine offered again.

"Back off," I spun and snapped at him. He leapt backwards and fell on his rump, but he did not go any farther forward or back. I turned around to my mate and took a steadying breath. At least if she were mortally wounded I would know. I stepped away from her, too, and gave her the space she seemed to need; but, I did not retreat too far.

I sat on the ground and assessed my own wounds. My blood dripped down the contours of my legs and I swiped at my face where the second wolf had latched on. I would probably have a scar from that one. The injury cut deep, and the skin folded where his fangs ripped through. My wounds were nothing compared to the pain I felt in my heart. Something was definitely wrong with Suma. She did not even tend to herself, but sat silent and watched me.

Then the truth hit me, stealing my breath. I clenched my fists and fought with the dark thoughts threatening to unmoor me. Suma had seen me kill a fellow wolf-man. Three times. A groan emanated from my guts and wove its way past my throat, and up into the night sky. I threw my head back to release my anguish.

I howled my torment and dug my fingers into the earth beneath me. Suma knew what I had been guilty of in my past, but for her to witness it? It was too much. I had fallen from her grace. To the white wolf, I was no better than the dull-toothed being who lurked naked behind me. I hung my head in shame, even as I longed for her forgiveness.

I inhaled and held the air in my lungs until they felt like they would burst. I released my breath through pursed lips until my nerves steadied. Suma would come around, I consoled myself. I felt it in my bones. She had just been shocked by the violence of my other life. My killing of those wolves was self-defense, even though I trespassed on their turf. The white wolf did not know those wolves as I knew them. If I had not slain them, they would most certainly have killed us. I had not acted without honor.

I looked at her then and leveled my eyes on hers. She did not look away in disgust, at least. In fact, it was me who wanted to look away from her stare. No doubting it. I had shaken her faith in me. I got onto my feet and trudged over to Kenrickey.

He sat with his elbows on his knees while he watched the scene between me and Suma play itself out. He raised his face when I approached him, and I knelt to his level.

"Give me your hands, porcupine." I held out my own hands for his.

He hesitated a moment, then placed his lashed fists into my palms. His seemed so small and delicate compared to mine. I caught him staring at them and cleared my throat. His eyes shot to my face, and even in the dark I could see him blush.

"It is all right. We are different," I reassured him. I unknotted the coil from around his wrists. "I trust that you will not stray, Kenrickey."

He nodded his head. "You just saved my life, I'm not going anywhere," he admitted. "Not when I'd bet the farm those three weren't the last ones out there."

"We are in their territory," I explained. "And we had better get out of here before more come looking. Grab your tools and let us go," I ordered. The porcupine jumped to his feet and unwrapped the rest of his leash from around his neck. Then he went over to his pile of things. I went to my white wolf.

"Suma," I whispered. She was gazing out over the little brook, the stars twinkled on its rippling surface. The white wolf turned her head toward me. "We need to get going. We will pick up Armand's and Eaen's trail and head in that direction."

She blinked but said nothing.

"We need to put as much distance between ourselves and Meron's pack as possible. Lars and his group will not be found for a few days, but once they are…" I knelt in front of her, and the hurt on her face prevented me from saying more.

"I am sorry you had to see that, little wolf." I kissed her under her white chin and withdrew. "Please, we must go." I stood up and walked back toward Kenrickey. My heart swelled and spread through my chest when I felt Suma step in behind me. We fell into a line and headed north again toward the young wolf-men.

* * * *

We stopped hiking at mid-morning, even though we were still in Meron's territory, but, at least we were on Eaen's and Armand's trail. Their scents were faint but identifiable.

Suma retained her wolf form so I knew she did not want to talk. I shoved away the nagging worry she had been injured and was hiding it. She acted physically healthy and I smelled no blood, except my own,

S. C. Dane

which had scabbed and closed the gashes on my stomach.

The porcupine plunked down onto the forest floor in a rounded heap and fell fast asleep as soon as we settled in. The removal of my collar would have to wait. I went over to the white wolf and knelt beside her.

"Do you mind my company, Suma?" She did not budge, but the tip of her tail thumped a couple of times in affirmation before she quieted it.

I made myself comfortable beside my mate, and she lay down with her chin on her paws beside me, but did not initiate contact. I respected her need for time to sort through her feelings, and did not speak beyond my initial request to sit with her.

I let my thoughts scamper through my brain on little mouse feet, visiting my fears and worries. I was sure that her seeing me kill another wolf-man had shaken her belief in my repentant heart. It was one thing for me to tell her about my past and how expertly I killed, and quite another for her to witness it with her own innocent eyes.

The death of a wolf was always a desecration, and I did not doubt t she saw me now as an offensive beast. I would not touch her.

My heart faltered, as did my faith she would want to remain my mate, no matter how much space I gave her. Had I not told the white wolf she could leave me anytime she wanted? I had been so sure of myself, then. I even thought I might find my brothers without there being any bloodshed.

What a fool I had been. In my happiness with Alec's pack I had forgotten just how low Meron's pack could drive a wolf-man. I murdered and felt justified. There lay the power of the silver wolf's pack, and it was why they still killed trespassers instead of just driving them away as any honorable wolves would do. I knew that, and still I brought my beloved Suma toward the danger. My white wolf's innocence had been stripped, and I was the one responsible for it.

I let my tears of loss drop onto my cheeks, and turned my back to the woman I loved more than myself. She offered me no comfort or consolation.

Chapter Twenty

The sun climbed up the eastern sky and still Suma slept. For one brief moment, the sight of her near me rekindled my hope. If she were done with me altogether she would have moved away. Yet, I bit off my thoughts for fear they would buoy my heart with a false promise of reconciliation between Suma and myself. I dared not even think of the bliss her forgiveness would mean to me.

I trained my attention on Kenrickey instead, who had risen to stretch his limbs. I unfolded myself and went to him. My heart felt too much like stone to greet him properly, so I began my inquisition without pleasure or goodwill.

"Porcupine, I have questions."

The human stopped stretching, and cast a wary looked at me.

"Ye-es?" he stammered, his muscles tensing. So much for all the stretching he had just done.

"How many humans came with you?"

Kenrickey sighed his relief. "Boy, for a second there I didn't know what you were going to ask."

I leveled my stare on him, but said nothing.

"Right. Okay, well. We were supposed to come with seven. You know, different people to record different things and take other information for anything else we might find interesting." The entire time he blabbed he moved his hands as if he needed them to talk with.

I interrupted him. I had no heart to put up with much. "How many, porcupine?"

"Three," he answered, and settled under my stare.

He did not lie. I only counted three when I scouted their camp earlier. I knelt down to get more comfortable and he copied my gesture.

"I can't believe you saved my life," he gushed with no prodding. "How did you know they—"

"Shut up."

He clapped his lips together. At least he could follow directions.

"What are the other two doing?"

"The other two? They're doing what I'm doing. Well, not really, because I'm here with you, and they're back..." The porcupine caught himself rambling that time.

I shook my head in amazement. "How did your species ever manage to kill so many of us?"

"Oh, that's easy. We—"

"That was not one of my questions, human," I growled, and let my snarl rumble along through my chest. "I know *how*, boy. I have seen your kind in action. What I want to know is what the other two biologists are up to."

"I'm sorry, sir." The young man hung his head, his ears burning red. I cocked my head at the sight of them. He was genuinely sorry, and my wooden heart twitched as if prodded by a summer breeze.

Without looking up, he answered my question. "The others are collecting data so they can establish what your territory is. That way they can protect it, you know, go to Congress and such to make sure that no one hunts you."

I raised my eyebrow on that bit of information, and my chest tightened as my heart stirred to life. "You are honest, porcupine?"

"Yes." He raised his face to look at me then, and I knew he spoke forthrightly. His face lay as open as an unfrozen pond in early winter.

"Where have they looked?" I pushed.

"We landed out by... Does it matter what the name of the lake is? I mean, it's some Native American name that I can't pronounce, anyway."

I shook my head. "No. I want to know what direction. Are you east? North?"

"We were looking south of north because that was where we

guessed that the wolves would be. Then we heard them, you, howling, and changed our direction to the west and north." He grinned as he added, "I guess we were right, huh?"

"Yes. Very clever." I responded without smiling. In spite of this human's inanity, he had managed to pinpoint us quite well. Great suffering, even the stupid ones were lucky.

"Have you seen others besides me and my mate, and the wolves I killed?"

Hearing myself utter those words *I killed* sent a shiver through my heart, but the porcupine gave me no time to dwell.

"No. When we caught you, uh, I mean when we caught the gray wolf, we…uh…"

"When you caught me," I encouraged the dolt.

"Yes. When we caught you we couldn't believe it, really. But Mark's a really good shot."

I arced an eyebrow and tensed. "Do not speak so lightly, human. That dart hit me. Now I wear a collar I cannot remove. Not very nice, would you say?"

He shook his head, and his ears flooded red again. "I'm sorry…"

"Grane. My name is Grane."

"I am sorry, Grane. I just find this whole thing to be…*incredible*."

"It is not so incredible from my perspective. I need you to remove this suffering collar from my neck." I coiled my fingers around its hard edge and glared at the young man in front of me. "Imagine yourself in my place, human. Would you appreciate this? Would you find this intriguing?"

He slinked down to make himself as small as possible, his submissive gesture checking me. He had signaled his subordination, and I backed off. I took a deep breath before I spoke again.

"Kenrickey, this collar puts everyone I love in jeopardy. Do you understand that? Once the world discovers us, we are dead. No action from your congress will stop that."

He sat silent as he stared at the ground, and I wondered if he would talk again. Without waiting to see if he would, I rose and left him to his thoughts, and returned to Suma. She stirred when I neared her, and my pulse quickened.

Sweet mercy, she owned every cell within my body. I could not stop the grin that grew from inside of me and spread to my face.

"Good morning, little wolf," I offered her my warm greeting, but I withheld from touching her. The tip of her tail wagged, and that tiny signal gladdened my heart. She rose onto her four paws and stretched and yawned. I waited for her to adopt her human form, but she did not.

I knelt down beside her so I crouched at her eye level, but I averted my gaze so I would not offend her.

"Suma, I want to keep moving now that you are awake. I do not want to hunt until we are well beyond Meron's territory."

The white wolf put her snout to the ground and circled until she picked up Eaen's and Armand's trail. She trotted north and Kenrickey scrambled to grab his equipment before he got left behind. I took it from his hands and had him go ahead of me. He was clumsy enough without having to carry something, too. Suma slowed her pace so the human could keep up, and before the sun set she stopped us at a thicket of raspberries.

Her thoughtfulness did not get lost on the porcupine. He wished the white wolf a hearty thanks as he stuffed the berries by the fistful into his mouth.

"Suma," I told him. "Her name is Suma." The sound of her name in the air itched my fevered skin as it did in the days before we had mated.

He stopped chewing long enough to compliment her. "That's a beautiful name for a woman, I mean a wolf…who is a woman."

"She is a wolf-woman, Kenrickey," I admonished him gently, and could not help but smile and shake my head with amusement. He was inept, but polite at the same time, and still potentially dangerous. He truly was a porcupine.

When I looked at Suma again, she had donned her pale, bare skin. Her name gushed from my heart, across my lips. "Suma."

Kenrickey stopped gorging himself to stare at her. I shot him a warning glance, and he bowed his head to resume his picking of the raspberries.

"Suma, are you all right?" I rushed toward her to sweep her into my arms, but her expression stopped me cold. Suma had averted her eyes from my greeting. I dropped to my knees and lowered my head.

"I am all right, Grane," she answered, but no lilt twinkled in her birdsong voice. I did not look up at her for fear of what I would see in her deep, brown eyes.

"I am relieved to see you are not injured." I bit my tongue before I uttered the word *mate*. I did not know for sure where I stood with her, and my heart tripped all over my chest so I had a hard time catching a normal breath.

"May I leave to hunt, Suma?" I raised my eyes to her then. "The human is rather harmless out here. I do not think he will hurt you. Unless, you would like to join me?" I offered her the hunt, hoping like mad she would accept because she wanted to be with me after all.

"I am not afraid of Kenrickey," she said, but added nothing more. Nor did she change back into her wolf, so I knew she intended to remain with the porcupine.

I backed away and slipped into wolf too easily. She had me rattled. I took off through the forest with my whiskers skimming the ground. At least hunting would distract my thoughts about Suma. I snagged a rabbit after a while, and doubled back with it. I dropped it at my Suma's feet and returned to the woods for my own dinner.

At least my quick trip back with the rabbit meant I could see how they were both faring. The human had been working with his gear, and Suma had sat close to him. Perhaps they even talked.

A pang of jealousy tweaked my heart for an anguished moment, and I knew I was bad off if I was envious of a human. I shed the thought to concentrate on hunting. I did not have much luck, and gave up, returning to our area with an empty stomach.

I headed for the raspberry patch to scrounge something to fill my hollow stomach, and it was then that I noticed Suma had not eaten all of her rabbit. I forced my body to heat and shifted to human, scooped up the rabbit and took it over to Suma.

She lay curled up in the shade of a maple tree. I knelt in front of her.

"You did not eat all of your dinner, little wolf." I held out what was left of the rabbit.

"I saved some for you," she spoke so soft she broke my heart, and I dared then to look upon her. As I had feared, no light glistened in her brown eyes.

"Suma, that was not necessary. But it is appreciated. You are always thoughtful," I added, hoping to spur some warm glow within her.

Her eyes shimmered as if she were ready to cry. I crept in close to comfort her, but she stiffened, and I was forced to retreat so I did not offend her.

Suma. I wanted desperately to erase her pain, to take it on myself, but I could not even get near her.

A shining teardrop plopped onto her pale cheek, and she stood up and strolled away into the woods. I did not follow her. There was no point. I chewed on the rabbit scraps without enthusiasm.

The porcupine, at least, had enough sense to leave us alone.

* * * *

That night, we continued to follow Armand and Eaen. True to his name, the porcupine stumbled around half blind and slowed our progress. Suma finally came to a frustrated halt.

"Enough, Kenrickey. We will sleep here until daylight, and then start out again when you can see where you are going."

I chuckled to myself. At least he was entertaining and he helped to lighten my mood. Otherwise, I would have sunk into my dark thoughts, and I did not need them right now. We settled in close together, and I positioned myself between Suma and the human. If he meant to try anything, it would be while we slept. I took no chances.

I had almost fallen asleep when he whispered in the darkness. "I'm nearly done with one of the tools."

My eyes sprung open, but I said nothing. Suma answered him, instead.

"Good, we will be safer when he no longer wears the collar." Suma said no more, and reading into her comment would have done me no good.

Eventually we all drifted off to sleep.

Chapter Twenty-One

I awakened and watched the stars get snuffed out by the morning sky. The sun peaked red above the tree line and a heavy bank of clouds sat in the west. I sniffed the air. By this afternoon it would be pouring, and we would lose the young wolf-men's trail. As soon as Suma and Kenrickey stirred, we would have to get moving. I wanted to at least figure out if the wolves turned south and east. If they did, they would have to be careful. That route put them very close to the biologists.

My heart sat cold at the thought of them. We still had the human and I still wore my collar. What would keep the others from using their antennas to track me? Us? And we were running out of time. Soon, they would miss Kenrickey if he did not return to them at the appointed time. They would come looking for him.

Suma stirred and stretched the sleep from her lean muscles. My groin thickened, and she rested her sleepy eyes on me. I offered her a warm smile, but did not break the quiet of the morning. The wolf-woman pushed herself up to her hands and knees and crawled over to me. My heart thumped mightily and my pulse raced. The sizzle of my spine heated my skin.

"Good morning, gray wolf," she lilted ever so softly and sidled in close. I opened my arms and pulled her against me. My throat constricted with the bliss of it, and I buried my face in the crook of her neck.

Suma.

She held her arms over mine so I would not release her. As if there would be any chance I would do such a thing. Except the heat that warmed my skin also seared my muscles. I took a deep breath and let it out slow.

"Do not," my mate pleaded.

I did my best not to change. I finally had her back in my arms, the last thing I wanted was to ruin that. But I had missed my little wolf, had worried that she no longer wanted me. I clipped off my thoughts. They were not helping, and I gulped another breath.

Suma spoke as if to distract me. "I smell rain. I love how the scents in the forest get heavy when it is going to rain."

I nodded, and breathed my reply. "Yes."

"The forest smells pungent."

All I could smell was spicy moss. I was not cooling down. "Suma, I cannot." I breathed again to try to cool the burn, but my muscles were roiling along my bones already. I slipped my arms through Suma's grasp and slid away into wolf. I shook myself and looked level-eyed at my mate and whined.

She gave me a shy grin, as if she knew she was responsible for my lack of control. I crouched up to her with my back rounded and kissed her under the chin, then flopped onto my back with my legs spread open. Suma reached down to tickle my exposed belly.

Utter bliss.

I let my head fall back as my mate ran her fingers through the thin hair at my abdomen.

"You were injured, gray wolf," she remarked as she slid a tapered finger along one of the scabbed gashes. "I knew," she confessed, "but I did not go to you. I am sorry." She did not look me in the eye as she spoke. Instead, she hung her head as if ashamed.

If only I could ease her remorse and tell her I had been injured many times during fights, these scratches were nothing. They were deep, but would heal before long, as had the hundreds of wounds preceding them. But with my wolf tongue I could say no such thing, and I wondered if telling her would only upset her more, anyway. The white wolf had finally gotten over the shock of seeing who I was, did I really want to add more details?

My train of thought got disrupted by the rousing of the porcupine.

He stood up and bid Suma a sincere good morning, but his ears reddened and his face flushed. I could smell his arousal, but I held back before I admonished him, just to see what he would do. The human dropped his eyes from the naked wolf-woman before him, and offered me a chagrined hello.

Reluctantly, I pulled myself away from Suma and trotted over to Kenrickey. He understood instinctively he should back down and knelt before me. Suma was my mate, and any outward show of physical attraction from him offended the both of us. He rolled his left shoulder back to expose his throat.

For a porcupine, he caught on quickly. I pushed my body into his space, and as he dropped his back to the ground I nudged him under his chin. His beard pricked my nose, but the nervous flush of his blood heated his skin. There was no point in being overly demonstrative about my status. He knew where he stood, and my spirits soared too high just then to inflict any kind of serious punishment.

Suma walked toward us and laid her warm hand on my back. I pushed my head against her thigh and she tugged my ear.

"Kenrickey," she said as she looked toward the ground at him, "we need to travel very fast today. There is rain coming and it will erase the trail of our brothers."

I barely heard her words, but wallowed in the trill of her voice. The porcupine sat up onto his buttocks and scrunched his eyebrows together, his confusion apparent. Suma, of course, picked right up on it.

"We have been following the trail of two wolf-men; that is why we have been moving along as we have."

"Oh." The porcupine looked from Suma to me, and then back at the wolf-woman. He remained seated on the ground, but his curiosity caused him to fidget. "That's neat. I thought you guys were just roaming around." He smiled at his misconception. "Is that normal, Suma? I mean, is that what wolf-people do? Chase each other?"

"No, Kenrickey. Eaen and Armand left our pack to lure you and the other biologists away from us so you would not find our den. They were trying to protect us. But doing so puts them in danger, and they are just boys like you. The wolves we encountered the other night would have killed them if they found them, so Grane and I have followed to make sure they are not harmed."

I pressed my shoulder into Suma's strong leg, and she twined her fingers in my ruff. My hammering heart pulsed the blood through my temples. She understood. My tail flagged joyously behind me, and the human noticed. He averted his face to stare at the forest floor.

"I won't be able to work on my tools then," he squeaked. "And Grane can still be tracked." At least the human spoke with honesty.

"You can work on them this evening when we stop. We really need to follow their trail as far as possible." She stepped away toward the metal pile and hefted the debris into her arms. Kenrickey rose to help her, and I crouched to change while he had his back to me. No point in startling him into another fainting spell.

They both turned when I approached them from behind. Suma shoved the human's metal goods into his arms, then pressed herself against me.

I enfolded her to my body and inhaled the scent of her. My Suma. I crushed her warm body to me and fluttered my lips across hers, begging for a kiss.

My mate lifted herself to her tiptoes to press her mouth to mine. I scooped my arm across her buttocks to lift her off her feet and cradle her to my chest. Suma clasped her arms around my neck, then clamped her hot mouth under my ear. My knees buckled and we dropped to the ground. The wolf-woman squirmed and twisted round to straddle for me.

Again, we stared straight at our guest, the porcupine. We heaved unified sighs and Suma's giggle flitted through the morning air. I smiled in spite of the intrusion, satisfied just to have my white wolf in my arms once again.

Kenrickey turned his back to us, trying his hardest to concentrate on his tool making. His ears burned fiery red in the early morning light.

I bent over and lifted Suma to me once again, and rose to my feet with her pale body nestled in my arms. She reached her face upward to feather a kiss under my chin, and I gazed down at my heart with the earth brown eyes. Then turned my attention back to the industrious porcupine.

"All right, Kenrickey, you can look now," I laughed, and Suma's warm body shook in my arms as she giggled more.

He turned around slowly, as if disbelieving my permission. He grinned, his relief shining forth, when he saw we were not mating, after all, and he stood up and wiped dead leaves from his bare knees.

"Come on," I ordered, suffused with good nature and exuding it like it had a scent. "We want to find Eaen's and Armand's new trail before it rains." I set Suma down and helped the porcupine with his things, and carried them for him again so we would not be slowed down. We hiked well into the afternoon.

The rain hit at about the same time the human began to stumble with fatigue and the heavy odors of Armand and Eaen enveloped our senses. They were close. Suma and I both took off at a fast run and left Kenrickey bumbling behind. The falling rain, for a brief time, pummeled the forest floor and released the wolf-men's scent into the damp air. Yet, as we homed in on where their odors pooled strongest, the stink of human wafted, polluting their pristine trail. We halted, and Suma turned an anxious look to me.

I wasted no time and shivered my spine to searing. I could not be caught in my human form. Suma crouched and shook herself into the white wolf. We trotted with caution toward the thickening scent of our brothers, and found the young wolves huddled in a thicket of alders.

When they saw us they bounded out of their hiding spot, nearly bowling us over in their exuberance. They were careful not to howl in their abandon, and they twisted themselves into panting knots as they exposed their bellies and throats, begging for forgiveness. The white wolf and I affected stern postures, but greeted them with affection, none the less.

My heart soared. They were both all right, and I plopped my heavy frame onto both of their prone bodies to mingle their scents with mine.

Then the porcupine came barging toward us from a thicket, and the reunion erupted into a scurrying of wolf bodies. Eaen and Armand both flipped to their paws and lunged toward the human.

I had no time to intercede, but Suma jumped in front of them in a flash, wedging her white body between Kenrickey and her brothers within seconds of their intended attack. She flashed her fangs and bounced on stiff legs to warn them off.

The young wolves grinded into a crumpled heap so as not to hit their sister, but they disentangled to circle around for another attack, even though their tails were crushed to their haunches in confusion.

Suma's interference gave me enough time to swing in beside her and face our brothers.

No!

Eaen whined in frustrated bewilderment, and Armand paced with bristling menace.

No!

I situated my flank against the human's quivering legs and raised my lip in warning, making it clear I did not want this human harmed.

Then the other human voices jabbed through the rain splattered forest, the bodies having finally caught up with their stench.

Kenrickey tensed and his mouth dropped open as if he wanted to speak, but then he snapped it shut and ducked so low I had to look down at him. I cocked my head in puzzlement and pricked my ears forward.

Yet wasted no time solving that riddle. Obviously, he did not want to be discovered, either. I shoved my head under his arm so he had no choice but to grab my fur, and I raced toward the copse of alders where Eaen and Armand had been hiding. Three wolves pursued, although the younger wolves shivered and squirmed to control their instincts. The naked human sat too close. We crouched lower in the foliage as the voices grew in volume.

Then I remembered my collar. My heart dropped to my paws, and I swallowed the whine creeping up my throat. I had no choice but to leave my little group in order for them to remain safely hidden. If the biologists had tracking equipment they would find us for sure. I threw a regretful look at Suma, but her brown eyes shined as she lowered her lids to show she understood.

I bolted, and two furred bodies and a bare one flinched and nearly sprang behind me in pursuit.

Stay!

They obeyed without hesitation, and I trotted north away from the others. The human scent remained strong. Kenrickey's friends followed, and I knew then they did have their own tracking equipment, and they would have discovered us all.

Now I was separated from the one who could help me, and I did not know when I would have the chance to double back to find him.

I continued trotting north and then cut east and south in the hope I could get close to the humans' campsite. Perhaps if they were close enough to their comfortable base camp, their fatigue would beckon them to rest and give up the chase.

If they took the bait, it would give me enough time to meet with Kenrickey and Suma to formulate a plan. My heart quickened with the memory of the porcupine's unexpected concealment. He had not wanted to be seen, which I could only take as his commitment to free me from the collar. What if he could not do it with the tools he was currently trying to fashion?

If I could not get this collar off, then I was going to have to keep running, and I knew it would be difficult to avoid a confrontation with Meron's pack. Once they found Lars and his cohorts, without Luna's protection, I would be hunted. There was no way I was going to risk Suma's life like that again.

If I managed to kill again before we were killed? I shuddered as I trotted through the rain. Suma had witnessed that already. I did not want to risk her seeing it all over again, either.

My heart weighed heavy and pulsed thick. For all of our efforts, for everything we already had to endure, we were right back at the beginning. The interfering humans were only a couple of days' travel from my family's den.

And it was all because of me.

Chapter Twenty-Two

The rain fell all evening, yet I still did not stop running. The wet weather acted as my ally in this game of chase, and I back-tracked toward the other two humans, who had been following me with their tracking equipment. Their trail cut southeast toward their camp, and my heavy heart lifted.

My hastily formed plan worked, and their fatigue and the weather had done the biologists in. I was free from them for the moment, and I raced back toward the area where I left my little group.

I sniffed them out from under a fallen spruce tree, yet my beloved Suma crawled out alone. Her spice filled my head as she smothered me with kisses and wrapped her pale arms around my ruff. I dropped to my back, and erupted my skin into flame.

Suma fell on top of me as my muscles contorted, yet I managed to hug her to me just the same.

"Hello, little wolf," I murmured through scratchy vocal chords.

"It is good to see you returned so soon, my gray wolf."

My gray wolf. Sweet thrill of the chase, I was her wolf once more, and her affectionate greeting proved it beyond doubt. I could have lain upon the soaked ground with her for an eternity, but matters pressed. I still wore a collar, and now Eaen and Armand had been introduced to a human.

"Suma? Are the boys all right? They have not eaten the porcupine?" I grinned at my joke in spite of the potential reality for just such a scenario.

My mate shook her head and bubbled an amused chuckle from deep within her chest. "No, our little brothers have not consumed Kenrickey. They are too intrigued by him for that."

"They are poking him with sticks?"

Suma giggled. "No, of course not. But they are poking him with questions. The three of them have not stopped talking since you left."

I smiled as I pictured the three young men out-doing each other with horrific, magnificent tales of their disparate worlds. I just hoped Armand's and Eaen's bad experiences with humans would be overlooked and not placed personally onto the porcupine. I voiced my concerns to Suma.

"Yes, as you know that was their first reaction. They were not easily convinced Kenrickey plans to help us."

We expected and accepted the reactions of the young wolf-men. Humans did not have much of a history of non-violence toward us, and both Armand and Eaen suffered personally. I would not have blamed them if I returned to find Kenrickey disemboweled.

Yet, they had heeded our warnings not to harm him, and were currently sitting knee to knee with an historic enemy.

"They are getting along?" I could not hide my astonishment at their generous turn of heart.

"That is to the porcupine's credit. When Eaen showed him his scar from the steel trap, Kenrickey shivered, paled, and nearly passed out. Eaen was too concerned for him to be angry. Plus, our little brother was a bit proud he survived such a wound in the first place." The black wolf's sister smiled with her affection, and the sense of well-being in reuniting with the young wolf-men surged through my body, tightening my muscles.

"I am glad we have found them, Suma, and that they are unharmed." I hugged my mate and lifted her off her feet. Then I slung my arm beneath her legs and cradled her in my embrace. "Suma, they are all right."

She laughed. "Yes, Grane. They are doing very well, even though I have a strong urge to knock them witless." She looked up into my face and her eyes darkened as her smile disintegrated. She brewed more than half serious about punishing them for what they had done.

I suspected her reasons why.

Suma spoke my very thoughts. "They have caused us, *you*, great harm, gray wolf."

She did not need to explain. I currently sported a very dangerous device around my neck. We had already been discovered by one human, and were lucky he had been so young and impressionable. The next time, our species would not be so fortunate. If I altered my shape before any more human witnesses? It was pure luck I had not when I had been sedated during my capture. We had every reason to be angry with the young wolves. I did not even want to think about the three dead wolf-men we left by the stream.

"We should speak with them now, Suma. Our pack leaders will be very anxious to see them, and they must return to face their punishment."

"Yes, and what of Kenrickey and ourselves?"

I inhaled and set my mate back onto the ground, but did not release her hands. I knelt and looked up into her pale face.

Her brown eyes narrowed with suspicion. "You are not leaving me behind," she stated.

I should have known the white wolf-woman would deduce my thoughts. I had not even uttered a single word about it. "Suma, I—"

"I know what you are planning, and you are not going anywhere without me," she repeated.

I tensed. As usual, she hit with eerie accuracy, but that did not mean I would give in to her. "You are not coming with me, little wolf. No. Absolutely not."

Her body stiffened and heated.

"Suma," I whispered my plea, and searched her eyes for understanding. "I almost lost you once because you saw who I am. I will not risk that again."

She cracked back as quickly as a snapping turtle. "I was a stupid lamb, Grane. I am lucky you forgave me for it."

I slid my arm around the backs of her thighs and pulled her into my chest, where I could rest my cheek against her taut stomach.

"There was nothing to forgive," I assured her. "Every wolf is taught killing is wrong. Yet, you saw with your own eyes how I have perfected it. My talent for killing my fellow wolf did not come about because I avoided confrontation." I inhaled and shut my eyes, even as I pressed myself tighter to my mate. "Little wolf, I have done things I am ashamed of. I do not wish for you to witness it again." I trembled with horror at the possibility of just such an occurrence if she accompanied me.

My sister's pack would hunt me down once they discovered Lars and his dead comrades. Suma would bear witness again, or be killed herself. My heart quivered in my chest and thumped its terrified staccato against my mate's flesh. Lose Suma to Meron's pack? The mere thought of it terrified me. We had come too close once already, and only survived it because we were not attacked by the scouts. I knew the next time we would not be so fortunate. They would search for us with poles. Our only salvation rested with living under Luna's protection.

Suma slid herself from my embrace and rested upon her knees in front of me, then leveled me with her ancient, forest-pond eyes. "You saved my life, Grane. Those wolves were out for our blood. They were not warning us away."

I shook my head. "True," I admitted. "But all the more reason for me to not allow you to come along."

I inadvertently stirred a stick in a hornets nest.

"Not allow me?" Her pale skin flared in my arms. "I was not asking for your permission, mate."

I took another deep breath to steady my nerves and back-pedaled. "I did not mean to tell you what to do."

Suma arced her brow.

"I just will not let you risk...Remember our wolf pup?" I offered lamely, as she demolished me even while she rescued my heart.

Suma grinned impishly and my spine sparked. She pressed her pale body back into mine and giggled. "No matter, gray wolf. You caught me with that one once, but not again. We stick together. Besides," she added, "I saw Kenrickey hide from his friends, and I think it is time we learned to trust a human."

She was dead serious.

My mouth opened but nothing came out of it, and I eddied around like a leaf upon a stream.

She nodded, and filled me in on her plan. At first, I stared at her with my heart flopping around spastically. As I listened to her I realized it was my beautiful white wolf in my arms talking to me. The same courageous wolf who could find the strength within herself to do the impossible for the sake of her pack. My ears tuned to the lilt of her voice as her words hooked upon each other in hauntingly sensible sentences.

She suggested we let Kenrickey go.

"You think he will lead the biologists toward Meron's pack?"

My adorable mate nodded her white head. "I do."

"Have you talked to him about it, yet?"

"No, I wanted to speak to you first. You are my mate, after all," she teased.

"Ha. Ha." But a genuine smile spread across my face, and I pressed her against me again, just to remind myself she was real. My little wolf was a witch in her own right, and she had me so caught up in her at times I could not think straight. This was one of those times. I felt my heart tattoo rhythmically against her warm body.

"Suma, you wreck me," I finally conceded. "We will talk with the porcupine."

She squealed and squirmed in my arms and then wriggled her way free. She clasped my hand in hers and yanked me upright. "Come on, then. Let us go talk with our new friend." Her laughter bubbled, and I felt no rain fall from the sky. I followed her like a nursing pup.

I could hear the young men talking as we approached. Kenrickey was regaling the wolf-men with fantastic tales of city life. Their eyes were spread wide in shock. I cleared my throat, and Suma settled in between Eaen and the porcupine.

I knelt to receive quick kisses under the chin from my little brothers, and then made myself comfortable among them. Armand showed no indication of being upset about me and Suma. I was sure my skin glowed with the utter happiness of that moment.

If not for the collar, our rainy evening would have been quite a pleasure. But there were serious things to discuss, and we did not have much time. By morning, I feared the biologists would be back out in the forest, and I would have to head toward Meron's territory if we did not go with Suma's plan. I forged right in and was sorry to ruin the good humor, even if having a human around made it surreal.

"Porcupine, any chance this collar can come off tonight?" As soon as I mentioned it all eyes focused on my neck. No gaze lingered out of respect, but Kenrickey hung his head in shame. I warmed at the sight of it, and Eaen reached over to console the human. Apparently, Suma had already told the young wolf-men all about it.

"I can try again with what I have," he offered, but his voice carried flat, without any lilt of hope to it.

"Do it please, Kenrickey," Suma pleaded softly. "If we cannot remove the collar soon, Grane will have no choice but to run back toward Meron's territory with your friends in tow."

Kenrickey blanched and darted his look toward me.

I nodded.

"But the wolves could kill you," he muttered.

Tact was not our porcupine's forte.

"Yes," I admitted.

Eaen and Armand tensed.

"Kenrickey," Suma murmured, "can you lead your friends away from here without them following the gray wolf?" She had her liquid brown eyes locked on his face.

He shook his head, and he barely whispered his answer. "I'm just a student. They're my teachers and I'm supposed to do what they say. I'm sorry." He dropped his head again, and Eaen and Armand leaned forward simultaneously to comfort him.

They awed me with their compassion for the human, and my chest tightened at their display. I cast a glance toward Suma, but she revealed nothing in her expression.

Yet, when she spoke, her voice cut clear and even. "Then try your tools. Now."

The porcupine hopped to his knees in an instant to obey her, spilling the rest of us to the balls of our feet in reaction to his swift motion. Kenrickey grinned his apology. Harmless or not, our wariness for humans coursed instinctual.

The porcupine held each tool up in both of his hands, and we settled back onto the ground. I crawled closer to him and exposed my neck so that he could get to my collar easier. The damned thing chafed against my skin as he worked on it, and his sighs grew heavier with every failed attempt. My three pack mates observed protectively in case the human tried something deceitful.

"Can we chew it off?" Armand asked in exasperation.

The porcupine shook his head. "No. This beauty was designed to last." He shot a look of regret at my little brother. "I'm really sorry."

Frustrated, I pulled away from his hands and hooked my fingers around the band at my neck. I was losing my patience, and the faces that surrounded me paled in sympathy.

Suma's brown eyes shimmered.

"Porcupine." I swallowed a deep breath before I spoke again. "Can you sneak into your camp and get the tools?"

"But I thought—"

"I know what I said earlier. But…" I rested my eyes on my mate and borrowed her courage. "But I trust you now."

Three young voices sang out their disbelief. "You do?"

I snorted a laugh and the room erupted in relieved giggles. This night was certainly the strangest I had ever spent. "Yes," I replied with a sheepish grin. "I do."

Kenrickey sat with his face hanging out.

"However, I am going along with you. To watch. If you tell anyone about us porcupine, I will gladly rip your lungs out of your chest."

He nodded, then promptly shook his head, too. He was comical in the confusing way he sifted through his reactions. He seemed glad he would get the chance to remove my collar, but he obviously remembered the fight he saw by the stream. Kenrickey knew I was quite capable of following through with my threat.

As entertaining as he was, however, it was time to leave. "It is settled, then. We go now." I turned my attention to the two wolf-men. "Eaen and Armand, Suma and I need you to go back to the den and tell the others what has happened. We have been gone too long already, and you know Luna. She will be frantic with worry, as they all will be. Tell them that Suma and I will return as soon as I get this collar removed."

"But Grane," Eaen protested.

Suma bit him off. "Brother, you and Armand left a very worried family behind. It is your duty to return to ease their hearts. Grane and I will not be long behind you."

We all rose and Suma hugged both of her little brothers.

"Go," she ordered. Her stern tone expected no argument and the young wolf-men gave her none. She was not ignorant, either. She stepped stiffly toward them and lifted her lip from her luminous teeth. "If I find out that you did not go straight back to the den, I will clean the hides from your flesh with my bare hands."

They shook their heads. "We will go back," Armand agreed readily. "But, will we see Kenrickey again?"

All eyes turned toward me for an answer and I shrugged. "I do not know. Much depends on what happens tonight," I confessed. I was being honest. I really did not know what I planned to do with the human once he freed me of the collar. The thought of killing him had lost its allure. I had grown rather fond of the critter, and hoped he would give me no reason to end his young life.

"We waste valuable time, little brothers. We all must go." I hugged each of them. "I am very glad that neither of you was harmed during your escapade, but please do not do anything like it again. I am sure Suma told you we met three of Meron's pack in our hunt for you. I do not want to do it again."

Armand wrapped his arms around me, and vowed he would not. He knew what his and Eaen's heroic foray cost me. "We will go directly back," he promised.

Eaen nodded his compliance, as well.

"Good," I gruffed. "Now go. And I will see what we can do about another visit with Kenrickey."

The young wolf-men crouched simultaneously and coalesced into their wolf forms. The porcupine gaped. Eaen put his teeth over the human's wrist in an odd display of affection and then turned on his tail. Armand bounded south into the forest, and the black wolf gamboled after him.

Once they were out of sight, I turned my attention back to Suma and Kenrickey.

"Are you ready?"

The porcupine's bleached skin glowed in the darkness. The young wolves had given no thought to changing shape in front of him, and his brain still grappled with the reality of it.

"Human." I snapped my fingers in front of his gaping face. He shook his head and focused his eyes on me. "Are you ready?" I repeated.

"Yeah," he breathed, then reclaimed his brain and recalled the task at hand. "Yeah, of course, I'm ready."

"Follow closely, then, and place your feet where we do," I instructed him. I had not forgotten how he stumbled in the woods at night. Plus, the rain had made everything slick. He would have a harder time of it.

I reached out for Suma's hand and lifted it to my lips. Then I knelt before her and shot the burn to my skin. I could not risk being seen in my human form. Suma dropped on her bare knees in front of me and buried her face in my mane. My tail fanned behind me, a banner signaling my pleasure. Being back in the sun of Suma's acceptance tripped my heart. She whispered her love in my ear and I squirmed and whined.

Suma!

Her giggled breath rippled the long hair of my neck and I trembled. She pulled away and rose to her feet. I followed her like a pet as she headed toward the east.

* * * *

By the time we made it to the campsite, we had only a couple of hours of darkness left. The white wolf crouched along the edge of the clearing while we watched Kenrickey sneak into the camp. He was doing well. We barely heard him.

Until he started rummaging for the tools he needed. My heart dropped to my paws when one of the tents lit up like the ass end of a lightning bug. Our porcupine had been caught, and our hope for my release from the wretched collar disintegrated.

I stole a glance at my mate beside me, but she continued to stare straight ahead. Was she doubting her decision to trust the human? If he spilled all that he knew about us? I minced my paws and pulled my tail tight around them. I had to keep my cool and my ears sharp. The muted voices on the damp night air were hard to discern.

There was a muffled stir from the tent directly after the rip of the zipper.

"Ken? Where have you been?"

The porcupine stood in the brilliant beam of a flashlight. And then a male voice exclaimed, "You're naked!"

194

Grane

Kenrickey dropped his chin to stare at himself. "Ah, yeah," he stammered. "It's raining and I got wet." He covered his genitals with his hands.

It was not the savviest excuse I had ever heard, but his human friend appeared to believe him.

"Well, welcome back. Did you get the data?" The human lit a cigarette and the match hissed in the sprinkling rain. The pungent tobacco smoke wafted heavily across the clearing. Suma wrinkled her nose.

"About that..." the porcupine fished for an excuse. I could see his brain working.

His friend sucked hard on his cigarette, but did not offer to share it. "Yeah, well, it broke. I was chasing the gray wolf far to the north and west of here, and I accidentally stepped on it. It's ruined," he lied.

Good boy.

"That's just great, Ken. That equipment isn't cheap and now we're down to one box. Good job!"

His angry sarcasm rankled and my lip lifted defensively.

The porcupine put a shirt around his waist to cover himself and dropped his head. His shame was obscene and unnecessary. I did not like Kenrickey's teacher. Suma's hackles lifted in sympathy. She was not fond of the other human either.

"Fine," Kenrickey's teacher continued. "We'll figure something out in the morning." He flicked his cigarette to the ground and squished it with his toe. A plume of smoke funneled out of his mouth and he turned back toward his tent.

Kenrickey balled up the cloth he had wrapped around his waist and threw it at his teacher's back. A boy's response, but I liked it nonetheless. The human never noticed, and as soon as he was zipped back into his tent like a turtle the porcupine resumed his rummaging for the tools.

Without warning, the turtle unzipped and the teacher burst out into the night again. "Ken," he whispered, excitement piquing his tone. "The wolf is here. He's here."

My heart froze. As did the blood in my veins.

The human teacher waved the wand of the antenna across the air in front of him and the box he held clicked to life. He pointed his finger at me like the barrel of a pistol. I spun and bolted. Suma raced at my heels, while we fled from the last shred of hope we had held for my release. And now we did not even have our human.

Chapter Twenty-Three

We did not stop running until the sun hung well above the tree line and had gained enough heat to turn the wet earth into steam. It was too muggy to continue at such a pace and we dug out the dark soil from a thickly forested spot and sprawled our bellies in its coolness. We both panted heavily, and shed our fur to stretch our bare skins across the freshly scraped forest floor.

"Grane," Suma uttered between breaths, "what will we do now?"

I had no answer for her, other than the one we had acted on. We had run straight for Meron's territory.

I laid on my sweating back and stared up at the clearing sky while I regained my breath. A hawk circled high above upon the air currents. My heart rate steadied, and I closed my eyes and listened to my mate breathing beside me.

"I think we need to lure our human out." I stared at the red of my closed eyelids.

"They will not send him out alone again. They will worry that he will break the last of their surveillance equipment," Suma whispered across the warm ground to my ear.

"If we are lucky, maybe we will catch him before they spot us. Me," I corrected.

"Oh no, gray wolf. *Us*. We can circle back, and if the biologists are without their boy, then I can go hunting for him while they hunt you."

"You would use me as bait, little wolf?" I affected mock surprise.

S. C. Dane

Suma giggled. "You would use yourself, wolf. I was just the first to suggest it." She stretched her arm out and I grasped her hand so we could twine our fingers together. My growling belly echoed in the still morning air, and Suma giggled again.

I basked in her merriment, even though the collar pressed into the skin of my neck and nagged its existence. "Shall we hunt, mate? It appears I am starving." I turned my face to her and smiled. She was already looking at me with a grin of her own. Her white hair glowed in the sunlight.

"You are beautiful, Suma," I breathed.

"You are mine," she promised.

I disappeared in her shining, earthen eyes. There was no heat, no collar. Only the white wolf-woman before me, who laid upon me the burnished eyes of redemption, peace, forgiveness.

"I love you, too."

"See," she smirked. "You knew what I would say before I had the chance to say it." Her lilting voice wavered sleepily.

"That one was easy," I whispered. My heart swelled in my chest as I watched her features relax as she dozed. I squeezed her fingers in mine and turned my face back toward the blue sky.

We would hunt when she woke, and would move from there. Knowing the humans, they would probably tranquilize me in the very act of searching for my breakfast. They had a knack for being disruptive. I just hoped Kenrickey would not say anything, even if I was captured again. I hoped he would not be around if I was. Suma had a good idea for catching him if he was out alone while I was unintentionally distracting the other biologists.

At least we would have the satisfaction of killing him if he had betrayed us. I slept lightly and I opened my eyes when Suma stirred beside me.

She rolled on her side to face me. I reached to pull her toward me, enfolding her into my arms. She suckled my nipple and my groin flexed with my need for her.

I shivered as my flesh prickled with goose bumps and draped my leg over her thighs to snuggle her closer. Her spicy, moss scent erupted around me as she heated, then she squirmed her torso so that her tight

198

buttocks pressed against my pelvis and I cupped her breasts in my palms.

She lay exquisite atop me, her flesh contoured perfectly against mine. I trailed my fingers along her supple waist, caressed her rounded hips, the soft shanks of her thighs. Her heated scent blossomed as she readied for me, and I entered her tenderly, savoring the slow drawing of her around me, the deliberate swiveling of her hips. She undulated along the length of me as I lay with my back upon the forest floor.

A sparrow twittered its discovery of a swarm of gnats and the wind soughed through the leafy branches.

My Suma.

Earth.

My life.

Her moan squeezed a spasm from me; urgency quickened the press of my hips to her buttocks, consuming me so that I cupped one of her bulbous breasts in my hand as my other pinned her to me at her core. I rolled our bodies so to press her belly to the ground, and buried my face into the fuzz of the soft hairs of her nape. The white wolf's breath carried my name and she spasmed deliciously, milking my seed as it pulsed into her.

After, I remained in her. To be with her. To be her.

I dozed while the spice of her scent curled its tendrils around my heart.

* * * *

We both awoke to the sun arching high in the sky. We had slept for some time, and still had not fed.

"We slept too long, little wolf," I warned her as I rolled away and stretched. I could not suppress the grin that pinched my cheeks.

Suma stretched languorously upon the forest floor. Right to her toes and tapered fingers. I feasted on the sight of her while she rested her doe eyes on my face. "You will have to change soon so the humans do not see." Her light voice dripped with regret.

I tilted my head.

"The humans run our lives," she explained.

I knew what she meant. I would stay in this spot with this wolf-woman for a thousand passings of the seasons if I could. Anger and shame gripped my guts as I rolled my fingers along the edge of the collar. The early autumn day lost its luster.

"It is not to be," I gruffed, answering aloud my private thoughts.

Suma rose and hugged me from behind. "No, it is not. But it will be."

I squeezed her pale arms and turned my head to press a feather-light kiss to her pouting lips. "Yes. It will be. But for now, let us hunt to fill our bellies. Then we will hunt a human."

We shivered the heat through our bodies without parting. We remained tangled until she nudged my chin playfully, then we unwrapped ourselves and trotted away with our muzzles to the ground and our stomachs growling.

Chapter Twenty-Four

We ate well enough considering we did not have the luxury of time. Eating a deer would have been better for our bodies, since the last time we had consumed anything that substantial had been back with our pack. Our bodies were showing the strain of traveling and dealing with the humans. Suma had dropped weight and that worried me. If she did carry a wolf-child in her womb? I shivered physically at the thought of it. I had never had a pup of my own before and the idea of it thrilled my heart into excited beating.

A pup with Suma.

My mate turned her furred chin in my direction and winked one brown eye. She had heard my final thought, and my ears tugged back in happiness. Let her hear. I would be the proudest wolf-man in the forest if Suma carried our wolf-babe, and I did not mind if she knew that.

But I clipped my wishful thoughts just the same, and refocused my attention on the job. We were back in the area where the biologists could find us, and I hoped we could find Kenrickey before we were discovered. I had to get this collar off or Suma and I would be spending a winter on our own. Not good, especially if she was pregnant.

The scent of the porcupine tickled my nose long before I located his footprints. My tail waved loose with anticipation. I smelled only him. A good sign. His scent increased the farther east we went. He was not far from the campsite, but now it became difficult to distinguish whether he was alone or not. I hesitated to go farther and Suma yipped softly behind me. I turned to look at her just as she nudged my rump with her nose.

No.

I would not lead us directly into the camping area. She could forget it. I sat on my haunches and refused to budge. The white wolf pricked her ears and nipped at my paws.

No!

But my tail wagged in spite of my stern reproach.

Suma shoved her snout under my rump and heaved me forward. I did not stretch my hind legs to stand and squatted on her head.

Our tails wagged in tandem.

No, Suma!

I let my tongue loll from the side of my mouth in a quirky grin.

She yipped again and licked my chin. I raised my front leg and pressed my paw to her head. She swatted back and nudged my chin again. I lifted myself up on my hind legs and plopped on top of her shoulders, while she scurried away and nipped at my back paws. She beamed a beautiful wolf smile, and I shoved my head under her belly to push her off balance, all the while my tail fanned crazily.

"Grane and Suma!"

We spun to face our audience, my heart lurching.

Porcupine.

Sweet pinecones, thankfully it was him who snuck up on us while we were busy being foolish. Suma, I suspected, would be spending the rest of her days turning me into a careless, romping pup. A fine endeavor. I let the prospect sit right next to the sight of Kenrickey in my heart.

We trotted over to him and he dropped to the ground in a proper submissive greeting. He wore clothing, so we approached with caution in spite of his meek posture. He was human, and clothing could hide any number of their weapons. I sniffed his entire body and Kenrickey did not flick a single muscle. Satisfied with his friendly intent, I greeted him with a couple of quick licks under his chin.

He chuckled and I cocked my head to the side. The porcupine was genuinely pleased with our reunion. So much so, in fact, that he started stripping on his own, as if he sensed my uneasiness with his human garb. I did not try to stop him.

Suma shed her own covering and crouched before the porcupine in her human skin. She watched him expectantly, until she could finally speak.

"Kenrickey." Her birdsong voice carried the hint of a scratch.

The porcupine stared at her briefly, then remembered his place. He dropped his eyes as his ears flared red.

"Kenrickey," she repeated. "Can you get the tools for the collar?" Her eyes widened in excited anticipation to his answer.

"Yes." He seemed as eager as she was, but then his face clouded. "But, Grane," he turned his attention to me, "my professors are out tracking you now. They'll find you here."

My hackles lifted, and the porcupine dropped to the ground again.

"It is all right," Suma comforted him, offering him a sympathetic smile. "His anger is not directed at you."

Kenrickey sat up, grinning sheepishly.

"How long have your teachers been out searching?"

"Since early afternoon, Suma. I'm surprised they didn't find you."

Maybe they had. For all any one of us knew, they were not far away. I whined.

"Go get the tools now, Kenrickey. Please." Suma understood my anxiety.

The porcupine leapt to his feet and Suma and I both braced ourselves defensively. He raised his palm in a quick wave, muttered an apology, and tore off toward the campsite. Naked.

I was pleased with the unfolding of events. Even with the imminent threat looming. The porcupine's honest displays of solidarity filled my heart with hope. We had a human ally. In my entire life, and especially since the death of Misha, I never thought my heart would welcome such a preposterous notion. The Luna and her entire pack had worked their sorcery.

Suma rubbed the length of her lithe body along mine. She wore her magnificent fur coat again, and my heart settled into a steady rhythm. At least if the other humans showed up, they would not see a wolf standing with a human figure. My little wolf had been clever to shift back into her safest form.

Kenrickey bounded toward us. He skidded onto his knees and panted, but he held up the tools like a victor. I wasted no time and crawled to him on my belly so that he could easily work on the collar.

Suma hovered anxiously.

And growled.

I stiffened and the porcupine's hands stilled.

The others come.

No! We were too close. I flipped to my feet, tipping Kenrickey backwards. He gripped his tools, slid his own feet underneath himself and shouted, "Run!"

The three of us bolted in the same direction.

The porcupine followed our path of escape.

I slowed my pace so that he could keep up with us if he ran hard. I did not know how far he could go at that speed, but any distance we gained would be helpful. My heart soared at the sight of the tools still in his hands. Suma flanked him for encouragement.

We did not get too far before our two-legged companion slowed. I could hear his lungs slaving for air. I stopped, and he fell to his knees and bent over his whistling lungs, but he waved me over just the same. He acted very valiant on our behalf.

I rushed to his side and crouched before him. We both panted and his hands shook, but he worked at the collar anyway. I ignored the pinching of the band as he twisted it to remove the bolts.

The porcupine mumbled to himself as he worked, talking himself through the procedure. No wonder the suffering thing would not come off easily. Humans and their contrivances. That collar had been fashioned to last.

My breaths finally evened, and still Kenrickey muttered and worked. It would not be long before we would have to run again. Too much time had elapsed since we first fled, and I was sure that the other two humans followed. If anything, the flight of their student would be enough cause to pique their interest. They would pursue us.

Finally, the wonderful metallic slide and click snapped in my ear. The porcupine wrapped his fist around the collar and pulled. Gently.

I twisted and ripped my neck free. The pain of its removal was nothing compared to the elation of being rid of it. Suma slammed herself against me in exultation and I threw my head back and howled my freedom at the sky. My mate threaded her song into mine and we yipped excitedly.

The porcupine, infected with our relief, hopped up and down and celebrated with us. He whooped, too, and then his cheeks and ears burned red with embarrassment. He cast us a shy look from under his brow. I threw my nose back into the air and howled an invitation.

He grinned and pushed a nervous squawk from his throat. Suma encouraged him with her own yipping, as she did with the pups to get them used to their own songs. Kenrickey latched onto her intent and offered his voice again, until each yip lengthened and stretched into a final, long wail. His bare chest expanded and he stood upon his toes with the effort. Kenrickey unleashed himself from his humanness.

I hated to end our celebration, but we were still with the collar, even if it was no longer around my neck. I yipped and spun away. Suma chased, but the porcupine did not follow. I halted, looked back, and yipped again.

What was I doing? I was free from humans, yet I was inviting one to come along? My mate and her pack had worked curiously upon my heart.

The porcupine's face erupted into a delighted smile. He had been waiting for an invitation. No longer needed to remove the collar, he doubted his role with us. Obviously he did not worry that I would kill him for knowing we existed. He leapt toward us eagerly, and followed along as we trotted farther away from his human companions.

We did not stop until our friend's lungs whistled as they strained. Dusk had settled, and I was proud he kept up with us for that long. I crouched, shivered, and contorted into my human form. Then, I wrapped my burning arms around the porcupine and spun him in an exuberant hug.

"Thank you, Kenrickey," I nodded once as I released him.

Suma stepped up to kiss his grizzled cheek. "Yes, thank you. You have saved us from having to spend a winter from our family."

The porcupine grinned shyly, but muttered his initial guilt.

"You were acting with a true heart, Kenrickey, in spite of the harm you caused. If you and your teachers can keep human hunters away, then your efforts were not without merit," I assured him. "But."

Kenrickey lifted his face and his body tensed as he waited for what I would say next.

"We are not typical wolves, as you know." I leveled my eyes on him and held his gaze in mine. "We cannot afford to have any humans in this area."

He nodded as his eyes clouded.

"They will keep coming," he whispered as he pushed his words through his throat. He had referred to the humans as if he were outside of them. A definite good sign.

"Yes. But if you could deter them? Sabotage their efforts?" I raised a conspiratorial eyebrow. The porcupine grinned and his face lit up.

"You mean, help you keep your secret?"

Suma slid her hand inside of mine and squeezed. I removed my gaze from the human in front of me to look down at my mate. She winked her consent, and my chest tightened. What I asked of Kenrickey effected the entire pack and I was heartened by Suma's approval. But, what would Beth and Alec think?

"You did not tell your teachers about us, I hope?"

The porcupine gasped in surprise. "Of course not. Are you kidding?"

I lifted my lip from my teeth, growled from deep within my chest, and had my hands clamped around the young man's throat in an instant. He toppled to the forest floor as I roared into his ear. "You did not tell anyone?" I snarled, and tightened my grip at his neck.

"No! No," he begged. The stench of his urine and his sudden sweat flooded my nostrils. He told the truth. I released my fingers from his neck and sat back so that the porcupine could get up. He did not move, but kept his eyes crimped shut.

"Kenrickey, open your eyes," I commanded gently.

He shook his head and kept his lids crammed over his eyeballs. His body trembled, and a pang of guilt pinched my heart. I hated to scare him like that, but it was the surest way I knew to reveal what resided in his heart. It was a trick I learned from Luna, and I had to admit it was very effective.

"Please, porcupine, I meant you no harm."

Suma crept in close to him and laid her long hands upon his sweaty back.

"Kenrickey," she whispered, and lengthened her arm across his

206

shoulder to pull his torso into her lap.

My stomach clenched at the sight of him cradled in her arms. Her song slid melodiously from her pale throat and my guts fisted. Not my Suma's song. Not for someone else.

But as my envious lament tore across my heart, her harmony dipped and she strung out a new melody for the human she held. My white wolf. Her compassion knew no bounds. She had woven a new tapestry for her young and fragile friend. The clouds in my heart dispersed as the wolf-woman's graceful spirit flooded through me.

There was no room for jealousy in my full heart. My eyes drank in her lithesome body as she curled around the porcupine. The knobs of her spine poked against her taut flesh as she bent her head to sing in his ear, while the muscles of her arms slithered beneath her pale skin as she caressed away his fear. Suma was utterly stunning, and I could not pull my eyes from her.

Her song wended its way through my head and my heart, and my pulse strummed with every clear beat in my chest until the strains of her song crooned familiar in my ear. I lifted my eyes to her face and she had her burnished, earthen eyes pinned on me as she sang. She held her friend, but she sang for her mate. My throat constricted and my chest swelled until I thought the muscles containing it would tear.

I let my tears fall without shame.

The wolf-woman's tears fell, too. But she did not remove herself from the boy. He had drifted off to sleep on the currents of Suma's song, yet she remained to comfort him. Her humming trailed off, and she spoke in whispers to me.

I nestled close to them as the darkness settled around us.

"Grane, my mate, you have decided with wisdom in your heart. Our pack will do well to have an ally in the human world."

I bowed my head with her compliment and offered my own. "White wolf, your pack does well having you."

She lowered her lids. "*Our* pack," she corrected.

I inhaled to control the burn that simmered within me, and Suma slid her warm hand into mine.

"Grane, I admit I was shocked to my core when I saw you slay fellow wolves so skillfully, so ferociously. I had forgotten to listen to my heart, and for that I will always be sorry. Gray wolf, my mate, I hold no doubts that you acted for the sake of your pack. You protected us and there is honor in their deaths." Suma held her gaze upon my face as she revealed her regret, her pride.

The white wolf laid the final shard of my heart into its true place with her words. My life reclaimed? I dared to look into the shining eyes of my Suma to see myself reflected, and I trembled under the weight of the promises revealed.

Freedom. To be wholly wolf.

Full of laughter, compassion.

To thrive within the bonds of true kinship.

With the family I loved and served with honor.

Kenrickey is reborn...

Kenricky

I lay on the cool ground, peering out from between the balmy arms that embraced me, and didn't dare move a single hair on my body. Not that I was in any kind of hurry to relocate. I mean, how often does a guy get cuddled by a wolf-woman? I sure as hell wasn't going to disturb her, and I sure as hell wasn't about to piss her off. Or piss off her mate, for that matter, who, by the way, was curled up on the forest floor with us.

I'd already seen what that wolf-guy was capable of, and if he wanted to, he really could snap my neck like a dry twig. On his own, he'd killed three mature wolves with his bare hands, or paws, whatever. He looked all innocent sleeping beside us, but when he attacked those wolves to protect his mate and me, *Christ,* he really could tear someone's head off to shit down their neck.

So, I was not going to disturb them, and was going to stay snuggled in until *they* stirred. The sun hadn't peeked up over the trees yet. It was still pretty dark out, but I could tell it was morning because I could see the tops of the trees against the lightening sky. If it wasn't for the heat the she-wolf radiated out of her like she was some kind of portable oven, I'd be freezing my balls off, because it's always coldest before the dawn, or something like that.

Our cozy little nest got even cozier because Grane, as if aware I was awake, unfolded himself from his wolf form and sat up as a human being. No shit. My head felt like it would pop off my shoulders whenever I witnessed the miracle of it. I mean, bodies were *shifting* in front of me. Crumpling, and growing hair, and tails and ears and *teeth.* Holy Lord, but these wolf-people had big freakin' teeth. Sharp, strong

209

and long. The wolf, who was now a man, rolled onto his side to muzzle his face into his mate's neck.

When I say muzzle, that's exactly what I mean. That wolf-man might have looked human, but he definitely wasn't. He exuded wild animal. Predator wild animal, too, not some little bunny rabbit that goes hopping through the forest, but pure he-could-turn-me-into-carrion kind of predator.

His mate pulled her arms from around me to reposition herself right into his waiting embrace, just like he was the safest place on earth. Instantly, the cold morning air wrapped around my naked body to chill it. I sat up and hugged myself to keep warm.

Grane pierced me with those hypnotic yellow eyes of his, and I plastered myself to the forest floor, then sure as hell made sure I stared off into the forest. *No direct eye contact.*

"Good morning, Porcupine," he whispered gruffly.

I swallowed, then cleared my throat before I answered him. Christ, he was un-nerving, and I tried like hell to always remember to move freakin' slow and keep my head low. And absolutely not disrespect his mate, Suma.

"Morning, Grane." The memory of his attack on me the night before rushed back like a hundred horses trampling my chest. He had not physically harmed me, just scared the literal piss out of me again. Good Lord, he could strip me down to a blathering two year old in a nanosecond.

"I am truly sorry I scared you so badly yesterday."

But then he could restore my ego by gobbling a healthy dose of humble pie.

He was beyond remarkable.

I was with wolf-people for jumped-up-criminy's-sake, beings who could morph from human to wolf, or wolf to human, and they were letting me hang out with them as if they liked me. My heart thumped so hard I had to gulp for air with the sheer miracle of it.

And the thing is, I liked them right back. In spite of the fact just being around them kept me teetering on the lip of sanity, I was drawn to them. Yeah, they were living marvels of nature, but my attraction went beyond that. These wolf-people were nice. Suma cradled me all night long like I was a baby, for God's sake. She even sang me a lullaby to comfort me after Grane had caused me to piss my pants. Well, I didn't technically piss my pants the night before because I wasn't wearing any. I was as naked as they were, which, by the way, I had done to comfort them. Nuts, huh?

But I'm rambling in my head and Grane definitely doesn't like babbling. What was it he was saying? Oh right. He'd apologized for scaring the crap out of me. I ran my hand through my hair and took a wicked deep breath before I answered him.

"It's okay. I mean, you had to know if I was telling the truth or not, right? I mean, I see where you guys—" I clamped my jaw shut because those freakin' yellow eyes *leveled.* I was rambling.

The white haired wolf-woman turned in her mate's arms so they were both facing me. She smiled softly, and man, she was gorgeous looking all dreamy like that. She had these deep brown eyes that reminded me of puddles that hadn't been disturbed; there were layers in her irises that just stilled me.

A low, nearly imperceptible rumble rubbed across my skin, and the hair on my entire body prickled. I averted my eyes to the tree line again and felt the blood rush to my head. Grane had caught me staring at his mate.

"Holy, I'm sorry."

He didn't say anything more because he didn't have to. These wolf-people communicated like nothing I'd ever seen before, except in the nature programs I grew up watching as a kid. There was no mistaking what their intentions were, and my body reacted. Instinctively.

Suma's giggle trilled like little birds, and I nearly looked straight at her again because of it. I remembered at the last second to lower my eyes. "Grane, the human is fine," she sang.

Her mate lowered his dark, gray head when she admonished him. Loving hell, the guy had scars covering his body like tattoos, yet he yielded to the woman in his arms as if she had all the power. Like I said, Grane was beyond remarkable.

"Kenrickey, you slept all right?" Suma's lovely voice warbled again as she directed her question at me.

"Yes," I practically stammered. The wolf-man's yellow eyes boring into me was no distant memory. "I slept great, thanks." I nodded, and kept my eyes focused on the ground. By this time, I didn't think either one would hurt me much, or kill me, even. But, I sure as hell didn't want to upset them. I was not exaggerating in any way when I said they had *teeth*.

My two bunkmates rose together, and like some kind of synchronized dance they stiffened and turned their faces away from the rising sun. Suma hopped up and down on her toes, and Grane's muscular body tensed and vibrated. They both thrust their noses into the air to assess their surroundings.

My goosebumps crawled back with a vengeance. They smelled something, or heard something coming, and if it was more of those wolves Grane had fought and killed, then *holy fuck.* I didn't get up, but I definitely got my feet under me.

Suddenly, Suma dashed toward the tree line, and I couldn't get my mouth closed before I gasped. The gray wolf-man turned to me and grinned.

"It is our pack leaders, Kenrickey. Stay low," he advised. I dropped my back to the earth like it sucked me there, and I sure as hell did not ask him to repeat his command. Around these guys, you didn't act like some stupid human being who asked questions for the sake of conversation.

I did look to where my new friends were focusing their attention, though. A red wolf and a brown one glided out of the trees to the west of us. *Sweet Jesus.* These two were not the ones I'd met a couple of nights before. Aside from the obvious difference in physicality, there was no fun and loose skinned jocularity in this pair. These two wolves were lethal. The brown one, the big one, was focusing his attention on our little group.

I swallowed the bile in my throat before it spewed into my mouth, because his golden eyes ate a hole in me. Freakin' right I was taking my protector's advice. I shoved my back into that cold dirt just so I could make myself invisible.

The gray wolf-man jogged toward the newcomers, too, and I stole a peek from under my lowered lids to watch how Suma and Grane greeted them. In spite of having human bodies, they dropped to their hands and knees and pressed their faces under the chins of their pack leaders. The battle-scarred wolf-man peeled his shoulders back and exposed his entire stomach, chest, and neck so that he was completely vulnerable to both wolves.

The red and brown wolves' tails swung in circles like the blades of a helicopter as they sniffed Grane and Suma all over, and then the four of them rubbed their bodies together like they were reclaiming their closeness.

Incredible. I was watching a reunion of creatures who loved each other and were glad they were reunited, there was no doubt in my mind about that.

Grane smiled like he sat on the front porch of heaven.

That lasted for about a second because that big-ass brown wolf refocused his attention back onto me, and his massive, furry body stiffened as his lips curled away from his long, sharp fangs.

Ho-ly. Shit.

I barely heard Grane introduce me through the pounding of my heart in my head, and my thoughts vanished in my panic. I tried my ass off not to even breathe, but I was gasping, and I clutched my genitals and squished my eyes shut. Dear God, I could hear the brown wolf getting closer. His snarling alerted every single strand of hair on my body and they stood to attention like a squadron of nervous little soldiers. He was going to kill me, and it was going to hurt.

A mewl squeezed past my constricted throat. I couldn't help it. Then a woman yelped, so help me God, she *yelped* the name Alec. My attacker bounced against his rigid front legs and stopped dead in his tracks. I know because his hot freakin' breath huffed across my bare, sweating body, he was *that* close.

"Alec, he will not harm you," stressed a woman's voice I had never heard before. I slid an eyeball in the direction of that voice, and watched a pair of naked legs stride to the side of the brown wolf. They bent, and a red-headed siren knelt down beside him and draped her arm over his back. She buried her face into his thick coat. The wolf-woman was beautiful and hot. Hot in the sense that heat blasted from around her in waves.

"Brown wolf, he has submitted," she purred.

Oh yeah, I had submitted all right. To the fact that I was going to die a gruesome death.

"Grane would not have let him live if he could harm us," she whispered without lifting her face from that sleek fur.

My would-be killer turned his wide head toward the scarred wolf-man, who had not budged from the spot where the reunion had taken place. My thoughts steamrolled back into my brain. Grane was a subordinate to the brown wolf and couldn't interfere to save my life. I was at the mercy of his pack leaders—the brown wolf and this red-headed wonder.

Ah fuck. Please oh please let this woman talk some sense into him.

I crushed my back further into the dirt of the forest floor, pulled my shaking hands from my genitals and splayed my entire body for the brown wolf to do as he would. It was the only hope I had of surviving this encounter.

Suma's voice warbled from behind the pack leaders. "Brother, the human helped us with great risk to his future. He deserves our mercy."

A snarl curled from the deep chest of the brown wolf, but the woman who held him whispered steadily. "We will need this one, Husband," she breathed, again without lifting her face from his flank.

The brown wolf whined.

Frustration? Was it possible he might decide to let me live? I panted with the sudden rush of the possibility, but absolutely did not move any other muscles. He could still kill me, and I was not about to offer him a single reason to do so. Christ, just my being here was reason enough for him.

Finally, Grane came near and spoke on my behalf, but not before he squatted with his head hung low between his muscled shoulders. "He freed me, Alec. I had been collared, and he freed me." The wolf-man's voice thickened with shame as he explained.

"I'm so sorry, Grane," I squeaked before I even realized it. I'd no idea that I'd tranquilized and collared a wolf-man, let alone one as noble as Grane, and my stomach shriveled in sympathy for him. I was learning pretty quickly just how amazing he was. I mean, after what I witnessed, he could probably physically dominate his pack leader, yet he didn't. The gray wolf showed only love and affection for his pack. It was a fucking wonder he hadn't killed me himself given what we'd done to him. I felt like a piece of crap, yet here was this awesome guy acting like he was to be blamed for something.

The red-head was quick to rebuff him, thank God. "Gray wolf," she corrected as she slipped away from her mate. "Give me your hand."

Grane's eyes watered as he breathed, *"Luna."*

What power did this woman have that could make Grane shiver like that?

Her voice flowed like cream. "Give me your hand, gray wolf," she repeated as she knelt down in front of him. That muscle-ripped man trembled like a puppy, but he placed his long hand in hers like he trusted her with every inch of his scarred skin.

"I see, mate of my sister," she murmured, "and our pack will benefit from your great sacrifice. My heart glows in your wisdom, and we anxiously await the gift of your offspring, the gift of your blood with ours."

Grane snapped his head up to look at the wolf-woman before him, and she smiled like an angel. I couldn't take my own eyes from her, until the brown wolf's warning growl sent my attention scurrying back to the tree line. I'd seen the look on Grane's face, too, and his tears of gratitude spilled unchecked.

I stole another glance. I couldn't help it, especially since the brown wolf left his post beside me. He joined his mate and Grane, and then Suma completed the group. They knotted and hugged and kissed and no one wasn't crying. Hell, even I started to.

When they finished celebrating the gift of a union, and a new life growing in Suma's taut belly, they turned their attention back to me. I remembered everything about subordinate displays, and lay back down with my face and throat exposed to the brightening sky. The sun was now over the tips of the trees, and the heat from it caressed my goose-flesh. Hope swelled in my heart in spite of the danger I was in.

The woman Grane called Luna approached, straddled me, and curled her long fingers around my throat in one graceful motion. Fire girdled my waist and throat, and I struggled to keep my eyes focused away from her even as her clutch shut off my wind.

"Brown wolf, *try,"* she coaxed with a voice that reminded me of ancient trees.

S. C. Dane

Try *what?* I squirmed, but waited only seconds before I found out. The pack leader minced closer with his head lowered menacingly and a growl that wormed through the physical barrier of my skin. Then the wolf yawned, exposing his lethal teeth all the way to his bone crushing molars. He spread his four iron legs and shook his gargantuan frame as if he'd been swimming. Then with a roar, he ignited into a bonfire while, *so help me Jesus*, those furred legs stretched and balded into human limbs. He lasered his golden eyes on me and glared with the human face that was Death. The fringes of my world blackened and blurred as I lost consciousness.

About the Author

S.C. Dane lives anywhere in the United States that her wandering feet take her. A student of Life, she learns from the seemingly impossible, the improbable, and the bizarre, as well as the commonplace. She has yet to be disappointed.

www. pararnormalromancebyscdane.co

Other works by the author with Melange Books

Luna, Book 1 of the Luna Chronicles

www.ingramcontent.com/pod-product-compliance
Lightning Source LLC
Chambersburg PA
CBHW031403250626
47155CB00004B/1393

* 9 7 8 1 6 1 2 3 5 7 0 0 3 *